THE WONDERLAND WOES

ADDIE J. KING

THE GRIMM LEGACY - BOOK 3

Loconeal Publishing

Amherst, OH

THE GRIMM LEGACY

Copyright © 2014 by Addie J. King
Cover Art by Melinda Timpone
Edited by Kathy Watness

Loconeal books may be ordered through booksellers or by contacting:
www.loconeal.com
216-772-8380

Loconeal Publishing can bring authors to your live event.
Contact Loconeal Publishing at 216-772-8380.

Published by Loconeal Publishing, LLC
Printed in the United States of America

First Loconeal Publishing edition: July 2015

Visit our website: www.loconeal.com

ISBN 978-1-940466-40-8 (Trade Paperback)

ALSO BY ADDIE J. KING

The Grimm Legacy
The Andersen Ancestry
The Wonderland Woes
The Bunyan Barter

DEDICATION

To Allison Jane Westcott . . .
My own little lost girl.

CHAPTER ONE

Coffee is the elixir of life. I cannot imagine starting the day without a big heaping mug of the stuff. I like sugar and cream, but in a pinch, I'll drink it black. It is cheaper that way, and a day without coffee is a day that feels like a slog through waist-deep mud in a rainstorm.

Yeah, I've got a bit of a caffeine addiction. I don't always trust my instincts until I've felt those first tendrils of wakefulness from the initial sips of coffee. Which is, of course, why I did a double take at the white rabbit my newest roommate was yelling for me to come look at—I hadn't gotten fully caffeinated yet.

"Janie, you gotta see this," Allie called. She stood at the sliding glass door in the kitchen, holding her own steaming mug and pointing toward the backyard.

I muttered something about early mornings and loud roommates as I crossed to the coffee pot, which was, thankfully, still mostly full. Yawning, I poured myself a mug of brown, steaming life-juice.

"Seriously, hurry up," she urged, waving with her empty hand as I shambled toward her.

"Someone is seriously too awake this early in the morning," I complained.

"Look," she said, jabbing her finger toward the window. "Stop complaining, and just go look."

I shuffled over to her and did what she asked; I looked. A white rabbit scurried across the yard in a most peculiar manner. Not sure of what I was seeing, I rubbed my eyes and squinted through the glass again. He would stop, sit up on his back legs, look around frantically, sprint a few yards away, and then do the same thing all over again.

As fascinating as it was, we did have places to be. It was probably some pet of the neighbor kid next door. I'd finally met the neighbors, and they had a ten-year-old son who had been begging for another pet. We kept finding his cocker spaniel all over the neighborhood. I groaned, thinking we were going to end up chasing this rabbit through the yard the same way we did when the dog kept getting loose. At this rate, the backyard was going to end up looking like something out of Wild Kingdom.

"It's gotta be Jimmy," I said.

"I don't think so," Mia said, coming into the kitchen from the patio. I hadn't seen her out there. "It's gone."

"Gone? What do you mean? It's not going to be burrowing into something in the backyard and leaving rabbit droppings for us, is it?" I asked. I really did not have an objection to animals, but Mia and I were in our second year of law school; Allie was trying to get her life back together; and our fourth housemate, my boyfriend, Aiden, was going back to school himself. He was trying to get a degree in my dad's old field, studying history and folklore at the University of Dayton. We had crazy schedules and tight budgets, so a pet wasn't on our list of priorities, and if having our own wasn't going to happen, we certainly didn't want to repeatedly clean up after one belonging to someone else.

"Relax. I saw it disappear into the drainage pipe that runs under the back fence. I think it's gone," Mia said. "I'll talk to Jimmy's folks this afternoon and make sure it went back to where it came from."

I was glad she'd volunteered to take care of it. I was looking forward to a relaxing Saturday, sitting at the picnic table on the back patio and staring at my laptop while I researched for a brief due for moot court in a week. It was a beautiful October day, late in the fall, and the weather had cooperated by providing a sunny day with unseasonably warm temperatures. I didn't think I'd even need a jacket to enjoy it.

I poured myself another cup of coffee as Mia and Allie began talking about their plans for the day. Their discussion reminded me I'd promised to take Allie to a group therapy meeting this morning before I began to dig into my work.

"Allie, what time do you have to be there?" I asked.

"Nine thirty, but I don't want to be late." Allie was eighteen, but barely. When I'd met her, just this past summer, she was a seventeen-year-old runaway living on the street and at the mercy of someone she refused to talk about. I'd gotten hints she had been a victim of human trafficking, sold for sexual purposes by someone who had taken advantage of her homelessness, so I had taken her to The Hope Project.

I'd heard about the group at the law school; they tried to provide counseling and resources for victims of that crime. It was a small group running on a shoestring budget, but Allie had done really well since she'd gotten involved, and Mia and I both felt like we owed her. She had saved our lives.

Mia and I both had an interesting family history. I was the youngest living direct descendant of the Brothers Grimm, and my stepmother had made a target of me just as Mia and I started law school last year. I'd gone up against Evangeline in the faerie courts and won. That had gotten me the house I was currently living in, as well as the car I'd be driving Allie to her therapy in—both the house and the Escalade had belonged to my stepmother.

Mia, on the other hand, was distantly related to Hans Christian Andersen, and her father, Tobias Andersen, spent most of his time protecting humans from serious magical and faerie court threats. She didn't know her father well because he was always traveling, but they'd reached an understanding after the Seawitch had tried to kill them both. Allie had been caught in the middle of it, but she'd protected us as well as she could. She'd refused to help the Seawitch get into our house and kept her mouth shut as to our whereabouts when we'd left. Mia and I had agreed we at least owed Allie a safe place to stay, rent-free, until she could get on her feet.

"I'd better go get ready," Allie said, putting down her coffee mug and heading for the steps.

I followed closely behind her, also going upstairs in order to change out of my yummy sushi pajamas and into a pair of jeans and a University of Dayton School of Law sweatshirt, my normal weekend uniform. Who was I kidding? It was my normal everyday garb if I wasn't doing anything for an internship or going to the courthouse for some reason.

The Hope Project wasn't operating out of its own facilities just yet. Instead, they met at Christ United Methodist Church in Kettering, a nearby suburb of Dayton. We lived in Oakwood, another suburb, which was just down the street from the church. It was also close enough that I could stop at Krispy Kreme, just a few blocks away, for donuts to take home. Since Aiden and Mia were both living at the house and paying rent, I could splurge a little more from time to time than I could last year, and I had a sudden taste for vanilla crème chocolate-iced donuts.

Intending to buy a dozen donuts to send with Allie to her meeting, as well as a few to take home, I pulled through the drive-through while the two of us talked. Allie chattered on about a book she'd been reading, and I made a mental note to take her to the library to get a library card; she'd been tearing through my meager selection of fiction fairly quickly.

The neon sign flashing "hot" in the drive-through window told me the donuts were fresh, and I ordered a dozen of them for her and an extra one for myself.

"Thanks," Allie said, smiling. "I know the donuts will be appreciated; some of the girls don't always get a lot to eat. Why don't you come in and meet them? I'm sure they'd like to say thanks."

I promised to come in, but still planned to leave quickly so they could get on with their meeting and I could get on with working on the brief. Allie would call me for a ride home when they finished, but that would give me a couple of hours to do my research.

I parked the Escalade in the parking lot behind the church and followed Allie in, carrying the distinctive white donut box in front of me. She led me inside, up a flight of steps, and into a Sunday school room with colorful pictures of biblical characters and stories on the walls. Four other young girls, mostly Allie's age, sat in battered folding chairs, and a middle-aged woman with a smart blond bob sat on a stool at the front of the room. Allie introduced me, and I handed over the box of donuts.

The older woman smiled when I produced the pastries, but her smile faded quickly when she opened the box. "What is this supposed to mean?" she demanded.

I gave her a confused look, and she turned the box around so I could see inside.

On each individual donut, stark against the chocolate frosting, were the words, "Eat Me," in white piping.

CHAPTER TWO

I had no idea.

"Obviously, some teenager at Krispy Kreme is having fun with us," I said. "I don't have a clue what it means."

Allie's mouth hung open.

One of the girls started crying. I tried to apologize, but I couldn't wrap my head around what was wrong. Finally, I just closed the box and agreed to take them away with me, leaving Allie to console her friend as I escaped to the car.

That was definitely odd. I'd have to apologize again when I went back to get her, but I wasn't sure my presence would do anything more than continue to upset her friends. I drove home, planning my call to the Krispy Kreme manager as I went.

I pulled in the driveway, parked, and walked up to the door of my house, only to find a large bottle of wine on the front step. Or at least, it looked like a bottle of wine. . My stepmother would have known what kind of wine it was; she threw all kinds of parties and dinners while she'd lived in the house and hired caterers to provide such things. I had never paid attention, as I wasn't much of a drinker, but now I wished I had. It was a smoky, dark green glass with no label, but a tag affixed to the neck of the bottle with two words: "Drink Me."

I opened the door. "Mia? Aiden? Bert?"

Bert was our fifth housemate, a talking frog and former human prince who'd been my helper and friend ever since I'd first had magic butt its way into my life. He advised me well, helped me study, explained legal concepts I didn't always understand, and had fallen hard for Mia the year before. It had taken most of the summer for him to start coming out of my father's study and be sociable once again, and Allie was the reason for it. She'd been hanging out in the study and going through the library there, and he'd been willing to talk with her about books. The two of them had become friends, and Bert finally started to act normal around Mia again.

It hadn't been Mia's fault; her affections had already been attracted elsewhere. She was currently dating a young starving actor named Jonah who, even Bert had to admit, was a pretty decent guy. I think the fact that Jonah was pretty likable actually helped Bert; knowing Mia was seeing a guy who treated her well made it easier for Bert to start to move on. At least he'd stopped moping around and hiding, or playing Nina Simone records into the wee hours of the night.

Speaking of Bert, my green friend hopped into the hallway as I put the box of donuts down on the hall table and turned around to grab the bottle on the doorstep. "What did you get? I'd kill for a maple donut. Is there coffee?"

"This isn't funny, Bert. Something weird's going on," I said, trying not to step on him as I balanced the bottle, donut box, keys, and my purse while walking to the kitchen. "We all need to see what this is."

"Maybe this is a serious enough conversation for a beer?" he asked.

He might have a point. It might be serious. I was beginning to think we were dealing with another magical something or other coming into our lives, and dreading it. It wouldn't be the first time a supernatural entity burst onto the scene for us. "Even if it is serious, Bert, it's not even noon. I'm not sure you want to start asking for beer before lunch, do you?"

He shrugged, hopping along behind me into the kitchen. "It's got carbs, and it's got nutrition in it. I'd say it counts as lunch."

Oh, wow. Had he gotten to that point with his drinking? Certainly, he was dependent on one of us to bring him beer, and I always tried to make sure there wasn't much alcohol in the house he could get into. He'd had one heck of a bender after he'd made a disastrous play for Mia's affections last summer, but I'd thought he was doing better. Maybe I'd been wrong.

"Is Aiden still here?" I asked, hoping to divert him from dwelling on the fact that I was not going to pour him alcohol . . . probably ever again.

"He's out in the garage looking for parts for something." Bert nudged the stepstool next to one of the kitchen chairs so he could make his way up to the seat and then onto the table. I had to bite my tongue. I'd asked him not to do that. It was the same thing as someone walking on the kitchen table, where we ate, in bare feet. It was just gross.

But he'd explained it was as close as he could come to being able to talk with us on a reasonably similar height level. Otherwise, he felt like a pet, a mascot, or just plain inferior. He was big for a frog—it took both of my hands together to hold him—but he still was at a distinct size disadvantage. I hadn't the heart to insist after dealing with a very heartbroken amphibian all summer, so I'd just invested in large, economy-sized containers of antibacterial wipes for cleaning up before dinner.

"Parts for what?"

"For another one of his magical gizmos," Bert said. "I don't know what he called it, but he was attempting to figure out how to magically imbue some kind of sword."

Aiden with a sword? That could potentially be a Very Bad Thing. The donuts and the wine bottle could wait a few minutes if he was about to mess with something sharp and pointy. I didn't necessarily want to be within reach of him when he held something with the potential to leave big holes through people, for my own safety, but I knew I was one of the few who could get him to stop when his head was buried in some whatsit he was experimenting with.

He was the world's biggest klutz. I'd seen Aiden trip over his own feet, wreck his car when it was idling at a stop light with no other cars around, and even fall up the stairs. Yes, I did say *up* the stairs. Didn't think that one was possible until I saw him do it with my own two eyes. If I didn't know the truth, I'd have thought he should see a neurologist to make sure there wasn't anything wrong with him. The reality was his genetics made him unable to stand still and chew gum at the same time. My boyfriend was only half human; his father was faerie court nobility. Aiden's heritage was a distinct disadvantage in the human world, but he'd long since made his decision not to go back.

I shoved the wine bottle and donuts on top of the counter where I didn't think Bert could get to them and then ran out to the garage. I didn't dare call out for Aiden for fear a distraction could lead him to drop a sharp implement and sever a toe or some other such emergency, but I was in a hurry to get to him before he could do something equally dangerous while his brain was otherwise engaged in magical theory and experimentation.

He could be the proverbial absent-minded professor: brilliant and insightful, but so entangled in his research at times that he would fail to notice the building burning down around him. Aiden normally would remember to tell someone when he was about to go work on something, so we could check on him periodically or remind him to stop for breaks, but it sounded like he had forgotten to do so this morning.

I slipped into the garage and saw him standing at Dad's old workbench with a wickedly sharp, strangely curved blade on the bench in front of him. He had his arms crossed over his chest, deep in thought, when I tapped him gently on the shoulder and then more insistently when he didn't respond.

He whirled around, a red blush staining his cheeks. It was the quick flush of a fair-skinned, red-headed man caught in the act of hiding something. What was he so guilty about? I wondered.

"Janie," he started to talk, clearing his throat, but stopped as I interrupted.

"What did you do?" I asked.

"Nothing! I swear. I'm just looking at this and trying to figure out how to make it work." Something about his expression made me even more suspicious.

"The pointy end goes in the other guy," I said. Keeping my hands up, I began to carefully edge my way toward the handle end of the sword just in case it got knocked off the workbench in the direction of my midsection. "It doesn't take a rocket scientist to figure out how a sword works."

"It's not just a sword. I think it could be a vorpal sword. And if it is, we need to figure out how it works in case we need it."

Why was he even working with weapons? Was there some kind of magical mayhem afoot? Up until today, I hadn't noticed anything. Did he know something I didn't?

"Why do we need a vorpal sword, and what does it do?" I asked. "Are we under an attack I don't know about?" I heard the edge in my own voice and cringed. It sounded very much like a nagging girlfriend voice, even if I felt like I had a valid point.

He flushed an even darker red. Okay, something was very definitely going on.

CHAPTER THREE

"What in the world is a vorpal sword?" I asked again.

"It's a sword that can cut through anything, whether it's steel, magic, a protective circle, or whatever we might need to slice through. I'm worried about protecting ourselves, and there's really no way to predict what kind of magical bad ass might come after us next," Aiden explained, reaching one hand toward the sword and tentatively touching the blade, as if it was a pet to be calmed.

He wasn't really paying attention to me; he was too busy staring at the sword, which looked like it had seen better days. The metal seemed dull, and I thought I saw rust at the place where the handle met the blade.

"Two questions. One, wouldn't we want something like this to be behind our threshold? Two, if it can cut through anything, should you be out here handling it by yourself without someone who can help if you drop it on your foot?"

I'd learned, the hard way, that a person's home has a kind of magical force field, a *threshold,* which prevented magical beings from being able to break in. Keeping the sword inside the house would mean a magical being couldn't sneak in and steal it or use it against us. It would be safe from a faerie being as long as it was in the house. I knew Aiden had laid a protective salt and iron circle in the ground surrounding the garage, but our threshold would be stronger protection.

He blinked, my words sinking in. "You're right. Maybe I should work on this in the basement instead of in the garage. I keep forgetting we had the portal down there closed. It would be a more secure place to work. For some reason, though, I'm not sure I trust it."

I knew why. It had nothing to with the portal itself and more to do with the unexpected visitor we used to get from time to time. Aiden's faerie father, Geoffrey the Tailor, was not exactly the most welcome sight in his son's eyes. Geoffrey wasn't all that bad for a faerie being. Many of them would try to trick one into giving permission for them to do all kinds of crazy things, or to obligate one to them by offering up food or drink or shelter or other needed things.

As long as I kept my wits when around Geoffrey and made sure I wasn't inadvertently making some arcane deal, he wasn't so bad. No question he loved Aiden's mother, Doris, in his own way, but it had been a relationship doomed from the start because of the pulls of their own respective worlds. Aiden held a grudge against his father, although I wasn't quite sure what all it was about.

"We haven't seen your dad in months. He can't sneak into the house anymore. But if he did show up, you know I'm going to offer him coffee, at least," I said, picking up the sword carefully from the fabric laid on the table. I was careful not to touch the metal just in case there was some goofy spell on it that would make weird stuff happen—I'd had a lot of that over the last year or so. I was hoping Aiden was too distracted by the conversation about his dad to realize I was removing the sharp, pointy object from his control and carrying it into the house.

Aiden followed me, almost bumping into me as he started off into space. "Why would you?"

I backed up, pushing him away just enough to get the door open and keep him from impaling himself on the blade while we talked. "For the same reason I pushed Mia to invite her father to lunch last summer. It's your father. You only get one." Mine was dead, and I missed him all the time. Aiden had helped me solve my father's murder, so it wasn't like this was news to him, but it helped Aiden to remember why I wasn't going to stop persuading him to at least have a civil relationship with his father.

Of course, there was the added bonus of pumping his father for information on the current state of the faerie courts. I could get all kinds of information out of Geoffrey, as long as I kept trying to convince Aiden to talk to him. I'd never rely on it completely, but it helped to have a conduit to whatever political machinations might be going on behind my back. And it would be nice to have a heads up should my evil faerie stepmother actually get released from Søborg Castle, the faerie form of prison.

"Anyway, not to change the subject too rapidly, but there's stuff happening I need you to consider. Something weird's been going on this morning." I filled him in quickly on the donuts, the bottle on the front step, and how upset Allie's friends had been at her meeting earlier this morning. "What in the world could all of this mean?"

Aiden stopped in his tracks. "I don't know a single fairy tale involving anything like that, Janie."

I walked into the kitchen through the sliding glass doors and put the sword on the kitchen table. I noticed the bottle was gone, but the white pastry box was still on the counter where I'd left it.

"What does that mean? We've never had anything come up that wasn't related to a fairy tale," I said, heading for the box to show him the message on the donuts. When I turned back to Aiden, I noticed the look of confusion on his face. "What's wrong?"

"Where's the bottle you mentioned?"

I knew who must have taken it. "Bert. Where'd that frog go?" It was only then I realized the pastry box wasn't completely closed. I opened it and saw there was a missing donut. "Oh, shit."

We ran for the swinging doors, both of us hitting them at the same time like something out of a Looney Tunes cartoon, before we stumbled through into the dining room. I heard a loud, long belch coming from somewhere in the vicinity of the living room. When I say loud, however, I don't just mean satisfied and rude. The walls vibrated.

We got to the living room just as I heard Bert sobbing.

He was *huge*. I don't mean he'd overeaten or had turned into a human. I mean Bert was the size of a dump truck, sitting where the coffee table had been in the living room. He took up most of the room, leaving just enough space to walk around him if one didn't mind stepping on the couch or the armchair and didn't have anyone else in the room to maneuver around.

That's a lot of frog.

Thank goodness we had a lot of living room. "Bert, what did you do?"

"I didn't do anything," he wailed as I heard a door open upstairs.

Mia hurried from her room to meet us, distracted from her own studies by the commotion downstairs. "Whoa," she said, as she got to the landing and saw Bert, bigger than an elephant, cringe and try to turn away from her.

I was just about fed up with Bert's broken heart. I *knew* something was off about those donuts. While I'd been talking to Aiden about his sword, Bert must have snagged the bottle and a donut to stuff his face with in private. He couldn't have waited five more minutes?

How did I fix this? Would we have to call in Aiden's mother and the rest of the F.A.B.L.E.S. guys to come mix up the kind of sludge I'd had to drink to fix my own magically messed-up hair growth last year?

Aiden ran for the phone, presumably to ask his mother exactly what I was thinking. Was it weird we were on the same brain wave at the same time? I'd have to ask him what he thought about it later, but right now, I was going to have to do something about the giant tears falling on my living room floor.

Damn that frog!

CHAPTER FOUR

I was mopping tears off the wood floor. My patience with Bert was wearing thin. Mia had taken off to call her father, Tobias Andersen, on her cell phone. While they weren't exactly close, Mia learning last summer that her father was some kind of Terminator/Van Helsing boogeyman to the faerie courts went a long way in healing some of her own insecurities and abandonment issues.

And the effort to create a new relationship went both ways . . .

He encouraged her to talk to him about magical stuff, and now that she was in the loop on his real job, they could have real conversations about his life without Tobias trying to hide things to keep Mia away from magic. I was glad she was calling him, maybe he would know something Doris and Harold and Stanley didn't about how we could get Bert back to normal. Mega-Bert was *not* my idea of how to decorate the living room.

With Aiden on the landline in the kitchen and Mia in the study, I was in the living room with Bert. He'd finally stopped crying when I'd gotten out the mop, but I couldn't afford to let the puddle warp the floor. Real wood parquet flooring doesn't do standing water well, and my budget did not extend to fixing them. I'd found that out when we'd had to do repairs to the house last summer.

We'd had more damage than I could afford to fix after tons of unexpected water damage due to the Seawitch. If it hadn't been for contributions from the F.A.B.L.E.S. group—of money and a lot of donated labor to get the windows, doors, and walls fixed, as well as the wood floors sanded down and refinished—the house would still be in wretched shape. Mia's dad had pitched in as well, tossing in a few bucks and hours of time on a ladder with hammer and nails to finish off the repairs on the upstairs windows.

But now I was missing a coffee table and had a giant frog in its place. This was so not covered by my homeowner's insurance, I was sure. "Bert, why couldn't you have waited until I gave you a donut?"

He sniffed, like a two-year-old with his hand caught in a cookie jar, and said, "Because I didn't think you'd give me one."

I just about lost it at him. "Have I ever refused you anything besides alcohol? And even then, I've only said no when you've had too much. I've never turned you down for food. I might not have had what you wanted, but I never kept food away from you. Why would you think I wouldn't give you a damn donut?"

He looked chagrined, if a frog could look chagrined. "You're right."

"You've been acting like a stupid brat! It's not like I don't get you've been depressed. Yeah, you lost the girl and she's with someone else. I'm sorry you didn't get what you wanted. I can't fix it for you. But Jonah's a good guy; you've said so yourself. You've got to move on. We need you around here. You know as much about this magical stuff as anyone else, if not more so. You still have contacts in the faerie realm. And you're my friend. Mia is still your friend."

"You're right," he whispered. "I've been saying I was fine, but I haven't been. And because I just wanted to drown my sorrows in wine and pastries, look what happened to me."

"Speaking of wine, where's the bottle?" I asked. I hoped he wasn't sitting on it. If we needed it to figure out who was pulling this crazy magic stuff on us, it would help if the bottle hadn't been shattered into tiny pieces.

"I saw it roll under the couch," he said. "I'm pretty sure it's still there."

I dropped to my stomach on the couch and leaned over the side to peer beneath the sofa, my shoulders wedged between the edge of the cushion and Bert's side. Sure enough, the bottle was there. I reached one arm out and snagged it, pulling both the green glass and a few dust bunnies from under the couch. How could anything have gotten dusty in the few minutes it had been under there?

Aiden came back into the living room just as I was straightening from my upside-down position, clutching the bottle in my hand. "Mom, Harold, and Stanley are on their way over here," he reported. "They were all at her house when I called."

Curious, I thought. *Why would Doris be entertaining those two at once without an official F.A.B.L.E.S. meeting?* They weren't scheduled to meet this weekend; were they forming a bowling league or planning a bake sale? I guess I just didn't know they socialized much outside of the meetings, and most of those had been held at my house over the last year. It made me wonder if there was something going on, if I was missing something the others had already figure out.

Of course, it could just be old friends getting together, but right then, I just didn't trust that things weren't all connected. Lately, life just had a funny way of continually supplying creatures who wanted to eat my face off.

Mia came in. "Dad's just on the other side of town. He's on his way." She didn't look the least bit happy.

"What's wrong?" I asked.

"He was at Mom's."

Tobias had been trying mend old wounds over the last few months. I thought maybe he would try to get back together with Mia's mother now that the Seawitch was more secure than she'd ever been, but there was no way to predict what Tobias might be planning. He was so closed off, he made a statue look emotional, and Mia hadn't mentioned anything, so I hadn't pried. The look on Mia's face at the moment told me now wasn't really the time, either.

Great. This was shaping up to be a wonderful afternoon. And it also meant I was so not going to get my moot court brief written today. Now I was grumpy, too.

"Hello? Anyone home?" I heard from the front hallway. It was Allie. She must have gotten a ride home. I was grateful, but at the same time, I'd wanted to apologize to her on my own, before we got back to the house. I guess it was a bit too late for that one.

"We're in here, Allie," I shouted back.

Allie came into the room, taking in Bert's size and the despondent look on his face, with an expression more of curiosity than frustration. I wasn't sure yet if that was a good thing, though it was certainly better than anger. I still felt bad about taking those donuts to her meeting.

"What in the world did you do, Bert?" Allie asked softly.

Why didn't she seem surprised?

Bert shook his head, as if he didn't want to tell her.

"Bert," Allie said with an odd note in her voice. It was as if she already knew the answer of what she was about to ask. "Did you eat one of the donuts Janie had?"

What was up with those donuts, and how the hell did she know that? I was starting to think Allie knew a lot more about the magical world than we'd originally thought.

Which meant, of course, she had a lot of explaining to do.

I crossed my arms over my chest. I was tired of playing catch up. I was going to get some answers, and it was going to happen before a magical shit storm landed on our heads this time.

CHAPTER FIVE

" **A** llie, what in the world is going on?' I demanded. Why was it that no matter who I met or what I did, magic always stepped in to hurt someone in my life?

She sighed, crawling onto the couch and tucking her feet up underneath her rear since there wasn't much room for her legs to squeeze between the couch and Bert. I saw her look around for the coffee table, as if she was looking to put her purse down on it, but it was gone. "I'd hoped I'd gotten away from it all."

"So dealing with the Seawitch last summer was not your first brush with magic?" Mia asked, her expression carefully blank.

Aiden also just stood there stoically, so I couldn't read his reaction, either.

"No, it wasn't." Allie leaned back against the cushions. "And I assume you guys want an explanation. You're entitled to one. But first, I think, we need to do something about mega-Bert, here."

"You know how to fix it?" the giant frog asked.

She nodded just as the doorbell rang. It was Doris, Harold, and Stanley, coming over to see what they could do to help. Of course, that meant Tobias couldn't be far away; Mia's mother lived just a few blocks away from Doris's house. As much as I was impatient to hear what Allie had to say and to get Bert fixed as soon as possible, I wasn't heartless enough to make Allie repeat herself over and over.

"We might as well wait for Mr. Andersen," I said, "and then we'll hear it all. You okay, Bert?"

He nodded, his own depression seemingly starting to lift. "It's my own dumb fault. I can hold out a bit longer if Allie says it won't hurt to wait."

"I don't think so," she said. "It's an easy fix."

I hoped she was right. She didn't seem all that worried about it. The living room was the only room really big enough to hold the gigantor-sized Bert, and as much as I liked having him around, I didn't want to spend the rest of my life with Bert hanging out in the living room taking up quite so much space. I'm sure he didn't really want to spend his life at a hundred times his normal size, either.

Doris hurried into the kitchen muttering something about some refreshments. I smiled. No matter what was going on, Doris would always worry about feeding someone. And we'd all eat well, no matter what she found. In fact, she'd probably loaded up her car on the way over.

The minute I thought it, I saw Harold and Stanley heading out to the car and bringing in pies. I went to the kitchen to offer to lend a hand. "I was baking when Aiden called," Doris explained before I'd even had a chance to ask. "I was just trying to get ahead for Thanksgiving and figured I'd bring them over instead."

I hugged her. "Thanks," I said. "I'll start the coffeepot again." I dumped out the dregs from the morning's brew and rinsed out the pot, the magical dangers hitting my emotions all over again. "Why does this stuff keep happening to us? Why can't we have a normal life? Why is it that no matter how much we do, no matter how far ahead we look, we can't seem to get through even a year without something magically hinky coming up, causing an issue, putting us in danger, or otherwise making us question our sanity?"

I just wanted to finish school and be a lawyer. What did I do to deserve this, and how could I fix it so I could have a normal life? I loved Aiden; maybe we'd like to get married someday and have babies, be a happy middle-class family, and go to soccer practices and drive carpools and attend PTA meetings—the kind of things I didn't get as a kid. I wanted to be happy and healthy with a mundane, but safe, life.

Or did I?

Doris was wise enough to shake her head and mutter something about life not choosing the less deserving to punish or choosing the worthy to lift up. I knew in my head she was right, but at some point, wasn't there a limit to what one person could expect? What one person could be expected to handle?

Wait a minute. *I* wasn't the one in the living room magically blown up to giant size, feeling like a fool in front of the person I loved,

waiting for everyone to show up and tell me again just how much I'd
screwed up. If there was one person who'd had it worse than me, it
was Bert. How many hundred years had he spent as a frog? I shook
my head.

It wasn't like I could hide from it. I had to keep going. There was
only one way through all of this, and it wasn't by burying my head in
the sand and pretending life was normal, or sane, or otherwise not
affected constantly by all the craziness that came from magic butting
its way, unwanted, into our lives and our home.

The coffeepot gurgled and boiled as I ruminated on all of this. It
wasn't fair. It wasn't right. I wanted my dad back. I wanted *him* here,
instead of Mia's dad. I wanted my mom here. I loved Doris, and she'd
filled a hole in my heart by acting as a surrogate mother for me, but I
wanted my own.

How selfish was that? I still didn't know Allie's story. I didn't
know what all she'd been through. It didn't matter how selfish it was,
though. It was how I felt. I swallowed it down and helped Doris slice
up a pie, waiting for Tobias to ring the doorbell. The things I wanted
were things I could not have. I could never have them, no matter how
unfair, no matter how much I wanted them, no matter if I deserved
them. I couldn't fix all the things that had gone wrong with my life,
my parents', my friends' lives, and everything else.

Aiden couldn't fix his own situation, at least not to exclude magic
from causing mayhem. Neither could Mia. Bert, well, he was hundreds
of years old. The people he missed were probably long dead and gone,
even if they'd had happy, productive, long-lived lives. He'd never
have a normal life, probably never get a girlfriend, no matter how
many dates he'd had before he'd been frog-ified.

And who knew what Allie would tell us.

The pie cut and ready, the coffee brewed, it was time to go back
and see what was going on in the living room. I noticed that Doris was
watching me closely as we silently headed back in. I hoped she didn't
have a clue about the direction of my inner monologue or my off-the-
cuff comments. Could the others understand why I felt so lost? The
life I always thought I'd have seemed like it was slipping through my
fingers, and it was because of magic. I'm sure they could understand

if I explained what I was thinking, but understanding wasn't going to fix anything, either.

Could I have the kind of normal, boring, bland, safe life I was longing for?

Not if I stayed in this house, where my stepmother had lived and killed my father.

Not if I stayed friends with Mia, who was rebuilding her relationship with the magical badass that was her father.

Not if Bert stayed with me.

Not if I stayed with Aiden. Magic and faerie court drama was part of who he was, and I didn't want to change him.

I'd have to give up everything that meant anything in my life and start over in attempt to get free of the constant worry about magic. Could I bring myself to do it? To cut ties with anything and everything and just leave? Right then, it was tempting. I wanted to just go to school, come home, study, and have the kind of cookie cutter life I saw in commercials. The ones with a car full of kids, a nice house, and my biggest worry being whether to put in stainless steel appliances or which preschool to send the kids to.

I can't lie. A part of me was tempted. Seriously tempted. I wondered if I went out, jumped in my car, and drove away whether they'd all deal with the drama and get on with their lives. My heart broke at the thought. I knew then I couldn't leave; I didn't want to know if Aiden could move on without me. And the truth was, running away would not make me, or any of the others, safer.

CHAPTER SIX

Doris and I carried in pie and mugs of coffee for the others as the doorbell rang. "Mia, do you want to get that?" I asked as I offered Harold a coffee. "It's probably Tobias."

I heard Mia answer it with a: "Hello, Dad."

They walked together into the living room, and I saw bruises on his jaw. "Been fighting?" I asked.

He smiled. "Yes. I didn't mean to, but it happened. Part of the job. Ooh, coffee," he said, gesturing for the tray in my hands without looking at the rest of the room. He didn't get far before he realized what was wrong with Bert. "Oh, wow," Tobias said as he stopped. "I must be under-caffeinated and overtired to have missed that one."

He did look tired—no, make that exhausted. Tobias looked like he'd gone ten rounds with a champion boxer and lost the fight. I could see that he was so weary, he had very little energy left in him for a new emergency. I'd imagine he'd have been about ready to keel over when we'd called, and I felt bad for keeping him from his sleep.

"Dad," Mia said, steering him to the chair. There was barely enough room for him to sit down, what with Bert taking up so much space, but he managed. I brought the tray close enough for him to snag a mug and waited for him to take a sip or two and let out a deep sigh before explaining why we'd called him.

"I've never seen anything like this," he said, looking at Bert.

Well, that was less than helpful. Doris, Harold, and Stanley echoed him.

Allie spoke up. "I said I know how to fix it."

Everyone turned to look at her.

She was slight of build, although Allie had put on a few needed pounds over the last few months of living with us and visiting Doris on occasion. Regular food and good nutrition had filled out her hollow cheeks and had given her a rosier look on her face than when we'd first met her, dirty and unwashed, living on the streets. The attention, however, caused her to blush and look down at her lap, hiding her face like a submissive waiting for permission to keep talking. I'd seen her do it before, but she'd stopped around those of us who lived in the house. She didn't stand up, she didn't look up, but she still did have the solution.

"Have him drink from the bottle with the 'drink me' label."

"That's it?" Bert asked.

"Yeah," she said. "It's a Wonderland potion. It would have shown up at about the same time as the donuts. They'll counteract each other."

"Are there side effects?" Tobias wanted to know.

"Shouldn't be," Allie said. "It might make him giggly for an hour or two, but that's about it."

Giggly I could handle. A semi truck-sized Bert vomiting on the carpet, not so much. I uncapped the bottle and tried to raise it to Bert's waiting mouth; it took a lot of maneuvering to get it done. Bert was barely able to raise a beer bottle in his normal frog size, but he didn't have any manual dexterity to manipulate the bottle to his mouth in the state he was in. I ended up sitting on Aiden's shoulders, pouring wine into Bert's mouth, while hoping Aiden could stand still and not fall while I was doing it. Somehow, we got enough into Bert, and he began to slowly shrink right before our eyes.

I could see the remnants of the shattered coffee table appearing under the shrinking frog, and I knew it was a loss. As he got small enough, Tobias reached over and picked Bert up to avoid him getting hurt on the glass and wood splinters fragmented all over the carpet. Doris went for the vacuum cleaner. Mia, Aiden, and I began picking up the larger pieces to put into the plastic garbage bags Harold and Stanley held for us.

Once we got the debris cleaned up and Bert straightened back around, it was time to ask a few more questions.

Allie had remained seated on the couch through the entire debacle without looking up or helping or otherwise pitching in. It was a bit annoying, but at the same time, there were a lot of people around, and I wondered just how bad the story would get.

The trash taken out, the carpet vacuumed of glass slivers, and pie passed around, there were no more excuses.

"Allie, how did you know about the wine bottle?" I asked. "How did you know it would cure Bert?"

"Because of my mom," she said. "She taught me how Wonderland works. I've had to deal with it all of my life because of her."

Things began clicking into place. "So the white rabbit this morning doesn't belong to Jimmy, does it?"

Mia piped up. "No, I went over and asked. His parents said he was banned from bringing in more pets at the moment. They denied getting him a rabbit."

"No," Allie concurred. "I wasn't surprised. I'm sure it wasn't the actual White Rabbit, but probably one of his underlings. He's looking for me. And I'm sure the donuts and wine were an attempt to scare me and get me to do something stupid so they'd be able to find me. It's happened before."

I knew Allie had lived on the street. I knew she'd done some terrible things for some men who'd taken advantage of her, and I knew she was scared of them. But the fear she'd exhibited in telling me what little she had wasn't anywhere near the level of horror displayed on her face at the moment.

I didn't push, but it did kind of annoy me that I'd invited her into the house without being told about whatever it was she was running from. Of course, I'd thought I was just protecting her from a street gang, as I hadn't heard her whole story. And what would I have done in her shoes? Would I have told? I didn't know, and probably wouldn't, until I knew everything.

Yet, did it matter now? She was here. Whatever danger she'd exposed us to wouldn't just go away if she did. We needed to know what we were dealing with.

"Okay, Allie," I said. "It's okay. If you're in trouble, we're here to help. What do we need to know to be safe? What kind of danger are we facing?"

She took a long, deep breath and raised her face to mine. I saw the same fear, but I also saw a bone-deep weariness in her face. I saw she had been beaten down, much deeper than I'd expected, so deep that it didn't seem like she had the resources to cry, even if she wanted to. She looked younger than her years, and yet older at the same time, small and vulnerable, yet wizened more than any teenager should be.

"My mom's name is Alice. She named me after herself. The story isn't fiction. It's all true. She fell down a rabbit hole and got stuck in Wonderland for years and years. She got out in time to meet my dad and get pregnant with me, but the White Rabbit's spy network found her and dragged her back in. I was born in Wonderland. She got me out, and I've been hiding from the Wonderland court ever since."

Wow. Didn't see that coming.

CHAPTER SEVEN

"I don't know how to begin, other than to say Reverend Charles Dodgson was a friend of my mom's family way back when," Allie started. "The story, however, wasn't a made-up one to amuse a friend's daughter. It was an excuse to use for why her friends didn't see her for months; she was always supposedly busy listening to his stories."

"It was even published under a pen name, Lewis Carroll. My mother cooperated with Dodgson to get the story on paper, and she warned him to use another name for his own safety and that of her family. The fact that her story was written down and shared, as well as profitable, is one of the crazier things I've heard, and if you knew my whole life story, you'd know it's an incredible scale to be on."

I thought of my own life. It certainly seemed unreal if I summed it up: my mother dead when I was a kid, my father married to a real-life evil faerie stepmother, his murder, and my own awakening to magic.

"Remember who you're talking to, Allie," I said. "We're not exactly strangers to the idea that life throws some really weird curveballs when you're talking about magic."

An unhinged little giggle erupted from Mia, and I saw Bert crack a smile. Yeah, it was exactly the right thing to say. Allie gave a wry grin and kept talking.

"As I said, my grandparents, who I never met, used Dodgson to tell people my mother wasn't available because she was engrossed in his tales. He told stories all the time when she was a kid. My mom and her sisters loved them. No one questioned it because the girls were known for begging him to tell a new story all the time. The truth was, she was missing.

"When my mom finally came back, she told Dodgson what was going on in Wonderland, and that's the story he published. He wrote it down and sold it; no one ever believed it was real. My mother wanted it to be written down and for him to publish it because she believed it would serve as some kind of warning for those who might be sucked into Wonderland. She wanted them to have knowledge of what to expect if they got stuck there."

"How old was she when she came back?" Mia asked.

"Seventeen," Allie answered. "She had been gone for six years according to the human world at that point, although it hadn't lasted as long in Wonderland. She came back older physically than she was mentally. She was home for about six months. Her parents consulted all kinds of physicians to explain why she was insisting on wild explanations for her true absence. Her parents thought she was crazy and wanted her to be treated.

"Of course, medicine being what it was at the time, I find it astounding that she survived the treatments and actually managed to get out of the house. She told me she met a boy, found out she was pregnant, and took off, trying to avoid more quack cures that could hurt me. And then the White Rabbit's team caught up with her, and she was sucked back in to Wonderland. She never came back.

"I was born in Wonderland. I don't have a birth certificate. So when she died and I escaped, there weren't a lot of options open to me. I didn't have a Social Security card. I didn't have a high school diploma. I couldn't get a job. Not even flipping burgers at McDonald's—not that I knew what McDonald's was at the time. I didn't know what a homeless shelter was. I didn't know how money worked here. I didn't know how to find soup kitchens, or anything else. I was not equipped to live in this world, yet I had to find a way to survive."

Wow, I thought. I had to give her a lot of credit for resourcefulness, in becoming as street smart as she was now. "How long have you been here?" I asked.

"A year and half before I met you," was the answer. She had been gazing down at her scuffed tennis shoes and didn't look up when she said it. "I was so naïve. I had no idea what those boys wanted when they offered me food, clothing, and a clean place to sleep."

No wonder she'd been so wary of Aiden when she'd shown up at my house. She'd seen me as someone safe because I was a woman, but the idea of accepting anything from a man had to have been hard for her. She'd gotten better and better about being around Aiden, realizing he was not a danger to her, but I understood now the level of fear she'd had.

"Did they give you food and clothes and shelter?" I asked.

"Sort of. They gave me a dirty mattress in a corner, some dirty clothes, and I got food when they remembered to give it to me. Then they sent me out to find customers. I had to bring the customers back to service them on the very same mattress they gave me to sleep on."

I winced.

Tobias shook his head. I wondered what he was thinking, as the absentee father of a girl who could have ended up in a similar situation. Thank goodness she hadn't. He cleared his throat. "Did you learn how to find things on your own?" he asked.

"Eventually, I learned where the soup kitchen was, and the homeless shelter, but if I went there and tried to stay the night, the boys would come and drag me away. I learned where I could beg without a panhandler's license. I learned where I could sleep away from them and out of the weather.

"I learned where I could earn a few bucks washing dishes or doing yard work if I needed something. I learned to squirrel away a few dollars and found ways of hiding it to prevent them from taking it from me. No matter where I went, the boys kept finding me and dragging me back, so I started looking for places farther away to get a good night's sleep. That's when you found me."

And when the Seawitch had found her as well, stealing Allie's voice to try to get her to sacrifice us. She refused, and it saved our lives. I hadn't thought about how much inner strength it must have taken for Allie to fend off one more threat, one more reason for her to give up. I wondered how I'd have reacted, and then I realized that even though she was so submissive in so many ways, she didn't seem to know how to do anything except to keep going and not give up.

Allie kept talking, faster now. "When I realized what you guys were dealing with, I was terrified. I thought for sure the White Rabbit's network would use your faerie court connections to find me, but then I realized you had nothing to do with it. You had the house warded from magic and experience fighting it. It was probably the safest place to be, and you offered to help."

Doris sat down beside her and put her arm around her shoulders. "You've been incredibly brave, and you have nothing to fear from us."

I nodded my head and saw the others all doing the same. No matter what misgivings I might have due to my own mental meanderings, I would not ever endanger the others. Then I realized I couldn't just walk away from them, either, because that *would* endanger them. I couldn't imagine being without any of them, whether it was Bert and his morose moping, Mia and her father and their attempts to re-establish a relationship, Doris and her pies, Stanley and his conspiracies with Harold to rein him in, or Aiden.

Just Aiden. With all his foibles and his lack of coordination, his cute smile, the way his eyes met mine just then as he nodded back at me. I realized I could not live without him. I knew I'd made a decision; I couldn't walk away, no matter how unfair it seemed my life had been taken over by magic. Allie had endured way more than I'd had to. I couldn't walk away if I could help, and I had no reason to complain in comparison to what she'd gone through.

"So, Allie, what do the donuts and the wine bottle mean?" I asked. The others seemed to be sitting there, letting her story soak in, and hadn't quite reacted yet. I needed to know the practical impact. What did we need to do to protect ourselves?

"I don't know."

"What do you mean, you don't know?" Tobias asked. "Haven't you ever seen anything like this before?"

She shook her head. "I've heard my mother talk about such things, but I've never really stayed the night in the same place for more than a week before. I've never seen it in this world. But I don't know if it's because the White Rabbit's spies never found me, or if it's something else from Wonderland looking for me. There's no way for me to know. I can only assume they've found me. And so, maybe I should move on."

There was no way I was going to let her do that.

CHAPTER EIGHT

Allie started for the stairs without looking anyone in the eyes. I let her go, knowing we'd see her if she came back down and headed for the doors. We could give her a break, a minute or two to compose herself after having to recite such a horrible history to us. I parked myself in the chair facing the stairs so I could both hear her footsteps and see her if she tried to slip out. I know, if it were me, I'd be thinking about sneaking away if I thought it meant saving the others. Heck, I'd thought about leaving altogether just an hour before.

Tobias cleared his throat loudly when Allie was out of the room. "I think there's even more there. I'm not sure she even knows it all."

"What do you mean?" Aiden asked.

"There were bite marks on the back fence," he said, pulling out his cell phone to show us pictures.

"How do you know it's not the neighbor's dog?" Mia asked.

"What kind of dog do they have?" he asked.

"Cocker spaniel," I said, "A little one. Probably eight months old, stands about this high." I motioned with my hand to a height a few inches below my knee.

"No way were these made by a cocker spaniel," Tobias said. "If those are teeth, then the mouth was at least as high as my chest, and deep enough that whatever made them had some leverage behind them when they bit down. They look deep enough to come from an African lion, rather than from a small domestic dog. That cocker spaniel would have to learn how to jump twice its normal ability as well as taking growth hormones strong enough to kill an elephant."

I looked closer at the picture, and though it wasn't a very clear, I could see exactly what he was talking about. It was the back fence, about twenty yards from the garage, not far from where Aiden had been set up earlier in the morning with his sword.

"Does it look like something trying to get through the fence? I don't see any breaks in the wood." I felt a cold shiver run up the back of my neck at how close Aiden had been to whatever it was trying to get through the fence. Would he have been able to defend himself? Would the sword have done whatever it was he was hoping it would?

"No, the fence looks intact in the picture. Maybe we should go check it out," Aiden said.

Tobias raised his hand. "It was still intact when I took the picture. Even if it isn't, we're all inside. I think we all learned last summer just how strong this threshold is, and we're safer inside until we figure out the next step." He was referring to the Seawitch's assault on the house last year, trying to get at Tobias and Mia, and he was right. However, we had an escape hatch in the basement last year in the form of the portal, which no longer existed. We'd gotten help through it, and who knows just how long the threshold would have stood if we hadn't been able to get help?

Bert spoke up. "That doesn't look like any tooth mark from any normal, non-magical animal I've heard of."

"What do you mean?" Aiden asked.

"It's forked."

On closer inspection, I noticed he was right. I could see indents in the individual teeth marks, showing there were either two points on each tooth, or the creature, whatever it was, had bitten the fence more than once in the exact same spot. I don't know what that meant, but I wasn't sure it mattered. The important part wasn't cataloguing the thing like a biology specimen—and I didn't like either scenario I came up with—but to figure out a plan.

"So what do we do?" I asked. "We can't just sit here and do nothing. What should we do?"

No one got a chance to answer me because that was when we heard an angry, animalistic roar coming from outside. It shook the windows and rattled the glass, so loud and permeating was its shriek. Everyone jumped up, running for the kitchen, with its glass sliding doors and clear view of the backyard.

"What the hell is that?" Mia exclaimed.

"I don't have a damn clue," replied her father, quite possibly the most knowledgeable amongst us when talking about faerie magic and the courts, the bad guys who could attack, and all the creepy crawlies that could come out of the woodwork. If he didn't know what it was, it was definitely time to be scared.

The thing outside howled again. What must the neighbors be thinking?

It didn't come anywhere near the house. It sat in the backyard, snarling and swiping at the garage, but the salt and iron circle Aiden had laid into the ground did exactly what it was supposed to do. It held off the swiping claws of whatever was sitting in our backyard.

And speaking of the thing the claws belonged to, I couldn't tell anyone what type of animal, vegetable, or mineral was crushing the rosebushes in the flowerbeds at the back end of the yard. It had the body of a dragon, a whiskered face that reminded me of a catfish, antennae on its head, and talon-like nails on its arms and its wings. The thing was even wearing a vest, although it appeared to be made of tweed. It looked like something I'd seen before, but I couldn't figure out where. I had an idea, though, and I was going to look.

"Is the threshold solid?" I asked Aiden, whirling away from the door.

He nodded.

I ran for the library, which held all of my father's books and bits and bobs related to his research on folk and fairy tales. Or at least those items my stepmother had not thought to throw away when she'd been in charge of the house. I was betting Evangeline didn't know what this thing was either and so had left the books and such I was now looking for.

I was right.

I slid into the library, Aiden close on my heels. I grabbed two slim books from the bookshelf and tossed them into his arms as I headed for the small framed paintings and drawings my father had collected but had never taken the time to hang. I gave a small yip of excitement as I found the one I wanted and pulled it out, motioning to Aiden to follow me back into the kitchen.

The others still stood watching the thing swiping repeatedly at the garage and yowling every time it did so. I took that as a good sign there wasn't any progress at damaging the garage, a sign we had time to try to figure out what we were doing. Time to see if I was right, if we were dealing with something out of the childhood stories my father had read to me, the same story Allie claimed to be the true story of her mother's life and abduction.

I had grabbed a copy of Alice in Wonderland and a copy of Through the Looking Glass. The framed drawing? It was one of the Jabberwocky done by Sir John Tenniel. I saw the name right there, on the bottom right-hand corner of the drawing. I laid them out on the kitchen table for the others to see as well. They crowded around, each looking at the drawing and then back out to the thing in the yard.

It was an exact match, as if Tenniel himself had been sitting in the kitchen and drawing from the life-sized thing in front of us.

"I'll be damned," Tobias said. "It's real."

CHAPTER NINE

"**O**kay, so that's all well and good," Doris said. "We know what it is. But what are we supposed to do about it?"

Good question.

"The poem says it was slain with a vorpal sword," Aiden spoke up, "and I think I've got one."

Everyone started talking at once. Doris was asking how he knew it was vorpal. I began clamoring that Aiden himself had no business wielding the sword in the mortal world because he'd slice his own foot off and I liked him with two feet. Tobias began yelling that he, himself, should take the sword and go out into the yard, and Mia began to shriek that it was too dangerous and he wasn't experienced with that kind of beast. Harold and Stanley began arguing about which one of them should sacrifice himself for the good of the group.

Bert didn't join in. Instead, he found a way to cut through the din with an ear-splitting whistle. When we all shut up and looked at him, he had a simple question. "Does anyone know where Allie went?"

"Went? What do you mean? She went upstairs," I said, not completely sure, because I'd meant to watch for her and had gotten distracted by the beast in the backyard. I had a sinking feeling as to what Bert was about to say.

"She slipped out the front door," he said. "She's out there, and for all we know, the Jabberwocky is after her on behalf of whatever it is in Wonderland that is after her. You know, she told us she was hiding from the White Rabbit and his spies, but she didn't tell us if there was someone the White Rabbit was working for. And the Jabberwocky showing up like this? I've never heard of anything like that, and I've been alive for four hundred years. There's far more to the story than she's told us."

He was right. I ran through the house to the front door, hoping to catch her before she'd gone too far, but she was nowhere in sight. I had no idea if she'd taken anything with her, but I hoped she had. I was going to go looking for her, but with all the weird happenings lately, I wanted to be prepared for, well, anything.

Aiden was right behind me. "We'll find her. And we'll protect her. You know we will."

"It's not just whatever she's running from in Wonderland. It's also those guys she talked about. She never really gave us their names. We don't have any way to call the police to look for them, or any direction to start looking in ourselves."

"She said she'd go to the shelters."

"But she also said she never stayed because they found her there."

"True," he said. "But that doesn't mean we won't find her. We've got an idea of what she looks for in a place to crash."

"What, are we going to hit all the patios and backyards in Oakwood? How about the other Dayton suburbs? There's no way we can do that!" I exclaimed as I heard Mia calling from the kitchen. We headed toward her, coming into the room to find all of them looking out the window once again. The creature was gone.

"Where did it go?" I asked. "Who fought it, and how did it disappear?" I guess I hadn't thought about how we'd handle that size of body in the yard if someone did fight and defeat the jabberwocky, but the property wasn't big enough to dig a sizeable hole to bury it in without a backhoe and some seriously curious neighbors. I was happy the creature seemed to have disappeared, but the lack of body convinced me it wasn't dead.

"No one fought it," Bert said. "I saw Allie slip behind it and disappear by the fence. The Jabberwocky looked around, but I don't think it saw her. It sniffed the air a couple of times, stopped swiping at the garage, and then it disappeared on its own. No one went outside. No one touched it. I think she may have gone into a different realm."

Huh? Did we seriously have another portal, or whatever she might have used, right on the property, that existed without our knowledge? How had Aiden missed it? Or Tobias, come to think of it? The two of them walked the property line on a regular basis, looking for any magical shenanigans and marks and other signs anything magical had tried to step foot on the lawn or to test the threshold. Nothing had ever been found.

Aiden and Tobias must have been thinking the same thing,

because they went outside, with Bert guiding them from Tobias's hands, pointing out where Allie had disappeared. I followed close behind them while Mia stayed with Doris, Harold, and Stanley, digging though the books for any hint or clue as to what we needed to know if we were going to look for Allie.

The only thing anyone found was a small hole near the fence, likely made by a gopher, groundhog, mole, or rabbit, and we only found it because Aiden nearly stepped in it. Bert was adamant that was where she'd disappeared.

Down the rabbit hole. Just like the book.

And I was going to go after her. I didn't say a word, but I didn't have to. Tobias did.

"We need to try to be prepared for this. Going through something like this blind isn't a good idea. And we need to be ready for anything. Do you have backpacks?"

I nodded, knowing Mia and I both had our school bags, and Aiden had the one he used for hauling research materials back and forth to F.A.B.L.E.S. meetings. Many of their research materials had made their way to my house, as Aiden had moved in and the group had begun meeting at the house rather than the warehouse where they'd met for so long.

We headed back in. I also found an old Hello Kitty backpack from junior high, which was still serviceable and free of holes. Aiden began sifting through research materials to determine what, if anything, we'd need to take along. Doris hit the pantry, warning us we wouldn't want to eat much of anything found in Wonderland. If what had happened to Bert was any indication, and if I remembered the story correctly, she was right.

Tobias put himself in charge of weapons and had a brief argument with Aiden about who would carry the vorpal sword. I was about to intervene and suggest letting Tobias carry it when the doorbell rang. I let them argue as I went to answer it.

It was Jonah, Mia's boyfriend. I'd forgotten he had wanted my help in surprising Mia with a picnic lunch today. He'd asked me weeks before, and I'd said I'd help surprise her, but it had completely slipped my mind. I swore under my breath, but he took it in stride, coming in with a picnic basket and a backpack, dropping them on the floor.

"Magical shenanigans? How can I help?"

Thank goodness he was so cool about it, but then again, he'd been in the loop last summer with the Seawitch debacle. I didn't really know what he'd thought about it all, but I'd heard long, impassioned discussions of the matter through the walls with Mia and Jonah hashing out what had happened with Bert, with the Seawitch, and with Mia's father. He didn't ask a lot of questions, just offered help, and that meant a heck of a lot.

I nodded. "Help me solve a dispute between Tobias and Aiden about weapons, and then maybe you can come up with more ideas of what craziness might come next in our lives. Another mind applied to the situation might get us adequately prepared."

"Prepared for what?" he asked.

"Wonderland."

CHAPTER TEN

Jonah came inside with his picnic basket and backpack and instantly settled the sword question. "It's not a question of who gets to use it. It's a question of who carries it. Tobias is used to carrying weapons. Aiden's clumsy until he gets into the faerie realm, and there's no guarantee the clumsiness goes away in Wonderland like it does in the magical realms he knows. It's a world of magic we're very ignorant about. That's not a slander on any person's ability; it's a practical concern." Even Aiden had to pipe down about it.

Doris raided the pantry and began packing cans and boxes of soup, beans, Ramen noodles, granola bars, Pop-Tarts, and crackers into the Hello Kitty backpack, as if she was planning to go with us. I thought about arguing, but her practical skills could come in handy in an unknown world. Who knew where we might end up or what we'd have to do? And this gave her a chance to spend more time with her son. Plus, I'd have never thought about all the non-perishables.

Jonah also dumped out his backpack. He had a thermos inside, which was filled with iced tea for their picnic. He found another thermos in my pantry and began brewing coffee to fill the second one. Stanley and Harold scoured the kitchen and pantry for water bottles from the gym to fill with water. Mia and I went upstairs with our backpacks to toss in an extra handful of t-shirts and pair of jeans or two. Who knew how long we might be gone or what we might need?

When we came back down, I found Aiden in the bathroom raiding the first aid supplies. With him living there, we'd accumulated quite a collection of gauze, band-aids, antibiotic ointment, tape, and other odds and ends.

"You okay?" I asked.

"I'm fine." Something in the tone of his voice, however, was very un-fine.

"No, you're not. Give me credit for knowing you that well, at least." I closed the door behind me, leaning against it as he crammed stuff in his bag.

He looked up at me, and I saw he was angry. We didn't necessarily have time for an argument, but there was no way I was going to let him go with me down the rabbit hole without getting whatever was chapping his butt into the open.

"Who appointed you my protector, Janie? Who gave you the power to decide that poor little Aiden couldn't handle himself, or weapons, without hurting himself? Who gave you the belief you could consign me to the sidelines with nothing to do except look things up in dusty books?"

Hooboy. That one had been building up for a while. He kept ranting and raving at me, yelling about how I was overprotective and I wasn't his mom, I wasn't his dad, and I certainly wasn't his babysitter.

"You want to know who gave me that power?" I asked quietly.

"You damn well know it!"

"You did."

"What?"

"You miserable fool, you did. You made me fall in love with you when I would have kept my heart to myself. You gave me someone to care for. You, and your mom, gave me what I haven't really had for years: a family. You think I'm going to let that go without a fight? If you think so, then you really don't know me well. I'm a fighter once I settle my mind on what I want. And I want you."

I reached up to cup his cheek in my hand and smiled a small, tender smile at him. "I want you alive, and holding my hand, and telling me about vorpal swords and jabberwockies. I want you whole and in front of me, hugging me and telling me it's going to be all right. I want you in one piece, protecting my house and my friends, and I want you to be the one I fall asleep with every night and wake up next to every morning."

I must have taken the wind out of his sails, because his shoulders slumped. "I love you, too, Janie. But I'm not fragile; I accept the thought that I might get hurt. I can't just sit on my hands while you sail into dangerous territory. I have to protect you. I have to help, because I need you with me, too."

I sighed. "I think we both have to remember that. It kills me to think of you getting hurt, but I know I can't automatically exclude you. You're right. I'm trying to protect you too much."

He nodded and drew me into his arms for big, enveloping hug. "We have to keep talking. We can't just assume anything. I know you want me safe. And I know you're not ready for anything more serious than what we are doing right now, but I want more. I want you to think about it. We love each other. We live together. Heck, we sleep together. It's not enough. I want a permanent commitment from you."

I gulped. I knew he'd propose sooner or later, as long as we stayed together and kept our relationship going in the direction it was going, but I also knew I didn't want it to happen in the guest bathroom while we were about to go into harm's way. I didn't know what my response would be—as he'd said, I wasn't ready for it. I had too much else on my plate.

I nodded. "Can we talk later?"

He frowned and then kissed my forehead. "As long as later means we'll actually talk about it, as opposed to saying we'll talk and the conversation never happens."

I leaned back in his arms and stood on my tiptoes to kiss him, my hand going around his neck and my eyes closing as I felt his lips against mine. I was glad he hadn't read my mind earlier when I was considering walking away from everyone to keep them all safe. Of course he was the biggest reason I couldn't do it, but to go from wondering about that to talking about marriage? I wasn't ready, and he knew me well; he was holding himself back from proposing right that second. He wanted a family, and I did too, but there was just too much going on to consider it at the moment.

"Janie, I want you to know something." He pulled away.

"What's that?"

"If something happens to me, I want you to know there's a letter in my dresser upstairs. Two, actually. There's one for my mother, and there's one for you. Don't look for them unless something happens to me, but I want you to know they're there."

I couldn't say anything. What would I say? I had nothing. I hadn't planned anything like that, and even if I had thought about it, the idea of putting pen to paper and writing anything for someone to read in the event of my demise was more than I could bear. I didn't think I'd ever be able to do it. What in the world did it say? How long had he been thinking about it? What had gotten him thinking of it? How long ago had he written it?

I nodded. "I'll take care of it."

He squeezed my hand. "Let's go see if the others are ready to go."

We left the bathroom, hand in hand.

CHAPTER ELEVEN

We got back to the kitchen to find Jonah, Mia, Doris, and Tobias slinging on backpacks to go with us. Tobias had the vorpal sword strapped to his back, under his pack, with the hilt sticking up behind his head. Mia had dug up some sleeping bags to take along in case we had to spend the night, and those were strapped to the backpacks, as well, with belts and bungee cords and, in one case, an old jump rope from the garage.

We'd certainly be a colorful bunch. My old Smurfs sleeping bag and the lavender unicorn one I graduated to when the Smurfs one wasn't cool enough had been strapped to Jonah's and Tobias's backs, respectively. Mia had her own green sleeping bag tied to her back, and Jonah handed me the blanket he'd brought along for the picnic he'd tried to set up for him and Mia. It was red and black checked, and I tied it to my own backpack.

Tobias handed us each a small weapon. "It's a risk to take iron of any kind into faerie, because it's one of the most dangerous metals to them. It's like smuggling a nuclear weapon into the US. Don't take it lightly. We don't know what the rules will be in Wonderland. I saw no indication that iron would be lethal there, but I also can't abide us being unprepared. We need to be sure we know what we're risking. I won't argue with anyone who believes it too dangerous to carry, but I also believe it's too dangerous not to be armed in some way."

He had a pistol in his own jacket pocket, as well as the sword, and passed out weapons that were easily concealed in pockets and waistbands. Mostly, these were hand tools; knives, screwdrivers, a heavy wrench. I had the same screwdriver I'd stabbed my stepmother with a year ago. It felt heavy, a reminder of what I'd done weighing it down in my hand.

Harold and Stanley had run to the store down the road while we were getting prepared, and they handed each of us a cylinder of Morton's table salt. "The same thing," Harold said. "We're not going.

Too many people will make your trip dangerous. We'll stay behind and watch your back. We're too old to be of much help if the magic of faerie doesn't exist there."

Magic in faerie realms generally took away their aches and pains from age and arthritis. If they were going to be slowed down by rheumatism and gout and dodgy hips and trick knees that kept them from doing all the things they wanted to do in the mortal realm, it made sense they didn't want to risk it in a realm they didn't know. And I could think of a whole lot worse people to be guarding our backs.

Stanley handed me a camera—an old, non-digital 35mm SLR model. I'd once been very interested in photography, but it had been a while since I'd had to work with one without any digital readings or automation. "Take pictures," he said. "We have no research on that realm. It might be important. And it would help if we could prove my theory."

Oh, God. What in the world could his theory be? I didn't ask. For all I knew, he'd believe Barack Obama and Elvis had cooked up a conspiracy involving the Oak Ridge Boys and Madonna to suck us all into a magic portal to gain some kind of weird mind control over the mortal realm with secret funding through the CIA. There was no arguing with him, though, and telling him no wasn't going to work. I took the camera and stuffed it into the top of my backpack before strapping the whole thing onto my back.

Stanley looked disappointed, as if he'd wanted me to ask about his theory, but I knew we'd never get out of there if I did, so I just kissed the top of his balding head and told him and Harold goodbye.

The others were already out the door and heading toward the rabbit hole. I saw Tobias disappear by putting one foot in it, and Mia followed suit with Doris behind her. Aiden and Jonah were waiting for me to catch up.

"What have I gotten myself into?" Jonah asked as he followed their lead.

Aiden leaned over and kissed my cheek. "For luck," he said and then stepped into the rabbit hole.

I took a deep breath, closed my eyes, and stepped forward. *What a leap of faith,* I thought, and then I opened my eyes. It was a true leap, as I was falling down a hole with no visible bottom. I saw bookshelves on the sides of the wall, but there was nothing to grab hold of, nothing to help slow my fall, and nothing I could do. I could see the others several feet below me, and I didn't see anything that could help them, either.

It seemed an eternity we fell, and I still couldn't see the bottom of the hole. I wondered how we'd get back out. If we scaled the bookshelves, it would be an awfully long climb, and we didn't exactly bring climbing gear. I didn't even think of it.

Eventually, I saw that a fluffy cloud had appeared below us. We fell through the foggy puffs, one by one. I couldn't see the others as they were enveloped by the mist, but I did see them after I passed through it. We landed on a crinkly, but fairly soft mass. It turned out to be a giant pile of dead leaves and sticks, as if someone had raked the largest yard on earth into a huge heap that stood nearly as high as the roof of my house in Dayton.

We were safe. And we were, supposedly, in Wonderland.

I slid down the pile of leaves to join the others, and there was a ton of tension in the air. Mia had her arms crossed over her chest with a sour expression on her face, arguing with her father. Tobias looked exasperated and was only half-heartedly arguing back. Aiden and Jonah, however, were laughing, and Doris . . . well, Doris was giving them all a very sheepish look.

"What's going on?" I asked.

"Well, he didn't want to be left behind. Said he needed to help make up for his own stupidity," she said, shrugging.

"You should have told him no," Mia said. "He needs to learn boundaries. He keeps getting himself in trouble because he doesn't know when to stop. Just look at what happened this morning. It's all because he decided he knew best. He decided what he wanted and be damned to everyone else. It's just because he didn't think he'd get his way. He's going to be nothing but a nuisance, and he's going to get us into trouble. Never mind what anyone here might think of him; they might find it an insult he's even here."

Oh, crap. Only one frog would do that. I looked at Doris's backpack sitting on the ground in front of her, and sure enough, the little brat was looking out of the top of the bag, balanced carefully on several packages of Ramen noodles and cans of soup.

"Bert, why didn't you just ask if you could come?" The reality was, even with Mia's rant, which was more than justified, I'd have asked him to come. I just hadn't thought about it, what with shoveling emotional baggage with Aiden before we left, but I was glad he was here.

"I didn't think you'd say yes." He stuck his lower lip out, like a two-year-old pouting over a lost argument or a dispute over a favorite toy.

"Well, you thought wrong," I said and then turned to the others with a sigh. "Bert's helped us in a lot of ways. And without him getting into the donuts and wine, I'm not sure we'd have gotten the entire explanation out of Allie. I've got a funny feeling she would have bolted, rather than tell us the truth, if she could have. Yeah, he's been acting like a spoiled brat, but he deserves a chance to redeem himself. And he's Allie's friend, too. We don't have a monopoly on that."

I could tell Mia didn't like the explanation, but the two of them had been very chilly toward each other since she'd learned Bert had fallen for her and was nursing a broken heart because she'd chosen Jonah. Even so, she nodded. "Fine. I reserve the right to say I told you so if he screws us."

I nodded. "So lead on. Who's got an idea of where we might go to find Allie?"

We all stared at each other. Apparently, no one had a clue.

CHAPTER TWELVE

W ow, were we dumb.

We'd packed clothes and weapons and food and water and blankets and other items, but we hadn't thought about a map. Luckily, we had brought the books.

Aiden skimmed through the first book, but said it was fairly skimpy on directions. "I see here there's the court of the Queen of Hearts. There's the Mad Hatter's Tea Party and the Tulgey Wood where the Jabberwocky is supposed to live, but the story doesn't seem to lend itself to a solid map."

"Because there is no map of Wonderland," said a voice I did not recognize.

"I'm sorry?" I didn't see anyone else. I took a few steps away from the leaf-pile and the group. I turned toward where I thought the voice had come from and saw a cloud of smoke. Behind the colored smog, I saw a giant caterpillar sitting on a mushroom as large as the couch in my living room.

"The Queen has decreed that no one shall map the land, and anyone who tries to do so will have their head removed," the caterpillar said before drawing more smoke from the mouth pipe of a large hookah. I'd never seen a hookah like that before outside of Hollywood movies, and the caterpillar was something that made Mega-Bert look small. He was almost as tall as I was and reminded me of Jabba the Hutt with the addition of a lot of legs.

I guess I should be polite, I thought to myself. *I wouldn't want to be forced into the gold bikini.* And I certainly wouldn't want Aiden to be frozen in carbonite or Bert fed to a sarlacc in a desert.

"So how do people know which way to go when they arrive in Wonderland?" Aiden asked.

"We don't get many visitors here, and we don't get many people asking directions. That's also an order of the Queen. We're supposed to report visitors to her."

A cold chill ran up my spine. "Supposed to? Does this mean you're going to tell her we are here?"

"That depends on you," the caterpillar said. "You see, there used to be more people who came to Wonderland, and more people who left. It wasn't unusual for visitors to Come and Go all the time, but the Queen put a stop to it because she felt it was hurting our lands. That being said, there are those here who sorely miss having visitors, despite her edict. There are those here who are unable to leave and go home because she had decreed it so. So I ask you, what is your purpose in visiting Wonderland?"

They all turned to me. I swallowed hard. Yeah, I had been the one to find a true path through the legal and diplomatic maze my stepmother had laid in front of me, but I was so not an expert. "We are here looking for a friend who has spent time in Wonderland in the past. She left some time ago, and she believed the White Rabbit was looking for her. We're here to find her and offer her our help."

"Are you planning to stay long?" he asked, taking in our backpacks and supplies.

"Only as long as it takes us to find her and give what help she needs, what help she asks for, or what help we are able to give." I'd learned about giving myself an out when negotiating with magical beings in the past. I didn't want to commit us to something we couldn't do, so I'd used the word "or." Even in a legal argument, a single word could be powerful, connoting a choice as opposed to a list of requirements or components.

He cocked his head as he considered my answer. "Clever, you are. And yet, you are here when you should not be. Who is the friend you are here to offer your help to?"

I looked at Tobias, who nodded. "She called herself Allie. I do not know if she has another name here in Wonderland."

I'd never seen a caterpillar look shocked before. "She's here? How did I miss her?"

"I don't know. She slipped past us and used the same Rabbit Hole we came through not long before we did." I estimated our delay as about half an hour and gave him our timeline. "I don't know if time works the same here or not. I only know the relation of how it was before we left, in our realm. We took time to prepare, and then we came."

He laughed softly. "How does one prepare for Wonderland? There is really no way to know what you might run into."

"That is very true, but at the same time, we wanted to be able to try. We didn't want to incur any debts of anyone here if we didn't have to, and we wanted to be able to hurry to Allie if we could. We read what we could and packed what we could carry."

"Smart girl," he said. "I did not see her pass this way, but if she is familiar with Wonderland, she would know how to scurry off without my noticing. I do so get distracted when it's lunchtime or when I need to refill my pipe. From what you tell me, it sounds as if your friend is very familiar with Wonderland, as well as very famous here. You might not be familiar with Wonderland, but it sounds like you are wise about visiting other realms.

"And you are right to worry about your friend. I cannot explain why, but she may be facing some serious risks by coming back to this world. She has been a friend of mine in the past, but I have not seen her in some time. She knows of the rules in Wonderland, and I have no doubt you will be unable to find her without help."

"Will you help us?" Doris asked, her eyes filled with hope.

"That's more than I can do. I cannot help with what I do not know. You may find others who are better able to assist than I. However, the Queen's edict about reporting visitors does not specify when or how she is to be informed of those visitors. It will take me three days to travel to her court, as I am a caterpillar who does not travel much these days. She does not specify I must send a runner, or otherwise speedily deliver the message. You have three days to find your friend and get her to leave, or report to the Queen."

I thought he was being incredibly fair, but I wondered if I was missing something. "Is there a catch?" Were we going to get burned down the road by some unspoken caveat, codicil, or clause to his promise we weren't aware of?

"No catch, but if the Queen crosses my path and asks me directly about visitors, I cannot lie to her. I'm not going to risk myself when I don't know you."

"Understood." I turned, and the others were nodding. It did seem fair. What else could we ask for? "Do you have any suggestions for where you think she might have gone? Any ideas of what direction she might take that would keep her from those who might turn her in? And do you know what she's hiding from?"

The caterpillar eyed me cautiously as he took another drag from his hookah. "I assume she ran away from me, but you could have figured it out for yourself. And I assume she's hiding from the Queen, who I know wants her presence, but you'd have to ask the Queen yourself as to why. No one knows the whole story, and I'd rather not guess."

"Is there anything you can tell us?" Jonah asked. "Anything you can help us with? Whatever information you can provide would be appreciated."

I wouldn't have asked, but he did. I wondered what the price would be, but I didn't say anything.

The caterpillar considered the request. "If you take a piece from the right side of the mushroom I'm sitting on, it can make you taller. If you take a piece from the left side, it will make you shorter. The mushroom regenerates, so there's no reason not to take it."

"What do you want from us in return?" I asked. I didn't turn around, but I could almost read Aiden, Doris, Tobias, Mia, and Bert's minds. They were all wondering the same thing. I didn't need magical powers to know what they were thinking.

"No. I want nothing. It gives me a break from sitting on this mushroom and gives me a reason to have it pruned. The Queen will get the message that we have visitors in due time, and I owe your friend a debt of gratitude I cannot repay. There is no price." The caterpillar slid down off the mushroom and headed away.

I blinked. I wasn't used to such gratitude and freely given help related to magic, but I'd take it. I asked Doris if she had any napkins in her backpack, and she did. I broke off a bread loaf-sized piece from the right side, wrapped it up, and gave it to Jonah for his bag and then did the same on the left side to give to Mia. "Don't forget which came from which side, guys. We don't want to waste it."

They nodded solemnly and packed away their mushroom pieces.

And then we all turned around and headed away from the mushroom, in the opposite direction the caterpillar had gone. Hopefully we were on our way toward Allie and not into the path of whatever it was she was hiding from.

CHAPTER THIRTEEN

W e walked for a couple of hours without saying much of anything to each other. What was there to say? We had jumped into a magical realm with about half of the story. We still didn't know what was going on, but at least with the help of the caterpillar, we had a better idea of what kind of rules the Queen had about visitors.

I was wondering about how to even start looking for Allie. If she was hiding, then she wouldn't be talking to people or staying in public accommodations, whatever those might be. We'd have to be very careful because it was already quite clear we didn't know what we were doing in this world.

I heard the sounds of horses on the path we were following, and I motioned for the others to hide in the woods beside the trail. We jumped out of the way just in time; a heavily ornate carriage decorated in large red hearts sped down the path. Aiden and I were hidden behind the same tree as we watched it barrel past.

"Is that what and who I think it is?" he whispered.

"Shhhhh," I hissed. "Watch where it goes."

We watched, but the carriage did not slow down. We waited several minutes to make sure it had time to get well past us before we popped out of the woods. Jonah had leaves in his hair, and Mia looked flushed. They must have been kissing.

Good for them. Their romantic afternoon might not be what Jonah had planned, but at least they were getting some romance in their lives. I wanted the best for my friend. Even though Bert wasn't happy at Mia being with Jonah, I liked him, and he made her happy. Tobias cleared his throat and looked away. I bet it was uncomfortable for him to think of his daughter being old enough to be in an adult relationship when he was absent for so much of her childhood. They'd argued quite a bit lately about him treating her like the little girl she had been when he'd left.

I heard singing coming from farther inside the woods and motioned for the others to follow me. The others treaded forward, taking great pains not to make noise on the fallen sticks and dry leaves. I'm not sure they were all that successful, but the singers didn't notice. Or at least they didn't hesitate in their song even once.

They were singing something old, something I'd heard somewhere before. Where had I heard it? History class. In high school.

Yes, we'll rally round the flag, boys,
We'll rally once again,
Shouting the battle cry of Freedom,
We'll rally round the flag, boys, rally once again,
Shouting the battle cry of freedom!

Seriously? I remembered this vaguely from watching movies about Abraham Lincoln, not about the faerie lands. What was going on? We inched closer to the noise until we heard another voice, higher, but still strong and passionate.

The Union forever! Hurrah, boys, hurrah!
Down with the traitors, up with the stars;
While we rally round the flag, boys, rally once again,
Shouting the battle cry of freedom!

A third voice, deep and resonant, cut in to add another verse.

Our Dixie forever! She's never at a loss!
Down with the eagle and up with the cross
We'll rally 'round the bonny flag, we'll rally once again
Shout, shout the battle cry of Freedom!

A fourth voice added a tenor to the din.

Would you have mansions of gold in the sky,
And live in a shack, way in the back?
Would you have wings up in heaven to fly,
And starve here with rags on your back?

"What the hell?" I mouthed to Aiden.

He shook his head and shrugged. I guess we were all out of our comfort zones. As I inched closer, I noticed all four voices belonged to birds. In fact, birds I'd never seen before. They had brown and grey feathers, yellow feet, and a black, yellow, and green beak that was strangely bumped at the end. The birds looked like a small, joke of a vulture, but they didn't look dangerous.

I had no idea what kind of bird they were, but they had strong, vibrant, and passionate voices. Tobias stood there staring at them, until his daughter grabbed him and yanked him behind a tree. Who were those birds? Did they work for the Queen, or would they be as helpful as the Caterpillar? Better safe than sorry until we figured out what we were looking at.

The birds hadn't noticed us in our shock. Instead, they merely kept chasing each other in circles along a sandy path around a tree stump, each shouting different verses of the same melody at each other, but none of them ever getting ahead or behind of where they were at in relation to each other.

As I listened, I realized the song was referring to the Civil War. Two were singing different versions of the Union verses, one was singing a Confederate version, and one was singing something about unions . . . the labor kind. None of them were listening to each other, but each one was adamant about what they were singing. Not one of the birds ever slowed down or stopped. I wondered how long they'd been doing this. Surely they couldn't have been doing this since 1865?

Should I ask? I grabbed Tobias's hand and leaned over to ask him.

"I've got no answers, Janie. I'm not even sure they'll stop to answer you. It seems to me this is something they've been doing for a long time," he said. Gee, no help from him.

Aiden had plopped down on the ground behind the tree and pulled out a book. No surprise there, but I wondered at what he'd found. "It's a caucus race," he said. "It's a race with no point and no resolution, with no beginning and no ending."

"Why would anyone do that?" I asked.

"I've heard of this," Jonah said. "I took a class on satire in acting school, and they talked about the caucus race in Alice in Wonderland being a wonderful comment on the pointlessness of politics. I think that's the point here, too, but why in the world would they be singing Civil War songs? Alice in Wonderland was written by an English Anglican deacon. How in the world would the two have come together?"

I thought about what he said, and then I wondered. Did time work the same in Wonderland? Had I hit on it as we talked to the Caterpillar? Did time in the mortal realm move faster while we were here, or did it slow down? If Allie's mother was the really real Alice in Wonderland from the story, then how could Allie only be a teenager? I grabbed the book from Aiden and checked. Sure enough, the original story was first published in 1865.

There were some pretty big questions to ask, but it didn't sound like we had a lot of time. Thank goodness it was a weekend, and a holiday weekend at that. No classes on Columbus Day Monday meant we had a bit more wiggle room, but if 260 plus years could disappear in the span of seventeen, we were definitely going to have to hurry up our search for Allie. We had to make it back without missing classes, because I knew just how hard it would be to catch up if we spent the whole week searching for her, let alone years.

Just as I was thinking about how much we needed to speed up, something happened to force our hands. Aiden, who had stood up when I took the book away from him, tripped over his own feet and fell right into the clearing where the birds were running in circles.

No question they saw him. They stopped what they were doing and stared.

CHAPTER FOURTEEN

"Who are you, and what are you doing here?" the first bird asked, coming close enough to sniff us.

I hoped everyone had remembered their deodorant earlier in the morning, because I'd hate for us to be offensive. "We are friends of a girl named Allie. We're looking for her."

"We know the girl you mean, but you're visitors to Wonderland, aren't you?" the first bird asked.

"We are," I answered.

The second bird made a loud squawking noise with its bill and asked its own question. "Why are you here?"

"To help our friend. We think she has been here before and came again with the hope it would prevent putting the rest of us in danger, but it doesn't protect us to be unaware of what might hurt us," Doris called out. I could tell she was nervous. Her voice shook as she said it.

The birds chattered eagerly amongst themselves, squawking and jabbering fast enough to be incoherent. It seemed like they enjoyed the bantering, but didn't come to a consensus so much, as they started hitting each other repeatedly.

Aiden, Tobias, Jonah, and I waded into the fray, each grabbing one of the birds and separating them, holding them until they quieted. "Shut up," I yelled. "We can't understand what you're saying unless you take turns saying it!"

They bickered at each other for a while longer, jabbering and contradicting each other, but we held them firm until they gave up. One of them finally asked a question we could understand.

"Do you have a prize for us? The last mortal lady had a prize."

"If you'll be quiet, answer us one at a time, and give us any information you have about our friend, we will give each of you a prize," I promised, thinking of the handful of quarters in my backpack, which I normally kept for the pop machine at the law school, parking machines near the school, or other mundane expenses that might come up.

They nodded in unison, and I nodded at the others. The birds sat down in front of us, and I whipped off my backpack to dig out the quarters. Each of them saw the coins, and their eyes went round.

"Oooh, shiny dimes!"

"Shiny dimes!"

"She's offered to give us shiny dimes?"

"My shiny dime!" the littlest one at my feet clamored, reaching up for my hand.

Maybe I shouldn't have given quarters if all they wanted were dimes, but it was too late now. Besides, how many places could one buy information for a dollar? "Each of you get one after we get information from you. We will each ask a question, and each of you shall answer each question. Once all the asking and all the answering is done, you will each get a shiny . . . one of these." *Aw, crap,* I thought. Now they had me about to call them dimes. "Question number one: Do you know who I mean if I ask about a lady named Allie?"

All four heads nodded in unison.

Aiden stepped forward. "Has she passed by here today?"

All four heads nodded again.

Mia stepped forward. "What direction did she go when you saw her today?"

Four wings all pointed in the same direction, away from the road and away from where we'd met the Caterpillar. I had to give it to Allie; she was at least being smart. She was traveling off the main road, going the rougher way rather than what was likely the easier route, in order to avoid being seen. The problem was, she had an advantage over us; we had no idea what the layout of this place was, how to get back out, or anything about the ground we were traveling over. I hoped we'd get some answers out of the dodos in front of us.

Doris stepped forward. "What do we need to know . . . I mean, are there things we might run into if we follow Allie?"

They looked at each other, from one to the next, and then they began to answer all at once, as if they'd forgotten the terms. I held up the quarters, and they quieted down. One of them cleared his throat, and they all looked to him. He—at least, I was guessing it was a he. I didn't know how I would tell, and it wasn't like I was going to ask—

spoke up. "You might run into the twins."

Another suggested, "The Mad Hatter and the Dormouse might be having a tea party."

The third indicated the White Rabbit's headquarters weren't far away, either. "He's had operatives in the forest all day. You might watch out for them."

The fourth shook his head. "And then there's the Queen. She doesn't like outsiders."

Jonah asked about the rules for visitors. They answered, again, one at a time, quiet and respectful and waiting their turns. We learned the Queen of Hearts had banned visitors from entering Wonderland and believed she'd sealed up all known passageways from the mortal world. The Queen had made those laws even stricter ever since Allie had left their world to seek out her fortune in ours.

I wondered what the connection between the two could be. Visitors were required to register with the Queen as soon as possible upon arrival and were required to have a pass to venture out of her castle walls once registered. The penalty for this was immediate expulsion from Wonderland. No idea how this would be accomplished, and I certainly didn't want to find out.

Tobias had the last question. He considered all the information we had and asked them about whether or not Allie was in any danger.

They all shook their heads. "We don't know," they answered. One told us he had no idea why she left and no idea what it was all about. Another thought it strange, but felt it was a sign of being more grown up. The third believed the Queen wanted Allie at the castle, but had no idea why. The fourth shook his head sadly.

"The whole thing is strange, and we have no explanation. We don't know why the Queen is looking for her. We don't know why the Visitor Laws were put into place. We are all confused, and the whole of Wonderland has been sad and quiet since she left."

I handed them each a quarter and they whooped and hollered and screamed about their good fortune. I shook my head and smiled. How long had it been since I'd been so excited about a whole quarter? Had it been when I was seven and helped my dad collate papers for his students and earned a coin?

The thought made me smile, and I realized my heart no longer hurt with a painful stab whenever I thought of him. I still missed him, and it still hurt, but it was much less than it had been the first time I'd been dealing with magic. Of course, I'd had another year to come to terms with his death, and I'd gotten some closure by getting my stepmother locked up after she'd murdered him.

We headed off in the direction the birds had pointed, trying again to walk through the woods without making tracks or noise.

It didn't take long before we saw something else.

And it was not anything I'd ever thought I'd see.

CHAPTER FIFTEEN

There was a man lying in the clearing, wearing clothes that had not only *seen* better days, but were *from* another day—the garments appeared oddly Victorian in style. He wore a fitted waistcoat and trousers with a high pair of riding boots. He had a pocket watch that dangled precariously from a small pocket just above his waist. Mud and leaves were spattered and smeared across his chest, his boots, and his face. He looked like he'd been in a brawl.

I heard a voice coming from Doris's backpack. "I smell whisky," Bert whispered.

I sniffed the air, and I caught the scent, too. There was a wet area down the front of the man's chest, just below his chin and just above the mud stains. It looked like someone had attempted to take a drink of something and spilled it down the front of their clothing. Sure enough, there was a bottle under one arm. The man snorted, let out a fart, and rolled over in his sleep.

"Ugh," I heard Bert say. "Do I look that bad when I'm drunk?"

Well, it was hard to compare a frog to a man, but they both looked as disheveled and degraded when they were sleeping off a bender. Then again, maybe Bert would clean himself up if he realized just how bad it was to clean him up when he was so far gone. I nodded at him and mouthed an apology.

"I'm never drinking again," I heard from the vicinity of Doris's back.

She grinned at me.

Aiden and Jonah looked at each other meaningfully. "Yeah, right," my boyfriend whispered.

A snore rose up from the man on the ground, and we began picking our way carefully past him. The idea was to get around him without waking him up, and it was working until Aiden tripped right on his legs, landing on top of him. It shouldn't have surprised me when Aiden fell in such an odd position, but it appeared his clumsiness hadn't gone away in Wonderland as it does in the faerie realm.

"Whazzup?" the man asked. "Whatyado that fer?" Did he have an accent, or was he still intoxicated? The stranger sat up as Aiden picked himself up off the ground, untangling his big feet from the man's boots and readjusting his backpack.

The man shook himself and hauled up the bottle from under his arm. He tried to take a swig, but the bottle was empty. He reached around, feeling the ground underneath where he'd been laying. "I dreamt I'd pissed meself. Glad I just spilled the bottle, but I'm gone to have ta look for another," he mumbled.

I still couldn't place the accent. Or was it just drunk talk?

"I'm sorry, sir," Aiden said. "I wasn't trying to wake you up. We were trying to go around so you could keep sleeping."

The man straightened himself and stood up, leaves and twigs mussing his hair, and he slapped a tall stovepipe hat on his head. He shook himself and rubbed his face before looking at us intently. "I'd take it as a kindness if you didn't tell anyone I fell asleep. I'm supposed to be on guard duty, I am, and the Queen won't take kindly to me falling asleep on the job."

Asleep? What would she say about dead drunk? I had to bite back a laugh, and instead, I pressed forward. "I bet we can work something out," I started. I caught a glimpse of Tobias's face, and I saw the approval there. I wondered what Mia thought of the whole situation.

"Wait a minute," he said. "You're not from around here. You're visitors. The Queen has outlawed visitors. I have to report you."

"And then we have to report you for drinking on duty while we're there. I've got a camera. I can take pictures. And then you'll have to answer for that one," I said.

I saw the panic on the man's face. He sputtered and floundered and acted like a fussy mother hen, talking about how there was no need to do such a thing and the mud and such on his clothing could be explained by Aiden's tripping over him.

Aiden was brushing himself off, refusing help from Jonah, and so I brought the man's attention away from Aiden's clumsiness and toward my own request. I laughed, earning a hard stare from Aiden, but I ignored it and kept talking. I had a plan, and even though Aiden probably thought I was laughing at his manic clown routine, keeping the man focused on matters at hand meant I had his full attention. Aiden's clumsiness wasn't even on his radar.

"You'd still have to explain why you were on the ground to be tripped over in the first place. And there's also the pungent odor of whisky permeating all your clothes. I think it might even be in your *pores*, it's so strong!" I exclaimed before realizing if there were other guards around, they might hear me and report us to the Queen themselves. I quieted down and said, "I think we can work this out and keep it just between us, don't you?"

He nodded, regal as he held his head up high, and winced from what I supposed was a hangover headache. I'd seen them on Bert enough to recognize it. "I'm sure we can," the man said. "My name is Alfred. I'm not much for guard duty, but the Queen's Edicts have drafted people into her service against their will and against their skills."

Alfred? I didn't think I'd ever met an Alfred. "Pleased to meet you, Alfred. I'm Janie. We are visitors, it's true, but we're here to help a friend. She's hidden herself in Wonderland, and we need to find her and make sure she's okay."

"I assume you will keep my secret if I help you to find your friend? Who is she?"

"That's about it," I said. "You help us find her, help us through Wonderland undetected, and we keep your secret. Deal with us honestly and truthfully and help us, and we'll be all out of your hair as soon as possible."

"Done," he said. "And I know where someone trying to hide from the Queen might find a place to stay. But you should probably take shelter for now."

"Why?" Tobias asked. "It's early yet. It should only be the middle of the afternoon."

"Yes," said Alfred. "And as such, it should be tea time, but instead, the Queen's Guard makes their rounds to check on everyone. It's generally to ensure there are no visitors and everyone is doing their jobs." He looked down at his waistcoat. "There's no hiding I've been drinking."

Doris sprang into action. "I might have a solution." She handed him a snack-sized bag of Funyons. When I gave her a questioning look, she shrugged. "I've been hooked on them lately, and since you had a few in the cupboard, I snagged them. They've got a strong odor, so if he eats them, it might cover up the scent of alcohol enough that the Queen's Guard might believe him wearing yesterday's drunk clothing as opposed to being drunk today. It's worth a try."

I shook my head and opened the bag for him. He took one gingerly and popped it into his mouth. "These things are like chewing stinky cardboard, but they taste wonderful. How in the world could I not have known such things exist?"

Oh, Lord. I was going to go down in history as the woman who introduced Funyons to Wonderland. I wondered how they'd make that look on my epitaph.

CHAPTER SIXTEEN

A lfred mowed his way through the bag of Funyons while taking us a short distance away to a cave. It was secluded enough that I hadn't even seen the entrance as we'd walked up. Unless I'd been looking for it, I'd never have guessed it was here.

We all climbed inside, as it was elevated a few feet off the ground. The cave wasn't large, but there was room enough for all six of us and a frog to take a seat and to get off the road long enough for a rest. Tobias suggested we all try to nap while we waited for Alfred to finish with the guard, and I thought he'd lost his mind.

"Look, Janie, we have no idea how long this trip is going to take and how long we might be sitting here. This could take a while."

"We don't have a while, Dad," Mia said. "We need to find Allie yesterday and make sure she's okay."

"And we won't be able to do that if we are exhausted, or caught by the Queen's Guard. We can't help anyone if we don't take care of ourselves, as well. We'll find her. We'll get her back. But we have to be smart about it. Take it from someone who's been on such journeys before. You rest when you can, eat when you have a few moments, and make sure to drink water. We brought such things along. Doris, something light, if you would."

She nodded and dug in her backpack. Bert hopped into Tobias's lap and closed his eyes, getting out of the way of Doris's rummaging in her supplies. She brought out two boxes of cereal bars, the ones I'd bought for on-the-go breakfasts when I needed to get out the door in a hurry. I realized I'd gotten cranky when my stomach growled at the sight of a NutriGrain bar. Maybe Tobias had a point.

We didn't unpack more than we needed to. The plan was to grab a quick snack, swig from our individual bottles of water, and get settled in. The air was still cool inside the cave, but we didn't get into the sleeping bags or blankets. The hope, of course, was that it wouldn't take quite as long as a full night's sleep.

I was tired, but I was also keyed up, listening for any indication the

Queen's Guard was coming toward us or Alfred would betray us. I just didn't trust the situation. There was no escape route from the back of the cave. There was no way out if something went wrong. I was starting to panic until Aiden hugged me tight and reminded me I wasn't alone.

I leaned my head against his shoulder and looked around at the group. Bert was out cold on Tobias's lap, and Tobias himself was already snoozing with his head tilted back against the wall of the cave and his legs sprawled out in front of him. He didn't even snore. I had the odd thought that the ability to fall asleep as Tobias had was an asset in his line of work.

Doris had curled up on the floor, in the fetal position with her head on her backpack, and was sound asleep. We had done a lot of walking, and it was probably more than she was used to. Taking a nap would do her good.

Mia was curled up with her head in Jonah's lap. Jonah was drawing her hair behind her ear and giving her meaningful looks as she relaxed, and I saw her eyes drifting shut. I felt my own eyes grow heavy, drifting lower and lower, and I felt Aiden's warm arm around me. It was about as secure as I could feel in this strange land.

My last thought, before I fell asleep, was about Allie and whether or not she was secure.

I hoped she was.

Aiden was shaking me awake what seemed like just a few moments later. Turned out we'd all gotten an hour or so of solid sleep, had gotten food in our stomachs, and I realized just how good Tobias's advice about resting and eating had been.

On Tobias's signal that Alfred was back, we began piling out of the cave. The cave hadn't been very comfortable, so we were all stiff as we crawled out. Alfred definitely smelled like Funyons.

"So, how'd it go?" Jonah asked.

He smiled. "It worked. Do you have any more of those things?"

It seemed we'd created a monster, one with a craving of Funyons. I shook my head.

Doris tossed over another bag. "We don't have many, but we do have a few. Thanks, by the way. I needed to rest. We've been walking for a long time."

He nodded. "Well, I'm not much of a soldier, myself. I'm more of a haberdasher."

"A haberdasher? What's that?" I asked. I wasn't ashamed to admit my ignorance, although it looked like some of the others actually knew what he was talking about.

He pointed to his head. "I make hats. Not much cause for them now, since the Queen has banned visitors from Wonderland. I have so many fewer clients that when the Queen was hiring for patrol and sentries, I didn't have much choice but to sign up. I'd lose the shop if I didn't, and I don't know anything else. Then I ended up with more shifts on patrol than I could handle and keep the shop open, but I couldn't quit because I needed the money. It's a vicious cycle, and I started drinking."

Alfred's hands were shaking.

"Are you carrying weapons?" Jonah asked. "I'm not trying to be insensitive, but if you're on patrol, carrying weapons, and drunk at the same time, that could get you in serious trouble in our world."

I cringed. He was right, even though I was sure there had to be a better way to ask.

Alfred started laughing, and once he got going, it was almost as if he couldn't stop. He stopped walking and bent over at the waist, tears flowing from his eyes as he laughed and laughed, holding his sides as he did.

"It's so sad, it's almost funny," he said. "I'm a haberdasher, but the chemicals used to make a good hat cause the shakes."

He held out his fingers. They were red and rough and looked like they'd been burned by chemicals. "I started drinking to even out the shakes. And then they started getting better when I wasn't making hats. But making hats was the only thing I've ever known how to do. My father's father's father's father made hats. We've all made hats. But the less I made them, the better I felt. This job, that I took to save my business, is making me better by not letting me do business. It's the world's sickest joke."

It was. I felt bad for him, but there was no question in my mind now as to whom we were dealing with.

It was the Mad Hatter.

And we'd asked a man with a reputation for a questionable grip on reality to guide us through a world we didn't know in search of a friend who was in a danger we didn't understand while hiding from a Queen we'd never met and didn't want to.

Somehow, I was starting to think he wasn't the only one with mental health issues.

Chapter Seventeen

I offered Alfred a Twix bar from my backpack. It was a little on the squished and melty side, but I figured if chocolate was good for a pick-me-up when I was feeling down, it couldn't be a bad thing for him. I was right. He perked up a bit. I maintain chocolate is a cure-all. Of course, putting something in his stomach besides whisky probably did him a lot of good, even if it was Funyons and chocolate.

He seemed like a decent guy, and fortified by food and a mission, it seemed he had a purpose to his day. I wondered how long it had been since he'd had that. It seemed to me like it was a good thing. I just hoped it was a good thing for us.

Alfred walked us through the woods, stopping to avoid patrols and working our way through a path only he seemed to know. I hoped he was actually taking us toward where Allie was. I didn't know how deep she might have hidden herself, or if she'd already been caught, and if she had been captured, there was no plan on how to get her back.

For all of our preparations, we'd been completely unprepared for our trip here. And traveling to other realms was becoming something we did on a semi-regular basis. I looked at Aiden and couldn't believe I'd considered leaving him just a few hours earlier in the morning. If it wasn't for him, I'd be lost in trying to figure all of this out. Even without all the magical hinky stuff, I'd just flat be lost without him. I needed him in my life. The more I thought about it, the more I was positive I'd made the right decision in staying, and I knew Aiden's sudden push for commitment was a response to my own fear. I wondered how much of my inner turmoil he'd guessed.

Aiden was oblivious to my current mental wanderings, even though we were wandering through the kind of forest one would see in a storybook. I started to pay attention to our surroundings as we walked, and at first glance, it appeared to be a normal run-of-the-mill forest.

I wasn't much for walking in the woods, but I'd done it with my father several times as a kid. He'd liked trying to teach me about toadstools and moss and such. I wondered if he'd had some reason to believe I'd notice something was off, or even magical, in a forest far from home. How had he known?

Because I did notice something. The toadstools, which were normally a dull, off-white at home, were gray with brown and black spots. I stopped and pointed to the toadstools at the base of a tree. "Doris, you have any idea what this is? Aiden? Tobias?"

Tobias went white.

Okay, if something was making the Billy Bad-Ass of the magical community go pale, it was definitely a Very Bad Thing.

"I know what that is," he said. "Don't touch it. It's deadly poison."

Doris had already been leaning over it. Alfred came running back, followed by Jonah and Mia. Aiden took a step back, pulling his mother away from it, as if merely breathing near it would kill them. She stumbled, nearly knocking him over. It was Doris, though, who kept them both from falling over, and it was a good thing, too. More of those toadstools were right behind them.

"What is it exactly?" I asked.

"It's the nightslip mushroom," Tobias said. "It's highly dangerous. I've only seen it in books. Its poison will enter your system through the skin if you touch it with your bare hands. It's one of the most expensive poisons known in the magic world, and there is no known antidote.

"There's some indication of things that have prolonged life after they have been touched or ingested, but nothing consistently enough to be a known and reliable cure. It works fast, too. I heard once of someone who touched a nightslip with one finger, and they lived for about two hours afterwards. At the end, they were writhing in pain, with blood coming from each and every orifice of the body."

"Yikes," I said. "Don't put me down for that one."

He chuckled.

Alfred waved at all of us. "Be careful. Don't step on them. There are some shoes they've leached through in the past."

"He's right," Tobias added. "Although the rubber soles of our tennis shoes and hiking boots should be fairly sturdy. Rubber isn't porous, so you should be safe, but we might want to roll up the hems of our pants a bit so they don't rub the mushrooms as we walk."

Alfred looked at him in amazement. "I didn't think to warn you about the nightslips. It's just part of living here, such that I didn't even think of it. I apologize. But are you honestly saying you have shoes that might protect one from the dangers of walking in these woods? They must be outrageously expensive, and you must be rich to even consider it. If you are, you must know Wonderland's economy is severely depressed. A bit of money spread around would do wonders in flushing your friend from her hiding place."

What a laugh! He thought we were rich! I looked down at my off-brand WalMart sneakers I'd bought on clearance just before school started. They marked me as rich? Then why did I only have five bucks in my pocket after buying donuts this morning? I snorted as I bent to roll up the hem of my pant legs, but caught myself when I saw Alfred didn't understand. I wondered if there was some way we could use it to our advantage somewhere. I filed it away in my brain and ignored Alfred's statement about our collective net worth.

"It's a matter of technology in our world," I told him. "I'm sure there are things here in Wonderland that we could use as well. And I'm sure there are dangers in our own world that none of us would think to warn you of, either. Lead on, good man." I put on a cheery smile and pointed through the woods.

Aiden and Alfred began a discussion about various bits of flora and fauna as we walked. How strange could one's life get? Doris and Tobias joined in from time to time, with Mia walking ahead and listening intently. Was she just trying to learn more about her dad and help with his work? Or was she trying to soak up information so she wouldn't have to call him in the future? Hard to tell.

It left me bringing up the rear with Jonah, and that reminded me there were numerous things I wanted to ask him about. I wanted to know whether he was getting serious with Mia. I wanted to know why he'd tagged along. And I wanted to know what else was going on; he'd been way too quiet. It made me worry, as he, along with Tobias, were the outsiders in our little entourage from the mortal world.

"So, Jonah, I've been meaning to ask you a whole lot of things," I started.

He grinned at me. "Is this the well-meaning best friend speech? Yes, I'm in love with her. No, I don't plan to hurt her. Are you going to tell me that if I break her heart, you'll have to hurt me?"

"Absolutely," I said with a smile. "But there's more. The magic stuff doesn't seem to bother you. You take it all in stride, without reaction or even surprise. You might have been mildly surprised to meet Bert, but it wasn't the kind of reaction I expected. Mia was nearly on the back of the couch shrieking when he first talked to her. You . . . well, it was as if a talking frog was pretty low on the surprise factor list for you. Is there some deep dark secret in your past I need to know about in order to keep her safe?"

He gave me a small smile. "I don't know who my family is, because I was adopted. They might be magic. They might not. I've seen all kinds of strange things over the years. I've thought about it over and over ever since I met you guys, and I've come to the conclusion that I didn't just have an active imagination as a kid. There might be something else there . . .

"It was a closed adoption, so there is no information about my biological family. My adoptive mom was pretty great. And my adoptive dad, well, he wasn't too bad, either. He wasn't around a lot, but he was an okay guy. Nothing magic about them, just two people who worked real hard and didn't always have the time to give a lonely, weird kid who talked to homeless people like he knew something and kept winning weird awards for gardening in the backyard. I could never explain it, and people always asked how I did it, and I'm wondering now if it was something more than just a green thumb."

And I'd thought my family background was mysterious; I at least knew who my parents were, even if I was still uncovering pictures and genealogy records. "Your family sounds normal, so why in the world would you know anything about magic?" I asked. "I want to know because I need to keep my friends safe if I can. Allie didn't tell us about herself, and now look at us. We're tromping through the woods of Wonderland with dangers we don't understand, because we believe she needs help and she deserves it. You're around enough; if you're with Mia, you're one of us. I don't want to make the same mistake with you as we may have done with Allie."

He sighed and rubbed one hand over his face. "Well, you'd think I'd know more about my own family, but I don't. All I know is that I can make plants grow. If I concentrate on a specific plant, I can accelerate its growth, so what would likely take years would only take an hour or so. I don't know where I got it. It was a bit scary when I first learned about it."

Whoa. He had powers? But my necklace, the one Aiden had given me to alert me to the presence of magic, never went off in his presence. I said as much.

"Well," he said, "it's not like I use it very often. I'd think if I was actually using that ability, your necklace would be going nuts. So would all of Aiden's magic-detecting gizmos. I've never experimented. It's not like there's much practical use for it."

I could think of several, but I just patted his arm. Now wasn't exactly the time for a pep talk. The others were stopped ahead of us, waiting for us to catch up. "Thanks for telling me. It might come in handy while we try to help Allie."

"Who?" Alfred exclaimed.

"Our friend?" I said. "The one we're here to help."

"Who is your friend?" he asked again.

"Her name is Allie," I said. "She's in danger."

"Oh, dear," he said. "There's only one place to go, then."

"Where's that?

"Straight to the Queen," he said. "She's looking for Allie as well."

CHAPTER EIGHTEEN

That did not really sound like the world's best idea. I said so.

"I know Allie and the Queen did not get along for a long time, and the Queen's the one who sought a reason for Allie to leave Wonderland. I'm not sure she's all that happy the girl's back, but I'm not sure what the dynamics were," Alfred said, wringing his red, shaking hands.

Okay, so maybe it was time to ask a few questions about the Queen. I remembered Allie saying the White Rabbit was trying to drag her back, and I assumed he was doing so under the orders of the Queen. So why had the Queen wanted Allie to leave? Was I convinced the Queen was evil because of the run-ins with my own stepmother? Was there a relationship between Allie and the Queen? What was going on?

I started to ask, but Alfred perked up his ears at something and shushed us. He was right. We were right on the edge of the forest, having come up to a small river. On the other side of the river was a dirt path, and we could see a guard unit, in uniform, marching in formation. I whispered, "I count about thirty."

"Thirty-five," Tobias whispered. "Where are we?"

"We're on the edge of the Queen's property. The river here is the border of the land that belongs to her, surrounding her castle. We need to go around her land. I doubt Allie would have come here," Alfred said. "But it's the fastest way I know to get where someone familiar with Wonderland might go to hide from the Queen."

I'd have to remember to ask more about where he was taking us later, but now wasn't the time. We tried to sneak quietly away from the guards and keep moving, but Aiden slipped on a loose stone on the edge of the river and reached out to steady himself. I grabbed for him, but it wasn't enough. I went down as well, dragged into the water when he went in. The current was strong enough to wash us farther down the stream, which kept us from being noticed too much from the guard right away, but the sound of something splashing and our friends trying to call to us from the bank did not do much to keep our activities clandestine.

The guards broke formation. A couple of them waded into the water, forming a human chain in an attempt to haul us in. Even so, Aiden inadvertently pulled the first one under as he flailed and floundered in the water. The guard came up spitting and sputtering, and I noticed our friends had taken the opportunity to slide back into the woods. I grabbed the hand of one of the guards, and he hauled me out without much trouble. I gave Aiden a hard look, and he winked at me.

He'd done it on purpose. That rat. Of course, I wasn't sure how much of the clumsiness this time was an act and how much had just happened, but he'd gone with it to create a distraction to keep the others from being found.

Of course, between the two of us, maybe we were the right ones to go into the Queen's court to try to find Allie behind the scenes if she was there, rather than with the entire group. They could keep looking with Alfred's help. We could go undercover here and make the best of it.

The guards pulled us to the bank, and we collapsed, soaking wet, with Aiden coughing as if he'd swallowed half the river. I crawled over to him and whacked him on the back repeatedly to keep up the pretense of the drowning victim. He coughed a bit more before putting one hand up and saying he was okay.

"Who are you?" the captain of the guard asked.

Hooboy. Didn't know how to answer that one safely. Aiden spoke up. "I'm Aiden. This is my girlfriend, Janie. Thanks for helping out. I didn't mean to fall into the river, and I sure didn't mean to take Janie with me."

"That wasn't what I meant," the captain said. He looked young, but definitely in charge of the men who'd been marching up and down the path just minutes earlier. His blue eyes were intelligent and wary. I could tell there was more he was asking for, but I wanted him to ask. I let Aiden take charge. He was good at stuff like this.

"Sir, I don't know what you mean," Aiden said. Okay, maybe not. I'd go with it for a while. I kept my mouth shut and hauled my wet bag up and onto my back. I hoped nothing was ruined.

Aiden stood up, and reached a cold, wet hand out to me. I took it and hoped he didn't want a hug. I felt absolutely disgusting, and being pressed up against him when we were both soaking wet and cold didn't really appeal at the moment.

"Are you visitors to Wonderland?" the captain asked.

"I guess we are," Aiden said. "We've not been here before."

"Visitors are not allowed in Wonderland without the express permission of the Queen," the captain said as some of his soldiers began to form a circle around us.

"Does your Queen ever leave Wonderland?" I asked. I couldn't keep quiet.

"Well, no, she doesn't," came the answer.

"So how are visitors supposed to get permission from her if she never leaves? That's impossible." Aiden crossed his arms over his chest, his soggy backpack still at his feet.

I could tell that the captain either wasn't very smart, or he didn't have a lot of autonomy. "Well, why don't you ask her?" he said. "We'll take you to her."

Time to be the airhead, I thought. "You're taking us to see your Queen? I can't meet a Queen looking like this! My hair! My clothes!"

The captain cocked his head. "I'm not buying it. I think you were trying to avoid coming here. Unless you've got the appropriate court attire in your bags, I don't believe you would have registered upon your arrival as you were supposed to. How long have you been here?"

"I don't know, sir. I'm not wearing a watch." And it was true. Aiden almost never wore a watch. He'd once told me he spent too much money replacing ones he'd broken than it was worth to keep a watch on his wrist. I only wore one when I had to dress up for whatever reason, whether it was during last summer when I'd interned with a judge, or when we'd had to have mock trials in our evidence class earlier this year. I held up my naked wrist to show the guards, in agreement with Aiden.

"Can you guess?" the captain asked.

I had to give him credit for not giving up when something seemed off. Maybe he wasn't stupid, just young and on a short leash. "No, we can't. We don't know if time works the same way here as it does where we live. We have no way of knowing, estimating, or even guessing."

He nodded at me, as if he wasn't surprised by the answer. "Well, that's above my pay grade anyway. But I still believe you intended to avoid registering with the Queen as a Visitor, which is a potential criminal offense."

Oh, great. "Are you going to lock us up?" I asked, ready to burst into tears if I needed to, to beg for sympathy if I felt it would work.

"No," he said. "The Queen's steward will decide what to do with you. You'll likely be given a room for a bit while the Queen decides whether you've violated her edicts on visitors."

Oh, goody. He asked us to follow him and then headed toward the castle. We weren't restrained or handcuffed or tied in any way, but there didn't seem to be any question that we weren't free to leave. They were armed, and we were outnumbered. We each had a small weapon, but it wasn't like I was going to fight off a whole squad of guards with a screwdriver.

Aiden wasn't much better. He had a retractable police baton in his pocket that had been a gift from a friend of mine, Mike, who was a former police officer in my study group at the law school. After I'd explained the truth behind the situation with my stepmother and stepbrother last year, he'd given me the metal baton as a means of self-defense. Aiden had taken it when we'd been figuring out weapons before we'd left the house for Wonderland. Had that just been this morning?

No wonder I was getting tired. I wondered, myself, just what time it was. We walked for several minutes before a thought occurred to me. "Who is the Queen's Steward?" I asked.

"Well, the White Rabbit, of course," replied the captain of the guard. "She consults him on all matters about the land, her edicts, and any other disputes that arrive at her door."

CHAPTER NINETEEN

That couldn't be good, I thought. The White Rabbit and whatever spies he had were whom Allie had been hiding from. I didn't know the White Rabbit's motivation for his actions, much less whether he would kill her, and we were on our way to see them.

What else could we do, though? We followed the guards, our wet sneakers sloshing on the dirt path and leaving wet footprints behind us. I wondered what the others were doing and whether or not they'd gotten away. I worried there might have been other guards patrolling, ones we did not see but who might have seen them when they tried to get away. It wasn't like I could do anything else at the moment.

The guards had weapons. The long barrels of their guns looked similar to something I'd seen in a Civil War film somewhere, but I was so not a gun expert. I couldn't have told anyone the make, the model, or the year they were made, just that they looked like something I'd seen in movies.

Their uniforms looked vaguely like something from the Civil War as well, which fit in with the song I'd heard the dodo birds singing earlier. What was going on? How many visitors had they had in the past, and how long had it been since they'd been cut off from the world? Why had the Queen done so?

I had no easy answers, and all the mental gymnastics weren't answering the question. We finally reached a stone wall higher than the roof of my house—which, with two stories as well as a full attic, wasn't anything to sneeze at—and as we passed through the gate, I realized the stones of the wall were nearly three feet thick. Someone had been thinking of serious fortifications when they'd built this thing. I wondered why, but like many other questions I had, I had no way of knowing.

The courtyard was bustling with activity. It seemed to be an active marketplace, with stalls and grocers and such. It looked a bit like a cross between Victorian London, a Renaissance fair, and a Civil War-era open air market. Or at least, it would be, except for the fact that many of the merchants were human-sized animals who spoke in a variety of accents.

There was a hedgehog as tall as I was, wearing a waistcoat and breeches with a white apron tied at his waist, a monocle squeezed into one eye, and carrying a hot tray of buttered buns, calling out for his customers. Kids clamored around him, waving what looked like copper coins and begging him for a taste. A female hedgehog was behind him, wearing a full-length calico skirt and white shirtwaist top, also with a white apron. She was probably his wife, and her basket looked like it was full of baked goods. I could smell them; they smelled wonderful.

There was a booth with a sign that said "Treacle Tarts," with a mouse asleep on the counter.

There was a pig walking on his hind legs, dressed in white, with a smear of blood on his apron, a sign above his stall advertising his services as a butcher. I thought that was just all kinds of sick and twisted, but hey, to each their own.

There was a candlestick maker, as well, with a giant bee sitting in a booth and drumming his antennae on the post beside his head, as if he was bored. There was a cat with herbs hanging from a rope above her head, as if they were drying in the slight breeze that was also drying our river-wet clothing.

Other merchants and storekeepers were lined up in the common area, hawking all manner of goods and services, from millinery to stove pipes to haberdashery to a tailor to weaving and baskets to vegetables and all sorts of things. I knew I was gawking, staring at them, but I'd never seen a market like this, much less staffed by walking, talking animals who wore people clothes.

Aiden elbowed me, but I noticed he was doing the same thing I was. We didn't have a lot of time to watch, however, because the guards brought us into the castle and took us straight to a bedroom. It was a simple room with a double bed and a dresser. It wasn't huge, and it wasn't what I would call luxurious, but the quilt on the bed looked clean. The walls were large stone blocks, and there was a heavy curtain hanging from the wall on one side. I wondered if it was a tapestry to keep the room warmer.

We walked inside, and the guards shut the door behind us. I heard a key in the lock, and I went to the door, knocking softly. "How much time do we have?" I called out. If I could wring out my shirt, that couldn't hurt. Everything I had was soaking wet, so it wasn't as if I could change, but I could at least do something about reducing the amount of water.

A guard called back that we had until the next change of the watch. I had no idea how long that was, but I didn't waste time. The room was without decoration, but there was a plain pitcher with water and a basin on top of the dresser. I set aside the pitcher and put the basin on the floor, whipped off my shirt, and began wringing it out, the water dripping into the basin. Aiden watched for a second before he pulled off his shoes and set himself to doing the same with his soaking wet socks.

I didn't really feel like trying to strip off my jeans, because they weren't going to get dry anyway, but I did as Aiden did and tried to get as much water as possible out of my socks. I hoped it wouldn't take long for our things to dry. What I wouldn't give for a roaring fire and a rack to hang my clothing on in front of it, but it wasn't in the cards at the moment. There wasn't even a fireplace in the room. And we had other concerns.

"So what's the game plan, Aiden?" I asked.

He took a long, deep breath. "I don't know."

"You don't know. What do you mean, 'you don't know'? You're the guy who comes up with the plans!" I exclaimed.

"I'm starting to think there's much more going on here than Allie told us or maybe even knows about. I'm thinking we should have pressed her for more information."

"I'm not sure we had reason to before the Jabberwocky showed up. I know I thought she'd be right there for us to ask questions, but things happened kinda fast. I didn't think of asking her what her relationship was with the Queen, because I didn't think we'd be in Wonderland just yet. As she was telling us about her past, I figured we'd end up here eventually; I just thought we'd have a bit more time to prepare."

"Well, we can't redo it; it's too late to ask more questions of

Allie. So what do *you* think we should do?" he asked. Pragmatic. What else could we do? It wasn't like we had other options right now. We could only go forward.

"Good question," I said.

He stood up, his bare feet leaving damp marks on the stone floor. He paced a bit, back and forth, and I could almost hear the gears in his head grinding toward a solution. At least I hoped so.

Someone knocked on the door. I pulled my shirt back over my head, just in time for two guards to enter the room. They gave us time to pull on our still-damp socks and our still squishy shoes, but otherwise hurried us out the door.

We tried to ask them what was going to happen now. They wouldn't answer.

I guess we'd find out sooner or later whether we'd be received as honored guests, or if we'd be clapped in chains and thrown into the dungeon as dangerous criminals.

CHAPTER TWENTY

We weren't shackled, and we had our backpacks. They hadn't searched our bags. They hadn't even asked what we had. I hoped that was a good sign.

We walked along a stone hallway, much like I'd envisioned reading about in my history and western civilization classes in college. There were tapestries on the walls, but they were seriously decked out in hearts of all different colors. Upon closer inspection, there were even hearts imbedded in the stonework of the hallway. No question, then, which Queen we were here to see. It was the Queen of Hearts. Then again, who else would it be in Wonderland? I'd never heard of any other queen in this realm.

Of course, I always had to leave room for the idea that I was far from an expert on Wonderland, on royal etiquette, or on magic, even though my dad would probably have known all kinds of things about this stuff.

We eventually came to a large set of double doors with intricate wooden scrollwork in the panels. It was incredibly lovely. Even though there were hearts everywhere, there was no indication that the Queen was anywhere near as cheesy as the Disney-version *Alice in Wonderland* movie had led me to believe. Everything here was understated and lovely, without being over the top. She had excellent taste, if she was the one who had done all the decorating.

The doors were opened in front of us, and we entered a large room with a rough stone walkway. If I had to guess, it was the throne room. The Queen sat on a gilded chair located up a few steps to a dais just high enough to look down on visitors who walked in. Again, it was tasteful. Romantic, without looking like something from a tacky honeymoon hotel in a commercially advertised spot. Yeah, I'd definitely seen the Disney version way too many times. I kept waiting for her to yell "Off with their heads!" and look like a deranged mental patient.

The woman on the throne was probably ten years or more younger than Doris, with lovely smooth pale skin and auburn hair drawn up into an elaborate do I was betting would take hours to style. I hoped it was a wig, for her sake, because that was a lot of time to sit still. I wouldn't have had the patience . . . . Yeah, I get all kinds of irrelevant thoughts crossing my brain when I'm nervous.

The guards brought us before her, and Aiden pulled off a fairly courteous bow without falling on his face. I bobbed into a curtsy, but it was awkward. It wasn't something I'd done before, but I'd seen it in the movies.

"I am Euphegenia, the Queen of Hearts," she said, rising from the throne. "I hear you are visiting our fair land. What is the purpose of your visit?"

We looked at each other, and I nodded at Aiden. He nodded back, and I responded. "Your Majesty, we are looking for a friend. We have reason to believe she may be in danger. We do not expect to stay longer than necessary, but we came to find her, to protect her if we can, and to see if there's anything we can do to prevent her from being placed in further danger." I really did not want to give Allie's name if I could help it.

The Queen pondered my statements for a moment before asking another question. "Is your friend from Wonderland?"

How did one answer that? I mean, Allie had said she was born here, but her mother had been a visitor much like us once upon a time. *Gah!* I definitely didn't need to be thinking in faerie tale wording. Once upon a time? Who thinks like that? I shook my head.

"No, she's not. She has been here before, though, and knows it better than we do. I believe she ran here to protect us from something dangerous. If she'd asked us for help, we would have helped her. We would have done anything and everything we could to help her if she'd just told us what was going on. We could not leave her to whatever it was she was running from. Friends don't do that."

She gave me a small smile. "How do I know you're not saying that to get into my good graces? How do I know you are actually her friend? Is there a way for me to know whether you pose any harm to her? And you haven't told me who she is. I could try to guess, but I assume you're keeping her identity from me to protect her."

I nodded. Aiden did, too. We looked like a couple of synchronized copycats, bobbing in unison. "If she did not tell us of the specific danger, it makes it hard for us to know whom to trust with the information that could lead to finding her. We want to keep her safe, not make things worse."

"You are wise, and a good friend, if what you tell me is true," the Queen said, stepping slowly down the steps toward us. Her dress had a train of rich red velvet, with imprinted tiny hearts throughout the fabric. I wouldn't have even seen them if the light from the window behind her hadn't hit a fold in the fabric just right.

"How can we prove it to you without betraying our friend? We don't know what might be overheard here in your court that might be dangerous to her. We don't know what dangers she is facing. We just don't know," Aiden added.

"Well, then, we have a dilemma," the Queen said. "How can I trust you among my people? How can I trust you are not a danger to them if we cannot trust each other enough to talk about our goals?"

We didn't say anything. She was right.

"This is why I have passed Edicts restricting visitors to Wonderland. Too many of our people do not understand the ways of other realms. We have, in the past, been overrun with visitors. Some of my most beloved court staff have been hurt by visitors. There are many who hate those from other lands and might do them harm because of problems from other visitors in the past. They are no longer allowed to Come and Go."

We didn't say anything.

She continued, "This is why visitors are supposed to register with my court when they arrive. This way I can determine if they pose a danger to our citizens and our land. Also, I can determine if our visitors will be safe in our lands."

I nodded. "I understand your purpose, but there's no way for a visitor to know there's a limitation when they enter your lands. There are no posted signs. There are no notices to those who may enter your world."

She winced. "You're right," the Queen said. "I had not thought about it, because we really don't get visitors these days. I've taken great pains to discourage it, and I thought we were all pretty safe, but apparently there are still ways for others to get into our lands that we were not aware of."

I smelled something rotten in her statement. I didn't trust her all of a sudden. If she was truly trying to keep people out, why in the world was she sending the White Rabbit and his minions, whatever they were, into our world, looking for Allie? If she was taking pains to keep people out, why was she looking to bring someone back?

Either she had no idea what the White Rabbit was up to, or she was lying to us. Either way, it didn't really put me in a mood to take her into our confidence. When I looked over at Aiden, he had a puzzled look on his face. Either he was confused, or he was thinking the same thing I was thinking.

But that didn't mean I had an answer of what to do next.

CHAPTER TWENTY-ONE

"If you don't mind, I have another question, Your Highness," I said.

"Since you've asked so nicely, yes, you may inquire," she answered, a smile teasing the corner of her mouth.

I had the thought she might be a whole lot smarter than anyone gave her credit for, with a sly wit and a sense of humor. I wondered if she'd failed to put up notices about her rules on visitors on purpose to give her a reason to detain anyone not from Wonderland and extract favors to permit their leaving. If so, she was a formidable opponent. Of course, we weren't quite ready to leave yet, but we hadn't exactly thought about how we would go about actually doing it once we were.

That might be a problem for another day. I had no idea what time it was, but I was getting tired of playing this game. "Why the restrictions on visitors? What happened? I would think the visitors to Wonderland might spend money with your vendors, with your merchants, and add to trade. There are always items developed on one world that might benefit another."

"Such as?" she asked.

Well, the soles of my shoes protecting me from the nightslip mushrooms came to mind, but I wasn't sure we should tell her about Alfred. Instead, I tried to think of something else.

"Well, for example, there are different techniques of handling fabric that tailors and seamstresses might share. Different shoes might have different technologies that make them better or worse to a new world's terrain. I don't know. My point is that the sharing of ideas sometimes improves life for the people who might not have thought about it before. I would think this would help people in more than one land, make their lives easier, and maybe make their lives better."

"What would you propose as a way to keep all people safe while we try make things better?" she asked.

I heard the interrogation in her question. Why was I worried about it? "Well, we don't know much about your flora and fauna in this world. What's dangerous to eat? To touch? To step on? To sniff? I don't know. But I do have these shoes." I pointed down at my feet to my off-brand sneakers with the rubber soles. They looked a bit worse for wear because they were still squishing a bit, but otherwise serviceable.

"They're comfortable," I continued. "They give me great foot support, and I can walk farther without my feet hurting or getting tired. But even better? Though my shoes are wet, it's not because it soaked through the sole, the bottom of my shoe. It soaked through the top. The bottom of the shoe is waterproof, and things don't really seep through it. If I step on something, they've got enough grip to make sure I've got good traction, but at the same time, they're bendy so as to move with my foot and not let dangerous stuff in to hurt me."

Her eyes widened. "You must be a rich and powerful person to have foot wear so pliable, durable, and magical."

Nothing magical about it. But she thought I had value. Or at least my shoes did. That could only help us in the negotiation department.

"I'd like to hear more about such things," she said. "But now is not the time. I have many other items that will take up my schedule for the rest of the day and other events upcoming in the court. We will meet again. I am interested in discussing some of the notions of free exchange you mentioned. I am always interested in change if it is in the best interest of my people. However, change has not always been kind to us in the past."

I nodded. I understood her point and her reluctance to dive in. She did have, well, people—and animals who looked and talked like people—to protect. What responsible political leader ever jumped into an idea with both feet without asking questions about whether it was a good idea? On second thought, maybe I shouldn't answer that one.

"In the meantime," she continued, "you are my guests. Please, make yourselves at home in my castle."

"While I appreciate the hospitality, I must inquire. Are there restrictions on where we can go, who we may talk to, or what we may do? I ask before we inadvertently break some rule we didn't know of, much like the visitor laws themselves."

Was I pushing it? Maybe. But at the same time, I didn't want the woman who had been immortalized in literature as a batty, homicidal megalomaniac who demanded "Off with their heads!" and would be dictating my every move to think I was trying to insult her. I liked my head very much attached to my neck, thank you kindly.

"My steward will see you to rooms that will be designated as yours for the length of your stay. I will have to ask you not to approach any of our citizens without one of our guards present. That's as much for your safety as for theirs. We just don't know who might hurt one of the villagers or kill one of them.

"I must also ask you not to criticize our leaders when you are out and about in public," she continued. "It's not very fair to our leaders, to our consumers, to our clients and shopkeepers et cetera, to hear someone undermining the very system that props many of them up. It is the system they live by. Some of them might become very protective. It's what they know."

I nodded. I understood what she was saying and why, but at the same time, I wondered if she was really trying to shield the citizens from something dangerous or from change? I didn't like how that one sounded, but *her house, her rules.*

The Queen pulled on a long red velvet rope hanging behind her throne, and a human-sized white rabbit appeared. "Steward, I need you to take these two visitors to the Visitor's Annex and assign them appropriate quarters for their stay with us. Make them comfortable, and also provide them each with a change of clothing since their wardrobe is still wet from the river."

I tried to protest that we could take care of it ourselves, but she would hear none of it.

"Miss, your clothing is soaked. It will take hours to dry, and I insist you be our guests at dinner tonight in the Great Hall. Your clothing is not appropriate for the event, even if it could be dry in time. If I insist on your presence when you are not prepared for such an event, the least I can do is to provide you with the necessary clothing. I would be a poor host if I treated my guests like poor relations. There's an event tonight that I wouldn't want you to miss."

She wouldn't tell us anything about it other than the food would be delicious and the entertainment would be illuminating to our knowledge of Wonderland. I hoped the evening's show didn't include the removal of heads . . . especially our own.

Illuminating. What a word. I wondered if she'd chosen it on purpose.

Almost without realizing it, we were ushered out of the throne room by the very being we'd been worried about since I'd seen the gigantor-sized Bert and gotten at least a partial explanation from Allie. Had that really been just this morning? And while I was on the subject, why in the world had they sent the donuts that had blown Bert up into the Frog who Crushed my Living Room?

CHAPTER TWENTY-TWO

We were following the White Rabbit down another stone corridor in the castle. How many freaking hallways were there in this maze of a place? The hall we were currently in was less ornate than the ones near the throne room where we'd met the Queen, but it was still a solidly made building. I then realized we hadn't seen a window in quite a while. Were we guests or prisoners? I didn't know, but I didn't like it.

The rabbit had a strange, loping gait, but we were able to keep up easily—with the exception being the backpack that wouldn't stay where it was supposed to on my back. I'd be glad to get to whatever room it was we were going to, because I'd just about had it with the wet clothes and the backpack sliding off and the cryptic diplomacy and not knowing what was going on with my friend, and all the unanswered questions in my brain. I was tired.

I heard a sneeze behind me. I wondered if Aiden was coming down with a cold. That wouldn't help anything. I turned my head, but I didn't see any sign he felt sick or that he'd sneezed. It had to be him, though. There wasn't anyone else behind him.

Finally, we came to a door that the rabbit opened with a large iron key.

I could not help myself. "Are you planning to lock us in?"

He shook his head no.

"Are you going to give us a key to our room?"

He handed me the key. "I will send a porter with clothing for you to wear tonight. You should have towels and blankets within so you can get warm, and there's a grate in front of the fireplace where you can hang your wet things to dry. Someone will be by to collect you for dinner." He took out a pocket watch on a chain. "Oh my, I'm late. You have about an hour."

Was he kidding me? A rabbit saying he's late? *If he tells me he has an important date, I will not be able to control the giggling,* I thought. "Thank you," was all I could manage to say aloud.

We went inside, and I struggled out of my backpack as Aiden closed the door behind the rabbit. When the door shut, my backpack sneezed. Or rather, something in my backpack sneezed. I opened it, and there he was.

It was Bert, shivering and sniffling.

"How in the world did you get in there?" I asked, yanking him out.

Aiden grabbed a towel from the shelf just inside the door and wrapped him up in it, setting Bert gently near the fireplace. There was already a fire going in the hearth, even though it was low. Aiden threw another log on the grate and stoked it with the poker he found leaning against the fireplace. Heat flared out into the room, and it felt wonderful. Bert let out a long, tortured sigh, wrapped in terrycloth. Aiden folded up another towel and laid it in front of the hearth, setting Bert on top of it to give him a soft place to warm up. I heard another pitiful sneeze coming from the pile of towels.

I could relate. We'd at least had the chance to wring some of the water out of some of our clothes, but Bert had gone into the river with my backpack apparently, and frogs weren't warm-blooded creatures by nature. He'd spent at least the last hour or so huddled in my wet bag, surrounded by a wet blanket, wet clothing, and the rest of the odds and ends I'd thought to bring. Not a one of them would have kept him warm. He'd somehow managed to keep his mouth shut, keep from sneezing, and hadn't even come out when we'd been in the room waiting for the Queen.

"What in the world are you doing in my backpack, Bert? I thought you were riding with Doris or Tobias."

He coughed, and it didn't sound good. "I came along to help. I want to help. Allie needs my help. I figured if we got separated, you and Aiden were more likely to be the ones to find her than the others, so I took advantage of the nap you all took and snuck into your backpack. How was I to know you two would end up taking an impromptu swim?"

He didn't look good. That trip in the river and the cold air afterwards hadn't done me a ton of good, but Bert definitely appeared to be ill. What was I supposed to do with a sick frog? "Bert, I wish you hadn't done that," I started, but he didn't let me finish.

"First of all, I kinda wish I hadn't done that either. I could do without the coughing and sneezing, and I can't get warm." He was shaking, even bundled up in the towel.

I looked around and found an old brick lying near the hearth. I wondered if it was used for a foot warming pan, like I'd seen in a colonial museum somewhere. It would do. I grabbed it and shoved it as close as I dared to the coals, trying to will it warm. If nothing else, maybe it would be warm enough by the time we went to dinner so I could leave him something warm to curl up with while we were gone. What I wouldn't give for a good, old-fashioned hot water bottle at the moment!

Aiden picked up the towels and hugged Bert to his chest, hoping some body heat would rub off, but he was chilled as well. I took Bert, in his towel cocoon, away from him. "Go take off that wet shirt and grab the quilt off the bed. We can hang up the shirt in front of the fire, and that way you're not getting his towel wet, too."

Aiden nodded and moved to do what I said. He stripped down to his boxers and wrapped up in the blanket. I passed Bert back to him and grabbed the wooden rocking chair in the corner, dragging it before the fire. Aiden sat down as close as he dared with the quilt trailing on the ground. I heard Bert stop making shivering noises within just a few minutes. It was worth it.

I found a small rack beside an armoire and set it up before the fireplace, hanging Aiden's sweatshirt, T-shirt, and jeans up to dry. I realized Bert was asleep in Aiden's arms, snuffling frog snores coming from somewhere near Aiden's chest. I smiled.

Was it just me, or was I picturing a much more domestic version of this? One not affected by magic, and Aiden maybe cuddling with our own child instead of a cursed, unlucky, pain-in-the-butt frog. I shook my head. I liked the idea of domesticity with Aiden, but I didn't like the distraction at the moment.

Were we prisoners? Were we guests? I wasn't sure, but I suspected the truth was somewhere in between.

Aiden looked up at me. "Strip down, Janie. Get out of your own wet clothes and under a blanket, too. Best thing you can do. That brain of yours can keep spinning while you get out of your things. I'm telling you, it's infinitely better to keep from getting sick while you ponder this one out."

He was whispering, but he needn't have bothered. Bert was actually looking a bit better, being warmed up and dry, and was drooling in his sleep. I wondered if we'd have an alcoholic beverage with dinner, and if so, I wondered if I could sneak some back for him. A good slug of something might do Bert a whole lot of good.

"What are we going to do?" I asked.

"I suspect we're going to thaw out, we're going to put on dry clothes, and we're going to go to dinner," he said. "And quite frankly, all of those things sound like a really good idea just now."

He had a point. I might have wanted everything to fall into place in my mind, to figure it all out like a puzzle that just needed one piece to fix the rest of it. Doris had said to me once that when one was lost, sometimes a good meal and a good night's sleep would put everything into perspective. It had worked before. I hoped we didn't need that long.

CHAPTER TWENTY-THREE

We let Bert sleep for a while, sitting in silence before the fire. The porter appeared with clothing for Aiden and me.

"Miss, I brought a court dress for you. Sir, here is a suit with waistcoat and tails. And for your friend, I have a bowtie."

The porter must have known Bert was there. We'd hidden him when the knock sounded on the door, but it sounded as if he was included. I still didn't think Bert was up to dinner, and I said so.

"Miss, I have instructions that all of you are to report for dinner. I do not believe the Queen wishes for anyone to remain behind, but if one is unwell, I can take a message to Her Majesty," the porter reported, folding her hands in front of herself and bowing her head as she curtsied.

I looked at Aiden.

He shrugged. "We'll bring him. However, his health may necessitate our leaving early should the festivities go long into the night. We cannot endanger him; he is a good friend whom we owe a great debt to. Can you please advise us if we will be insulting anyone if we need to make our excuses and leave due to the potential for his illness?"

She nodded. "I was aware you fell into the river. The Queen is of the opinion that all should be well and no chances should be taken with one's health. I do not believe it should be a problem, as long as you are present for the entire dinner and the entertainment. Dancing may go on into the night, but I can ask the Queen to excuse the three of you before the dancing begins."

"Please inquire of the White Rabbit or the Queen, as you think is wise. We do not wish to sound ungrateful or to insult our hosts, but we do have grave concerns regarding our friend." Aiden, as usual, knew exactly what to say. He might not be able to walk a straight line and chew gum at the same time, but that brain of his and silvered tongue? Made me smile and reminded me why I needed him in my life.

The porter laid out the dress and dropped into a curtsy as she finished. "I'll do that and will report back to you on the answer when I collect you for dinner. I'll also bring fresh blankets for your bed for tonight."

I nodded my thanks. The porter left as I was trying to figure out how in the world to get into my dress. It was a shimmery blue, slinky garment encrusted in sparkles and crystals. After examining it, I realized I could pull it on over my head. I slipped into the dress, and it was a perfect fit, hugging my hips and making me look like I was more Jessica Rabbit than a law student with a penchant for too much coffee and dessert.

There were moderate heels and fancy jewelry. I felt like I was playing dress up in clothing my stepmother might have worn in her younger days. I'd seen her in society matron finery, but never as someone at a dinner in this type of dress.

On a dresser in the corner of the room sat a hairbrush and a collection of pins. I brushed out my hair and did what I could to sweep it up off my neck, gathering it into a French twist to bare my shoulders. At last, final touch, I dug into my backpack and pulled out the necklace Aiden had given me the year before, the one that would protect me from the effects of magic. I didn't wear it much, but it was beautiful and a nice touch with the dress. It had protected me from magic when I was in danger from my stepmother. I figured it was a good idea to protect myself in the presence of the Queen.

Aiden nodded at me when he saw me put on the necklace. I thought he looked particularly good in his all-black suit, quite nearly a tuxedo, with white bow tie. He winced, because the shoes pinched his feet, but otherwise, they'd gotten the fit almost perfectly right for him as well.

We waited until the last minute to wake Bert. He opened his eyes groggily, and when I finally got him looking me in the eye, I realized his were glassy and almost feverish. I couldn't do much for him, other than to unwind the towel and set it with our now-damp blankets in a corner of the room and fasten the bow tie around his neck. We kept him sitting near the fire as the porter came in and informed us the Queen understood our concerns for Bert and was willing to excuse us after the entertainment if we felt it necessary for health reasons, as long as we agreed to stay as long as we could. I nodded.

The porter wheeled in a cart piled high with blankets and towels and indicated she would bring in a pitcher of water and basin later. I wondered just how much of this hospitality was normal and how much was setting us up somehow.

The porter gestured for us to follow her, and we did, with Bert wrapped in a new towel and riding in Aiden's hands, my arm tucked into Aiden's elbow. Despite the fever-brightness of Bert's eyes, we looked good and we knew it. We'd never taken a night to dress up and go out before. Maybe we'd have to try to do it again when we got back to the real world.

"Bert," I whispered. "We're supposed to be having dinner. I know there is an issue with eating and drinking in faerie realms. What do you know about doing so in Wonderland?"

He pondered a moment. "I've never heard of the same thing here. It's been a long time since I've heard of anyone coming here, but I've never heard of anyone being enslaved by any reason other than by their own actions. No funny business that I'm aware of, but watch the others at dinner and follow their lead."

Good advice, and not just on figuring out which fork to use, but also to see if we could recognize any other visitors and what they might be doing at such a dinner. I wondered if there was anyone present who might be able to tell us anything about Allie, and I whispered as much to Bert, although I was careful to leave out her name.

"I saw her," he replied.

"What?" I stopped walking, almost tripping Aiden. He stopped as well, and the porter didn't get more than a few steps ahead before she stopped, turning around and motioning for us to keep going. I could tell she was listening, but I wasn't sure I cared.

"I saw her this afternoon in the open air market you walked through. I was watching through the mesh opening at the top of your backpack. I saw her talking to someone. I didn't see who, but she looked like she'd gotten a change of clothing."

"Why do you say that?" Aiden asked.

"She was wearing a skirt, a long one that went all the way to the ground. It wasn't a fancy dress, like the one Janie's wearing now. It was rough material, maybe broadcloth or corduroy; I couldn't tell from the angle I had, but it wasn't upscale. She had her hair pulled back, and she was wearing a big floppy hat, but I caught a look at her face. It was her, no question," he said.

"What was she doing?" I asked. I hoped she was buying food, or talking to a friend, or otherwise socializing and doing something completely safe and innocent, but I had a funny feeling the truth wasn't anything like that. What Bert was describing sounded like a disguise. What was she hiding from here? What in the world was going on?

The porter was tapping her foot at us and acting as if we were holding her up.

I guess we were.

We'd have to talk more later, when we could actually take our time and hash it out.

I doubted Allie was still in the market, and from the hubbub I could hear through the doors in front of us, it seemed like no one else was at the market at the moment, either. It sounded like they were all at the party.

If this was the case, maybe Allie was here. I brightened at the thought and took Aiden's arm again, motioning him forward.

He nodded, and we headed off to the party.

CHAPTER TWENTY-FOUR

Without a better idea of what to do about the sighting of Allie in the courtyard, we were left with being ordered to a party. I don't think I'd ever been a party animal, but I had a million and one other things I'd rather have been doing than going to this one.

The doors opened in front of us, held by two court sentries dressed in brilliant red armor. They held red and black banners on long poles reaching above their heads, decorated with simple graphic hearts. As we came into the great hall, there were red and black draped fabrics, table décor, and all the Valentine-y goodness most Hallmark stores were draped with every February. For as tasteful and delicate as the rest of the castle had been, this was a gaudy, ugly representation, as if Cupid himself had vomited cheap hearts and flowers all over the inside of a castle.

I couldn't believe what I was seeing.

Servants were dressed in different shades of red, black, gray, pink, and fuchsia as they bobbed and curtseyed and otherwise toadied to the Queen, who sat on a giant pile of pink and maroon and red pillows on a huge throne at the far end of the hall.

Two giant cats with big, cheesy, dental office advertisement kinds of smiles lounged on either side of the Queen's oversized throne. As we walked in, one of them winked and disappeared, or at least he disappeared except for the big, cheesy grin. It made me smile back, from reflex, but it was all kinds of creepy and wrong.

However, this party wasn't quite as big as I'd have thought from the sounds behind the door. There might have been thirty people, and I did mean people, as opposed to the anthropomorphic animals from the market. There was a hum of conversation as we walked in, but the hall itself echoed to make it sound as if there were more people than there actually were. I was somewhat disappointed.

We were directed to one table with a couple of empty seats, room enough for the two of us and Bert to squeeze in without trouble. We were sitting near an older couple who gave each other very significant glances as we sat down, but they didn't say anything. There was a blond woman with a scar across her face sitting across the table who didn't react at all as we sat down. I realized within a second or two that she was blind, and there were so many people around that she probably hadn't heard and couldn't see us sitting down in front of her.

She looked vaguely familiar, but she didn't appear as though she was upset, or lost, or otherwise being hurt or tortured to be here. The scar on her face looked old and had healed cleanly. Whoever stitched up the wound had done a decent job. It seemed as though she'd gotten medical attention somewhere, because the scar didn't look like it caused her any pain or discomfort, but may have contributed to her vision problems. She had to know it would be one of the first things a new person would notice about her, but she did not act as if she was trying to hide it.

As I looked down the table, I saw several others, all at least twenty years older than Aiden and me, and none of them gave the impression they had been compelled or otherwise forced to be at this dinner. Not one of them looked malnourished or like they'd been mistreated, but none of them actually looked happy, either.

What was going on?

I leaned over to the man beside me and asked, "Is this a regular feature for visitors to Wonderland, or just for the newbies?"

He snorted. "This is something the Queen does to make it appear as though she likes visitors."

"Why would she worry about that?" Aiden asked. "We weren't aware this was actually a tourist destination. Who would be concerned about it if she did treat visitors badly?"

It was a good question, but the man shrugged. "I don't know. All I know is that she doesn't want people walking around and talking to Wonderland citizens, she doesn't want anyone to leave, and she doesn't really want more visitors coming to stay. She's convinced someone, somewhere, has spread the word that Wonderland is a wonderful place to visit and then visitors will somehow ruin her lands."

Paranoid much? I wondered. And then it hit me. It was about Allie and her mother. Something fishy was going on. Something about

Allie's mother and her initial visit to Wonderland might have made it easier for visitors from other lands to come. But why was that such a bad thing? I winked at Aiden, trying to signal to him to follow my lead, but he just gave me a very confused look. We were going to have to work on our signals.

"When did this start?" I asked. "Even better, what happened? Has she ever allowed visitors to wander around Wonderland? Why is she worried about it?"

Before he could answer, the Queen grabbed hold of a giant staff and banged it on the ground. "No more questions!"

The hall fell silent.

Had she heard us? What was going on? Aiden and I looked at each other, but I had no idea what he was thinking. The Queen stood up from the throne and all of the pillows, reaching over the pet one of the large cats on the head. It purred and disappeared from sight.

"All of you are here because I have requested your presence. You are here because my citizens need to be protected from you, from outside influences and sicknesses. They did not want anything to change until someone put ideas into their heads. They were happy, healthy, and otherwise ready to go on about their lives. They were obedient; they were productive. None of that happens now. But I am not a monster. I feed and clothe all our visitors. I do no harm to them."

A gentleman at the end of the table stood up. "But you do not let us leave. We all have families and children and homes and lives we have not been allowed to return to. Though it's true you don't actively hurt us, you keep us here. But how long can we live in seclusion without the seclusion itself becoming a mode of torture? All we can do is sit here, day after day, and wait, hoping you'll change your mind and let us go home to whatever parts of our lives are left."

She shot out one hand, pointing at him. "I shall call you my Knave, good sir. You are not being a good guest, and I shall not allow you to taint the others around you. You have been so well-behaved, I wonder at why you are acting out in such a manner."

Oh, dear. She was unhinged. She was cray-cray and completely off her rocker. The man had been rational, reasoned, and calm as he spoke. She had ignored him completely and started talking about etiquette. Something was truly wrong here. It reminded me strongly of someone.

My evil faerie stepmother. But it wasn't her; the Queen in this realm didn't look anything like her. I recognized the crazy, though. It reminded me too strongly of someone with absolute power with absolutely no idea of what it was like to be subject to that power.

Did she have a sister I hadn't known about?

CHAPTER TWENTY-FIVE

The whole hall had fallen silent. Everyone sat and stared at the man, who was still standing but had not said anything else. Everyone else seemed to be staring at their plates. No one was eating, although there were all kinds of different tarts all over the table. Fruit tarts, savory tarts, spiced tarts, every kind I could imagine were heaped on giant serving trays.

The man at the end of the table didn't follow everyone else's lead; he had something to say, and the oppressive, scared silence didn't stop him.

"I'm tired of tarts. It seems to be the only thing you will feed us. Tarts all day, every day, morning, noon, and night. Is there nothing else to eat in this place except your tarts? You say you do not mistreat us, but you hold us in lonely cells with monotonous food, and our only crime is not being from Wonderland itself. You have to understand that we are willing to make promises for silence, for obedience, for all kinds of other things if you give us just a bit of hope."

The whole place remained quiet. I wanted to ask a million questions, but I didn't know what would happen if I stood up and asked them, so I didn't. Instead, I waited along with all of the others.

The Queen made her way over to the man, sashaying in such a fashion that the train of her gown trailed perfectly behind her on the cobbles of the stone floor. Her hair was styled above her head in an intricate birdcage of a design that hinted at a heart, with the shape of her face being accentuated to look more heart-shaped as well. I suddenly wondered if she tweezed her hairline to give herself the widow's peak to form the top of the heart for her face. As she minced her way past me, I watched the train and realized it formed the bottom peak of a heart. I wondered what she'd done to the front, but I wasn't here for style tips or fashion advice. We were in serious trouble if she was going to make us stay here forever with Bert.

She picked up a tart, delicately, with two fingers, holding it out before her as if it was a prize to be won. "Are you saying you wish to decline my hospitality? You wish to decline life in the castle?"

He gulped. "What happens if I decline?"

She ignored him and again asked if he wished to decline her hospitality.

He kept trying to ask questions to find out his options, but she refused to answer, just smiling politely and waving the tart in front of his face. "Are you hungry?" she asked him.

He nodded, and she held out the tart. He tried to reach up to take it from her, and she danced back, out of his reach.

It was like a kid taunting the neighborhood dog. No matter how well-behaved the dog, no matter how pleasant and how well-trained, there are only so many times one can wave a treat in front of a dog when it's hungry. Sooner or later, something was going to happen. The man was going to do something . . .

Only he didn't.

He instead stood there with way more self-control than so many people would have had. Heck, he had more self-control than I had. I'd have snatched the damn thing by now, except for the fact that I didn't want to eat any food she offered. I didn't trust it, and we hadn't been here long enough for me to be starving or desperate. I wondered if any of the food Doris packed had made it into my bag or Aiden's and whether it had survived the trip down the river. I was looking forward to getting back to our room and checking. I hadn't seen what Doris had packed for everyone, but I hoped she'd spread it around a bit.

The wait went on, with the others staring down at their plates still empty of food. Aiden and I couldn't look away from the show between the Queen and the man who wouldn't be cowed by her. Bert was sitting on my lap, but he wasn't high enough to watch, and he kept bumping my leg, over and over, as if trying to get me to tell him what was going on.

I leaned down and shushed him, but he wouldn't settle, so I moved my dishes over to sit on top of Aiden's plate and lifted Bert onto the table. It wasn't like he was going to be able to eat from where he was sitting on my lap anyway. Of course, once he saw what was going on, he couldn't keep completely still.

"Janie," he whispered.

I looked down. "What?" I mouthed, trying not to breathe a sound.

"I know who that is," he stage whispered. Luckily, his voice didn't carry very far. Aiden heard it, though, and tore his attention away from the Queen. He turned to Bert, who looked all kinds of awkward in his sequined bow tie. "It's Benjamin Bathurst," Bert said.

That was supposed to mean something to me? "Who the hell is that?" I asked.

"He disappeared in Germany during the Napoleonic Wars. Everyone offered rewards for information leading to his return, even a prince in Prussia, but they never found him. Everyone thought he was murdered by one of Napoleon's agents, but Napoleon always denied it. At one point, they found a skeleton in a house not far from where he disappeared, and many believe it was him, but his family was unable to identify the remains. It happened before DNA, before fingerprints, and before modern coroners and forensic science."

"How do you know it's him?"

"I recognize him from the papers back in the day. I never thought anything of it, never thought it would be magically related."

Wow. I was impressed with Bert's memory, but at the same time, something was bothering me about this.

I watched the Queen bounce and flounce and tease and cajole Mr. Bathurst, and I realized what it was. Hey, I'd paid attention in my history classes. I couldn't have told anyone what house was which in the War of the Roses, but I did remember the Napoleonic Wars came before the Civil War . . . which meant Mr. Bathurst's disappearance happened well before Alice in Wonderland was published. That meant he was likely here when Allie's mother was in Wonderland the first time, and he'd been here since then. Or had he?

Either way, I wanted to talk to him in a very serious way. Maybe he could fill in a lot of the blanks Aiden and Bert couldn't. I knew they were getting frustrated because they couldn't answer anything, but what could we do? We were stuck sitting here until the Queen got done playing with Mr. Bathurst, whatever he might do.

Soon, the Queen tired of her game and simpered her way out of the room. The two creepily smiling, dentally perfect cats followed her, grinning the entire way out. I was happy to see them go. The guards went with them. There were still servants on the edge of the room, but they weren't close enough to hear us talk if we kept our voices low.

I turned to the people on either side of us and asked, "So, how does this work? Are there rules we are expected to follow? How long do we have to stay?"

The blind lady looked up. Well, she moved her face, as if she'd be looking up if she'd been able to see. "We never leave. We follow the rules Euphegenia set out for us. And we live here all the time."

"You never go out into Wonderland?" I asked. There was something else here, something I just didn't understand yet, and it might come in handy once I figured it out.

"It is forbidden. We eat, we sleep, we live the way the Queen dictates to us. That is all there is."

"Have you ever asked? Has it been just understood, or something she has specifically forbidden?" Aiden asked.

"We have not been allowed to leave for years. She does not permit it."

The others began to get up, mill around, and talk softly, but they did not eat. No one did. There was a ton of food there, and no one touched it.

"Something wrong with the tarts?" Bert asked.

"Yes," Mr. Bathurst said, coming over to us. "She does not allow us to eat unless she has given permission. She did not give us permission; therefore, we cannot eat."

Damn. I saw Bert eyeing one of the pastries and snatched him up before he could sink his teeth into the nearest strawberry tart. We didn't want to cause a problem before we'd figured out what was going on.

One would think that frog would have learned not to eat something just because it looked good.

CHAPTER TWENTY-SIX

M r. Bathurst gave us the skinny. He'd gotten to Wonderland because he had gone through a rabbit hole outside of an inn. He'd tried to escape again, several times, but he'd never found a way to get out of Wonderland. Bert told him about the skeleton. Mr. Bathurst said he was never at the house where it was found. He seemed genuinely upset that his sister had to look at a corpse and try to figure out if it was him.

"Back to the Queen," I said. "When did she get goofy about visitors? Was she always this way?"

"No," he said. "I was here a number of years before she started rounding up visitors. Wonderland was a literal wonderland of experiences—some good, some bad, some just downright funny. The people are wonderfully naïve, but good-hearted, and they were always genuinely interested in other lands, other people, and other places. Then a little girl showed up."

That had to be Allie's mom.

He continued without me saying anything. "Well, no one ever figured they could leave once they got stuck here. We all tried to make the best of it. We tried to re-establish our lives here, working with the local population, but then all the anti-visitor laws started. We weren't allowed to open a business without a license. Then we weren't allowed to sell to certain classes of Wonderland residents. Then we weren't allowed to buy supplies for our businesses from residents here; we could only buy them from ourselves. Then we weren't allowed to travel. It kept bringing us into a smaller and smaller circle, until we were finally brought into the castle. We have not been allowed to leave since."

Apparently the rules kept getting tighter and tighter, but there hadn't been any new visitors in many years until we showed up. They had questions, about what year it was, about current events. One or two asked where we were from and were disappointed to learn we were from Ohio as opposed to wherever it was they were from. I could tell they wanted to ask about families and loved ones, and I hated being unable to answer their questions.

The only one who didn't ask anything was the blind woman. She waited until the commotion of the others' questions had died down and then asked Mr. Bathurst if he could help her come over and talk to us. He took her arm and helped her to a seat next to where we'd sat during the party that had never become a party. She reached one hand out, and I caught it in mine.

Her hand was soft and warm, and she placed her other hand on top of mine. "He knows most of it, but does not know all."

"What do you mean?" I asked. "What else is there?"

"He's not telling you about the girl who left."

The others all tittered and whispered behind their hands.

"They don't want me to tell you about her," said the woman. "They're scared. I don't blame them, but you need to know the truth. I wish I knew the whole story, but I know enough of it for them to be worried."

"What's the truth?" I asked. "What is so scary about someone actually leaving?"

She shook her head and smiled. "It's because of the level of anger the Queen would display if she knew we were talking about her."

How bad could it be? She might be mad, but what would she do? Then again, if it had been my stepmother, it could be pretty bad. Maybe it was just the whole crown and throne thing, but I wondered if they were related in some way. I asked about consequences.

"She likes to humiliate us if she is in any way embarrassed, but the severity of the punishment has more to do with how much loss of face she suffers from our behavior. If it's bad enough, she does like beheadings." One of the older people who hadn't said much contributed this in a voice barely above a whisper.

They were terrified of the Queen. It wasn't hard to see. So what had driven Mr. Bathurst to open his mouth and speak out? He had done it when other Wonderland-ians were not around, but at the same time, it still didn't seem like a smart move. Didn't he fear retribution like the others?

I asked the question, and he sighed, shrugging his shoulders. "After a couple of years, does it really matter much anymore? It isn't as though she's going to make our lives less miserable. We exist here, day by day, but it's not like we're actually going to ever get out of here. Is it worth being punished yourself, to hopefully make things better for the others involved? Is it worth ending the never ending boredom of being forced into a life where nothing ever changes and nothing ever gets better?"

I understood, but probably not in the way he thought. I had the opposite problem. My life was a little too exciting, in a way that always had us scrambling to come up with a solution to yet another dangerous mystery with someone I cared about at the center of the controversy. A part of me welcomed the idea of monotony with Aiden, to figure out why it was so attractive to me, but I still didn't know how magic or time or anything else actually worked here. I didn't want to spend a day or two and then finally get home and find out two hundred years had passed back home. That would really put a crimp in my plans to graduate and take the bar exam before I officially turned two hundred years old in the real world.

I looked at Aiden, and he had the same look of concern on his face that I was sure was on mine. "So how long do we have to stay in the hall?" I asked. "It has been a long day, and Bert was running a fever earlier."

Two of the ladies immediately began fussing over Bert in a way I wouldn't have thought he would mind, but he was trying to brush them off. I explained about our impromptu swim, and the blind lady asked what promises we'd made.

More about promises, then. I'd been smart to ask about specifics before we'd agreed to dinner. My stepmother had been caught up in her own promises, all her inconsistencies and lies, and she was now in the faerie court version of jail, Søborg Castle. The Seawitch, who'd been after Mia, was also bound by the promises of her sister, the Snow Queen, who vowed to keep us safe from the Seawitch's vengeance against Mia's family. And here we were again. Maybe I had a promising future in negotiating contracts after I got home, finished school, and became a lawyer.

"I promised to stay for dinner and the entertainment. We had permission to leave once the dancing started," I explained.

"Then you're as stuck as we are," the blind lady explained.

"Because we aren't allowed to eat yet. I don't know what she considered entertainment, but the dancing does not start until she allows it. If you're not allowed to leave until after dinner and dancing, but she withholds her permission for those things, then you don't yet have permission to go."

Oh, crap. She was right. We were stuck.

CHAPTER TWENTY-SEVEN

Well, we were sure screwed.

We couldn't leave. We couldn't eat. And we couldn't go looking for Allie or for the rest of our friends, or ask questions of Alfred, or anything else we wanted to do. The reality was I did still have concerns about Wonderland, but I had other things I wanted to do more. I was hungry, but that could wait. I'd had breakfast that morning, and I'd had a granola bar earlier. My stomach might not like it, but I could wait a bit for more food.

I didn't have a choice. I'd learned the importance of keeping promises in magical lands. We took advantage of however long we were stuck with the other visitors by asking questions about magic and all kinds of things pertaining to Wonderland. It was definitely a land that had seen better days.

Apparently, time sped up and slowed down depending on the mindset of the person involved. There was no way to predict if we'd lost two hundred years or two seconds; it fluctuated based on whether or not the person in charge of the clock was seeing time stretch forever in front of them, or if they were hurrying to get somewhere.

This was where the story about the White Rabbit looking at his watch had come from. He had been the one to keep track of time until more and more humans found their way into Wonderland and the time status quo got thrown off. Apparently, humans had more innate control over time than the Rabbit did, even though he had years and years and centuries and millennia of practice, due to our own expanded consciousness. The other visitors also thought the Rabbit had stopped paying attention to time when he'd taken on extra duties for the Queen.

He'd obviously been promoted at some point, if he'd gone from Court Timekeeper to Court Everything Guy. No wonder he'd kind of lost track of time.

Well, here was hoping our own impatience at trying to find Allie would keep time running in our favor; I had work to do before I went back to school on Monday. I just wanted to find my friend, make sure she was safe, and help her if I could. Speaking of helping Allie . . . . Maybe these people had an idea or two about where to find her? I didn't want to ask much about Allie herself, in case the Queen's servants were listening. I had no idea whether it was a good idea for the Queen to know about Allie or her mother or our connection to either one, and I didn't want to inadvertently put our friend in more danger if I didn't have to.

But I *could* ask about more general things a new visitor might be expected to ask about. "You said something about a little girl?" I asked. I could hear the sharp intake of breath. "You made it sound like something happened to her. Did she manage to leave?"

They all sat, or stood, in front of us and stared very intently at their own belly buttons. What was so scary about a little girl? "Look, I was curious if she was okay, but my bigger question isn't really about the girl. I don't see any little girls here at the moment. I assume she left. I want to ask about how she was able to leave. If she was able to leave, then maybe there's a way for the rest of us to get out of here."

Mr. Bathurst came forward again. "What year is it, currently, in the mortal realm?"

I told him. It was 2014. I gave him the date and time we left to step through the rabbit hole in our backyard. He slowly shook his head, and I saw a tear in his eye as he spoke. "There's nothing for us to go back to."

"What do you mean?" Aiden asked.

"Time speeds up or slows down. It does not go backwards. The little girl, well, she left once. She came back. She was here for three months the first time, but when she returned, she told me she'd missed six years in her own life. She then came back a week later, and she was eight years older. That's when we started figuring out the time differential. That was when we started to learn that time only went forward, and most of our families were already long dead."

"Many of us have nothing left. Our spouses, our parents, our children, are dead and gone. We know no one in the mortal world. We've all uprooted our lives at least once. How many people can do it twice? And none of us did it the first time because we wanted to. We landed here. We made it work. How many times can one person be forced to start over, from scratch?"

Why didn't he know more about the girl who left? And why was he talking about Allie's mother? Why wasn't he talking about Allie as the girl who also left?

Allie's voice was ringing in my head. She'd not been able to get a job because she didn't have a birth certificate or a Social Security number. She couldn't prove her own identity, and even the types of agencies that might have been able to help her would have asked for a social security number in order to sign her up for services. Children's Services, food stamps, cash assistance, a medical card, emergency shelter, rent assistance, foster families, work programs, and food pantries all had databases these days that many of them shared in order to make sure no one person was hogging all of the resources available and to ensure they could help as many people as possible.

Doris told me once about volunteering for a local food pantry and the types of limitations and such to prevent abuse. If Allie had such trouble finding and getting help when she wasn't ready for that kind of roadblock, what kind of help would these people need? How would they acclimate themselves to modern-day life? My house wasn't set up to take care of this many people, and neither was my budget. How could they all get help without committing major amounts of fraud? What could we do?

But I couldn't leave them if I was able to get out of Wonderland. I had to find a way to take them all with me if they wanted to go. I'd find someone, somewhere, who could help. Maybe Tobias knew someone. Or Doris, or Harold, or Stanley.

What could I do?

At the moment, nothing. And I hated feeling helpless.

Bert filled in the gaps for us. He started asking questions about the marketplace we'd seen on the way into the castle. Leave it to Bert. He'd found a way to ask questions that might lead us to Allie without asking about Allie herself. They told us the market was open every day, and sometimes, as a reward for good behavior, the Queen would let them walk out into the market and browse the stalls. They were not allowed to buy food, as food was provided for them. They were not allowed to buy clothing, as it was also provided, but they were allowed to buy trinkets and crafts and items not necessary for day-to-day life. They were also allowed to sell their own items from time to time, in order to earn the money they spent at the market.

"Are there any planned excursions into the market coming up?" Aiden asked.

That might be our entrée into the marketplace to look for Allie, or to try to figure out what she might have been doing there. I hoped we wouldn't have to wait long. I wasn't exactly known for being good at waiting for things, and I was beyond impatient to find her. Patience was only a virtue when I didn't have to wait for it.

The blind woman smiled. "We are allowed out in the mornings, unless something has happened to prevent the entire group from stepping out. At most, Mr. Bathurst might be prohibited from going with us, but the rest of us are still looking forward to the outing. Trust me, that's likely to be the extent of the punishment for his outburst."

Well, I hoped she was right. I wanted to get on about our search and see what we could do for Allie. I hoped the Queen was consistent and we would be allowed out as soon as possible. I didn't really feel like being patient while I waited to get on with looking for our friends.

"What happens if someone tries to escape?" I whispered.

"If they're caught?" the blind woman asked.

"Yes, if they're caught. I'd assume if they weren't caught, they'd go on about their lives, whatever they were escaping to," I said, impatient.

The blind woman laughed, a cynical laugh, that held back a century of pain, tears, and loneliness. "That's the problem. It's rare to escape and actually get away, and the Queen goes searching for anyone who does. She doesn't want anyone to escape. She wants to control everything. She's gotten more and more unhinged over the last several years, however, because there is one person who has gotten away and who has not yet been caught. I hope she never finds who she is looking for, but I can't say she won't."

"What happens if she's found?" Bert asked.

"Why, that depends on the Queen's mood at the moment the girl is found. If it's a good day, then she might eventually end up here with the rest of us. If it's a bad day, the Queen might cut off her head to make an example of her to the rest of us. Either way, the Queen is not predictable on the subject of escapees," the blind woman said.

"How do you know that?" Aiden asked. "What has she done in the past?"

"I've seen a man who escaped once before. He kept telling the Queen she should open her doors to tourism, to 'capitalize on the wonders of Wonderland' as he called it. He was put here, with the 'rest of the humans,' and the rules were explained to him. He escaped the same night, and when he was caught, he took an attitude with the Queen, telling her she was stifling her economy and punishing her people. He told her she was evil and a bad Queen."

That didn't sound like a pleasant scenario. "What happened?" Bert asked.

"She cut off his head."

CHAPTER TWENTY-EIGHT

W ell, put me down for something other than that. I'd prefer my head to stay right where it is, connected at the neck. And I'd just been telling the Queen outside influences could be good for Wonderland. I still believed what I'd said was true, but this maybe explained the odd behavior in response to my statements as well as the lack of real discussion about the idea. Apparently she didn't like outsiders getting involved in her realm's internal issues. Well, I didn't plan to bring it up again, although it appeared her basic objection was to anyone who questioned her own ideas.

It seemed like the native Wonderland denizens were all kinds of happy . . . as long as they kept her happy. Except they weren't happy, and it didn't appear there was any consistent way to keep the Queen happy, either.

When did Alfred's drinking start? It seemed, from what he'd said, it began when the policies about outside visitors began affecting his business. But that didn't make sense. If the Queen's policies were consistent, then it wasn't like the visitors would have made up much business for the hatter before he'd had to take up guard duty to make ends meet. But then why had he blamed the Queen for the policies against visitors? Was it the rambling of a drunk looking for some other excuse for his drinking, or was there something we weren't being told? If the latter was true, I wasn't sure the people here would actually know the difference, as they'd been so sheltered from the truth of the Queen's influence on Wonderland.

"So, are we the only humans in Wonderland?" I asked. "Or are there other castles with other humans? Are there any human settlements, or pockets of free humans, or other beings from other realms?"

They all began looking at each other, as if somehow the answers would be written on their faces rather than in their memories.

Mr. Bathurst was the one who spoke up. It was definitely appearing as if he and the blind woman were the leaders of the group.

"We don't have any way to know. We haven't seen any other humans. We don't have contact with any other humans. As far as we know, we're it."

I had a funny sort of thought that started niggling its way around in my brain. "Has there ever been a request for any special leave from this place, for any special dispensation to travel the land? Has anyone ever visited Wonderland who was able to gain the Queen's permission to be here, and if so, how did they get it?"

No one acted like they wanted to answer. There was a lot of shuffling and clearing of throats. They knew something, and apparently no one wanted to be the one to cough up the answer. That told me no one was willing to risk talking in front of the Queen's lackeys. I wondered if we would ever get the chance to talk without her retainers in the same room.

We were stuck in the hall for what seemed like hours. We had no way of knowing how long we'd be there, or if we'd ever get out of there and back to our own room. I was ready to pull my hair out of my head by the roots from sheer boredom before the porter finally came and told us the rest of the party was cancelled and we should all head back to our assigned quarters. We did as we were told, the shuffling of our footsteps on the cobbles the only noise as we went back to our cells.

Aiden, Bert, and I got back to our room and found a pleasant fire burning in the hearth, and we had a fresh pitcher of water on top of the dresser. A small pallet had been made up on the hearth, presumably for Bert. So why did I feel so uneasy about closing my eyes?

Aiden must have felt the same way, because he flicked the lock behind us and checked the latch on the wooden window shutters to make sure they were secured from the inside. Our clothes were dry on the racks before the fire, so I folded them up, leaving the still-damp sneakers before the fire. Those would take longer to dry out the rest of the way.

Our backpacks did not appear to have been touched. They were still slightly damp and still tied tightly enough at the drawstring tops to be obvious if someone had untied and retied the wet strings. I opened mine and found not only the change of clothing I'd grabbed for myself and Aiden—which, of course, were wet and needed to be laid out on the racks where our other clothing had dried earlier—but some food and bottles of water. I could have wept; it was such a beautiful sight.

Doris had been smart enough to stash a few items of food in our backpacks, real food and not Wonderland food. We each had a fork, a couple of cans of Spaghetti-Os, and some foil-wrapped packages of blueberry Pop-Tarts zipped in plastic sandwich baggies. Apparently she had thought about the possibility of our getting drenched and had planned accordingly.

Stanley's camera, on the other hand, had not fared so well with the dunking in the river. When I fished it out of the backpack, I had to pull off the lens and pour water out of the body of the camera. The film inside was wet, and the battery to the flash attachment was ruined. I shook my head and hoped I'd be able to find a repair shop that could clean it all out when I got back home . . . if I got back home. I'd hate to have been the one to ruin Stanley's camera. Then again, I had a funny feeling he would be unhappier with the thought I couldn't take any pictures for him than the fact that his camera was inoperable.

We stripped out of the dress clothes, and I pulled on my dry shirt. Aiden followed my lead, changing into his own dry clothing. I took apart all the pieces to Stanley's camera and set them out on a clean, dry towel to air out for the night. Aiden wrapped Bert in another towel and tucked him into his pallet. It was getting late, and there was no question we'd end up at least spending the night here. We needed to get the rest of our things dried out. We needed to regroup. And our one lead to find Allie was in the market, which was closed for the night.

We needed to follow Tobias's example and get some sleep when we had the downtime to do it, to rest whenever we could. And we needed to conserve what food we had in order to prevent getting desperate enough to take those tarts. I had a funny feeling that even if they didn't *compel* behavior like they would in any other realm, the pastries might be a way of *controlling* behavior. The Queen could be feeding them substances hidden in the tarts to reduce a desire to escape. Aiden and I couldn't risk anything that might prevent us getting outside of the castle in search of information, or leads, or anything about finding our friend.

We split a package of Pop-Tarts and each drank some of the water. The water wouldn't last long, but we'd make it stretch. Morning was time enough to figure out what to do next, especially if there was an outing in the market planned.

Bert curled up on his pallet and fell right to sleep, snoring and drooling. I bet the day had worn him out, and the healing power of a good night's rest beside a warm fire, in dry blankets and pillows, would likely do him a world of good. I know I was looking forward to it myself, if only to get to the looking-for-Allie faster.

There wasn't much we could do but try to get warm, get some sleep, and hope morning came quickly without incident. I stood by the fire, rubbing my shoulders absently, and Aiden put his arms around me, as if trying to get me warm.

"It's okay, Janie. We might be stuck here for a bit, but we have each other, and we'll find a way out. It's okay." He kept repeating himself, as if he was trying to reassure me, but somehow, it just made me more and more worried about what was going to come next.

"Aiden, I know we'll figure a way out. I refuse to give up. It's not okay; it's not anywhere close to okay, but there was a lot the other visitors were trying to tell us without saying it explicitly. There's more to what they know. I wonder if we could get them to tell us, if we could talk to them without the servants hanging around and eavesdropping."

He leaned back and looked down at me, his arms still around me, but an expression of confusion and disbelief was on his face. It was as if he'd given up; that wasn't his personality, and it definitely wasn't mine. Something hinky was going on here.

"Regardless of what we might think about the situation, there's a potential here for information that we had no way of getting access to in any way other than being in the castle. I think the visitors knew Allie's mother, and I think they knew Allie herself. They know *something* about her. I wonder if she grew up in this castle . . ."

If she did, how did Allie learn to be so resilient? How did she learn to adapt to such a radically different world as our own if she'd never seen anything new, or different, or challenging, day in and day out, for her entire life? I was betting Allie hadn't been solely confined to the castle, that she'd either had permission to leave, or had snuck out of the castle without asking. Of course, there was also the possibility of other human settlements, as I'd asked about earlier. I hoped I hadn't endangered anyone by talking about those possibilities, but I didn't know what else to ask.

Something truly fishy was going on here, and I wanted to know what it was. I *needed* to know what I was missing, as it might be the final piece of the puzzle I required to find my friend. Allie had to have contacts in Wonderland, or she'd have been right here, with us. She had to have some idea of how Wonderland worked, or why would she have gone down that rabbit hole to protect us from whatever was after her? If she had no experience in the rest of Wonderland, this would be her home. We'd have seen her at dinner and been able to ask all of our questions on the spot. She hadn't been there.

So what was she hiding? *Where* was she hiding? And how were we going to find her?

CHAPTER TWENTY-NINE

There were no real answers to be had. I brought up my concerns with Aiden, and he nodded. "I was wondering the same thing. We have to do what we can, pushing the boundaries of those laws if we must, to find out what Allie thought she could accomplish by coming here and why. She had to have known about the visitor laws. I can't believe she didn't. So if she knew, why come back? This isn't exactly a glamorous life."

He was right about that.

We couldn't come up with any real solutions, so we crawled under the covers. It took me a while to fall asleep because my brain was twirling and swirling with ideas like kids on a Tilt-A-Whirl. I couldn't stop thinking . . . but fell asleep anyway.

I woke up the next morning with a start, bolting upright in the bed, my hair standing up from static electricity. "Alfred!"

Aiden sat up, yawning. "What would you think if I sat up suddenly in bed and shouted out another woman's name? What do you want with that guy? He's probably drunk."

"He might be," I said. "But he's both technically human and a Wonderland native. In other words, we might be able to talk to him when others are off limits."

"Good plan, Janie," Bert called out from his pallet on the floor, yawning and stretching. "But how do you plan to get a message to him if he's with the other half of our group? Certainly you don't want them to be ensnared and brought here to the castle to sit with you, do you?"

He had a point, but if we saw Alfred in the courtyard, we might be able to talk with him. After all, he was on guard duty at least part of the time and might be around.

A knock sounded at the door. We hurried to dress in our spare clothes, stuffing our things back into our packs. I didn't want to leave anything behind. Within minutes, we were ready to go, with my hair shoved back in a ponytail, Aiden in a beat-up-but-dry baseball cap, and Bert perched in the top of my backpack so he could look over my shoulder and around behind us. It was time to head to the market.

The porter who had come for us was not exactly excited to see us packed up. "Miss, sir, there's no need to carry your belongings in the market."

I smiled at her. "The backpacks allow us to carry things without our hands being full. And it gives Bert a place to ride. I don't want him hopping around on these stones after he caught his chill last night, and this way we can take turns carrying him without having to switch a pack back and forth." Neat, rational, and a good excuse should we have an opportunity to slip off. I hadn't ruled that one out yet, either, but I was all about leaving my options open.

The porter didn't question us too much about it. Either she was going to tell the Queen we were planning something, she believed my crazy story, or she didn't want to be in the middle of it. The porter could be being deliberately obtuse, or she truly didn't care what we did. I was hoping for the latter. If she was putting on an act, it was hard telling who she was actually working for, and I didn't want another mystery to figure out on top of finding Allie, finding a way home, and doing whatever I could to keep everyone safe.

Bert acted like he was seriously shopping, pointing to things as we came out of the castle, into the market, and into the sunlight. He kept asking if we could look closer at some of the goods and crafts and other items for sale. The porter reminded us we were not to buy food or clothing, but if we wished to stock items we could pursue as hobbies to pass the time, we could.

She handed us each a few copper coins and told us these were the currency being used. I took them and put them in my pocket, but I had a sinking sensation in the pit of my stomach about accepting something from someone in a magical land. If it hadn't been for Bert whispering in my ear it was okay to take it, I probably would have tried to refuse.

Even if we ended up leaving Wonderland, it would be a good souvenir, and if we only got out of the castle, but not out of Wonderland, having money of some kind couldn't hurt. I was wearing the necklace I'd been given by Aiden last year to detect magic, but it didn't do anything to warn me of the presence of magic. I'd sniff the coins later and see if I could smell anything. I'd have Bert and Aiden do the same.

Magic smelled enticing, and it was individual to the person doing the sniffing. I smelled old books and peppermint, which reminded me of my dad. Aiden said he always smelled licorice and freshly mowed grass. We'd have to put it to the test and hope we'd be able to tell if it was actually dangerous. Meanwhile, I didn't have an excuse I could think of to turn it down, and we might actually find something interesting at the market.

The porter was watching us, but not actually holding our hands or walking with us in the market. I saw the others from dinner the night before also walking around, and none of them were being escorted by porters either. Plenty of servants in the Queen's livery were milling around, however. It was clear they'd see any purchases specifically outlawed, but I was pretty sure none of them would overhear conversations. At least, I hoped so.

With Bert whispering in my ear, we made our way through the stalls toward a booth at the edge where he'd seen Allie the day before. The shopkeeper took one look at us in our jeans, sneakers, and sweatshirts, and I saw a look of recognition on her face. "You must be the ones she was talking about."

I picked up a basket and pretended to be staring at the weaving, leaning in as if asking about its make and other details. The shopkeeper, a hedgehog with a raspy voice and intelligent eyes, leaned in as well, pointing at the bridge and the handle. She whispered to me that Allie knew we were in Wonderland and she'd left a letter for us.

I had the irrational and hysterical thought that Stanley would eat this up. All this cloak and dagger stuff was right up his alley. He was convinced Dick Cheney was to blame for portals in the mortal world. He also thought George Bush the First had arranged it in order to be able to insert CIA operatives through the faerie worlds and out again in places without the military drops that could be tracked by satellites. Of course, there were days I wondered if he was wearing a tinfoil hat, but Stanley was mostly harmless.

Had I read any spy thrillers lately? Maybe Ken Follett or Tom Clancy or Robert Ludlum would have known what the proper steps would be to get a message from someone without being seen. I always got caught passing notes in school, so I had no idea what I was supposed to do next.

Mrs. Hedgehog winked at me. "It's okay," she whispered. "I've hidden the letter in a small basket of craft supplies I know is approved for visitors. They don't search it if they've given prior approval, and they have. If you pay me with the coins I know they gave you, I can sell you a basket with the letter inside. If you just act normal, they won't think anything of it. And even if they did, I've read it. There's nothing in the letter that would give away her whereabouts or implicate her in any way."

I heard the unspoken meaning in the way she said it. It might not implicate Allie or lead anyone to her, but if Mrs. Hedgehog was caught with the letter, it may implicate *her*. Being in possession of it might also implicate us in doing something other than shopping for mundane craft supplies. In other words, having a fireplace in our room might turn out to be a good thing once we'd read Allie's note.

I reached into my pocket for the coins the porter gave me, and pulled them out. I looked over and saw the porter watching as she talked with another servant, but she wasn't paying us close attention. It looked like she was doing some of her own shopping, so I handed over a coin and received the small basket in exchange.

Bert kept his mouth shut and Aiden didn't say anything as we moved on to the next stall to keep shopping. I wanted to pull out the letter and start reading as quickly as I could, but I was going to have to wait until we got either out of range of our keeper, or back to our own room. As we looked at fabrics and hats and yarn and woodworking tools, we made a few selections to keep our purchases varied.

Even so, the few small coins we'd been given went a long way. I wondered at the strength of their economy if they were selling their wares so cheaply, but I didn't know if this market was representative of Wonderland as a whole. And we weren't exactly here as economic tourists.

Finally, our interminable morning in the market was over, and we were herded back to our room. The porter pointed to a basket of tarts in the room and indicated we were to eat dinner on our own. I guessed the Queen wasn't partial to seeing her visitors or allowing them to socialize. I was okay with that. As much as I had a million and one questions for the others, my biggest concern was figuring out what in the world Allie would have risked putting in the letter.

CHAPTER THIRTY

Once we were finally back in our room alone with the door shut, Bert off his perch on the top of my backpack, and were convinced no one was listening on the other side of the door, we tore into the basket for the letter.

Janie,

I was sorry to see you followed me. I was hoping to keep you all safe. The others are fine, though I am not with them, and I am working on a way to get all of you out of Wonderland. Please talk to the other visitors there and tell the blind woman I'm okay and will try to see her soon.

Don't eat the tarts.

Tomorrow night, after the visitor dinner, watch out your window for a message from me. You'll know what to do.

Allie

It sounded like she had a plan. I hoped it was an escape plan, but I'd take any plan at the moment. Today and tomorrow were going to be long days, but I could make it if I knew what was going on, if I had something to look forward to. Was that why Mr. Bathurst had snapped? Because they had nothing to look forward to, nothing to make their days less dreary or less . . .

I didn't even get the chance to finish that thought because a siren went off in the background. Where did they have a siren? I hadn't seen anything resembling a loudspeaker in the market.

Aiden peered out the window. He'd read Allie's letter over my shoulder. "Do you think she meant she'd send us a message tonight? What if this is it?" he asked, obviously as eager as I was to get the heck out of this place. He'd been pretty quiet for the last couple of days. I knew I'd been living inside of my own head, but he'd been awfully introspective too. It was uncharacteristic for the two of us to go through a day without some conversation, and it was throwing me off.

"Allie must know how all of this works pretty well," I said. "She seems to understand how the visitors are treated, how they are fed, and even what we are allowed to buy in the marketplace. She had to have known we wouldn't get the message until today. And we're not having a visitor's dinner tonight. I would assume she would know that as well." I headed to the window, though, to make sure. I wouldn't want to miss a message from her just because I misjudged her.

The window was one from a medieval castle. There was no glass, just the wooden shutter and a heavy curtain to close against the weather. Bert sat in front of the fireplace with the letter as Aiden shoved the curtain aside and pulled the shutter farther open, into the room, so I could get a good look as well. From where we were, we could see Mr. Bathurst in the square with his hands tied behind his back. Something was definitely going on, but I was pretty sure Allie hadn't arranged this one.

I heard the sounding of a trumpet and saw a white mouse as tall as Aiden blowing on a horn with a tapestry pennant hanging from it. The market noises all settled to quiet as the merchants and patrons stopped what they were doing to watch the mouse. He tucked the horn under his arm and turned to the assembled crowd, calling out as if he was town crier.

"Hear ye, hear ye. This visitor stands accused of high treason and theft from office! The Queen has pronounced sentence and—" He was interrupted.

The Queen was making her way across the courtyard and called, "Off with his head!"

"*No!*" I yelled before I could stop myself.

The entire courtyard seemed to turn at once to look up at my window. Even Aiden turned to look at me in surprise. Heck, even I was surprised.

I saw the Queen's mouth harden. She was angry. Even three stories up, I could see that. She leaned over to a courtier, who looked up at me and then took off running for the door.

"The letter," I started, and Aiden headed for the fireplace.

"Already on it," said Bert.

I'd somehow missed that he'd knocked over the poker leaning up against the wall and was attempting to nudge it into the fireplace, rather ineffectively smooshing ashes around, rather than poking the embers to life. I could see a small corner of white from the letter still sticking up, but it burned as I was watched it. God love that frog for thinking so quickly. Aiden ran over and grabbed the poker, finishing the job.

Heavy footsteps sounded outside the door, and I heard a loud, thumping fist banging on the door before it flew open. "Your presence is requested in the courtyard," a deep-voiced guard announced.

"Requested?"

"I'm being polite," he droned in a deep monotone.

Wow. What had I just done? But I couldn't keep quiet at a man being railroaded. I'd spent every free minute I'd had over the last year and a half reading and writing and talking and debating and eating and sleeping constitutional rights and criminal law and courtroom procedure and evidence and . . . and . . . it was basic.

"What were you thinking?" hissed Aiden.

Apparently we were sharing the same brain wave.

"I can't let someone get executed without a fair trial. That's part of why I went to law school."

"But you're not attending law school in Wonderland, Janie!" he bit out.

He was right, but the time to have that conversation was not now. I was ushered out the door by the guard, who had a buddy waiting in the corridor. Each of them took me by an arm. It felt like my feet barely touched the ground as I was hustled outside, and my upper arms felt like they were being squeezed in two separate vises. It hurt, but I wasn't going to let them see my pain.

I'd stood up to the magical powers that be before. I'd won. I had to be smart and on my game, to show the Queen she was wrong. Or at least we'd have to demonstrate there was a better way for her to prove she was a fair queen who cared about her people.

The system I was studying wasn't a perfect one, but there were safeguards built in to protect people. It worked, at least most of the time, and guaranteed due process rights and procedural due process.

The problem, for me at least, was that Mr. Bathurst wasn't even getting a trial. And I, who was about to dedicate my professional career to the idea that a fair trial mattered, couldn't let him go down without a fight.

Of course, I had no idea if he was actually innocent, but he himself had grown up in a time when people fought for those rights, who bled and died for the promise of being able to claim them. He was British; he'd had many of those rights. And he would be counting on some form of system for justice, not just automatic execution. I was the closest thing around to a qualified lawyer who would demand a fair trial. He grew up in a situation where they had lawyers, and they had trials, and they had a system that dated back to the Magna Carta.

He deserved to at least talk to someone before they cut off his head.

CHAPTER THIRTY-ONE

As I was frog-marched down the steps and into the courtyard, I'd made up my mind. I had a plan. I just hoped it was a good one; I didn't want to get my own head lopped off without a trial alongside Mr. Bathurst.

The Queen was in all her finery, holding the front of her red gown just off the dusty cobblestones while two pages held the train behind her off the ground as well. She had a heavily starched ruff around her neck, and her hair was arranged in a highly elaborate birdcage. I was strongly reminded of Queen Elizabeth I; she almost looked ridiculous and did look drunk on power.

I had no doubt she believed, on some level, that she was, somehow, doing something good for her people and for Wonderland in general. She'd been too much the caring, considered, compassionate leader when we'd talked earlier. How much of that had been an act? And if it was a complete act, if she was an absolute loony bird, just how far down the rabbit hole had I just jumped with both feet?

I was dragged right up in front of the red-faced sovereign, who looked as though she was about to boil over like a teapot left on the burner too long. I was seriously starting to look for steam whistling out of her ears when she finally asked why in the world I was questioning her authority to punish a criminal.

"Your Majesty, I am not questioning your right to punish a criminal. I am, however, questioning whether he is one. And even if he is one, isn't he entitled to some discussion about his rights, to some form of representation, and the knowledge of who accuses him? In short, isn't he entitled to have the charges against him proven in a fair trial before moving to the execution stage of the proceedings?"

Please let there be some sort of justice system, I thought over and over in a mantra. *I'm so screwed if there's not.* And Mr. Bathurst would be even more so, seeing as his head would be detached from the rest of his body.

She took a deep breath and said, "I'm the Queen. I'm the one who assures my people they are safe, I am able to care for them, and ensure they will be taken care of. Families who rely on their goods being sold will know that thieves who steal from their children, who take food out of their children's mouths, will be dealt with. That thievery ends more lives than one sentencing against an outsider-thief who had no reason to steal!"

"What happens when one of their children stands accused of being a thief? Should they turn the other cheek? What if you execute innocent citizens? Innocent visitors? Innocent children? Do you care if they are actually guilty, or are you more concerned about appearing like a protective Queen? Look around you. They are more scared of you punishing them for falling out of line than they are about petty theft or property offenses."

I had to give her credit. She actually looked. The bound Mr. Bathurst was staring at me, his jaw hanging open. I'm sure he didn't expect anyone else to stand up for him; he looked like he was used to standing up for others and not getting much support in return. I wondered, briefly, how he'd gotten away with it when the others seemed so convinced they couldn't, but that was a question to ponder later.

"In our world, people fought and died for individual rights. They laid their lives on the line to earn the right to be individuals, to have certain unalienable rights to protect them from overreaches of power from their government."

"Are you saying I bully my people?" The Queen had started calming down, but with this statement, the ugly red flush and whistling teapot impression started to creep back into her face.

"No. I'm saying your people deserve a government that allows them to express their concerns about their lives as well as the places they live and work without worrying about backlash from their government. They need to know that if their neighbor decides to accuse them of something they didn't do, they will have a process they can turn to, a fair one, that at least gives them the forum to say they didn't do it and be heard. They need to know that if they are convicted, the punishment fits the crime . . . or at least doesn't dole out a hundred dollar punishment for a five cent crime."

Boy, I hoped that metaphor translated.

She did not look happy, but there also wasn't steam pouring out of her ears anymore. I hoped that meant she was listening. As long as she was listening, I could talk about justice and fairness and all that for a long time.

"Look, our world has a system. It's not perfect. Mistakes are still sometimes made. But our system gives everyone a voice, a way to defend themselves in case they are accused of a crime, a way to air their grievances in a fair field. When a storekeeper opens up a bakery right next to a muffin shop and the two start fighting over stealing each other's recipes, they have a forum where they both can be heard. They can both feel like they got a fair hearing, even if they don't like the outcome. It's a way for citizens to feel like their government works for them, and let me tell you, citizens who are active in their government start feeling a sense of pride that is beautiful to see."

"You're advocating turning the asylum over to the inmates."

"No, I'm advocating letting people take pride in their lives, in their government, and the ability to be themselves without fear."

She turned away from me, at least giving the impression she was considering my statement. I held my breath, hoping she'd heard every word and took it to heart. Of course, I think my heart had stopped as well.

I felt bile rising in the back of my throat, that sour-sick taste of adrenaline, and I knew I'd picked the right profession. I was going to end up being a trial lawyer, and I knew it. I was getting experience at advocating for others, and for myself, before I ever sat for the bar exam. I hoped that meant the bar exam would be way easier than I was anticipating, but I had the funny feeling it wouldn't. Of course, I had a couple of years before that became a concern.

The Queen turned back to me, and I waited to hear whether I'd swayed her or not. The guards seemed to be holding their breath along with me, and when I glanced around, I noticed the shopkeepers and patrons in the market seemed to be doing the same thing.

Then I saw it.

The expression on the faces of the Queen's subjects was something I'd never actually seen in my own lifetime, but it wasn't hard to read what they were thinking, what they wanted, what they needed. They needed a leader, not a dictator. They needed something to rally behind in order to have pride in their lives, in their homes, and in their choices. It was written all over them. It wasn't just hope. It was the desire to hope. It made me proud to be the one trying to show them how to be fair, and free, and democratic.

There were butterflies. Big ones with very strong wings beating frantically, as if they were going to escape from my stomach just from the sheer force of their own will.

"Your Majesty, if I may," I started, but then had to clear my throat. "Your people don't want someone else to lead. They just want to know you hear them; that you consider their personal struggles as mitigation of their actions as you formulate a fair verdict, and that they have a way to access the system they live under. You have no idea how empowering it is to be able to say you have a voice and that it's heard. They don't even need you to agree with them all of the time; they just want you to listen. Is that so much to ask for?"

It seemed like the silence of the entire place was going to bear down and crush us all before we could even get started, then the queen finally deigned to answer.

"Well, miss, you've been talking about finding a more open way of governing. You've been talking about giving people more of a voice. Prove it to me. Prove to me this is something more than a pipe dream for people who just want to complain."

"Don't get me wrong. There's going to be some people who complain just to complain. Even so, complainers can sometimes give you a heads up that there's something else going on, even if you don't buy their complaint. It's a great big old pain in the neck, but at the same time, you end up with people who will do anything for you because they have become personally vested in their own process."

"Prove to me this is a good idea," she repeated. "You want this thief to have a trial? You want this man to have what you think is right? Fine. Let's have a trial. Work with the White Rabbit. Starting tomorrow, you will be representing this slime in front of a jury of Wonderland peers."

I considered for a moment. Allie's plan wasn't to go into place until after dinner the next day. I didn't know what else I'd do all day the next day. Was I supposed to count the number of stones in the walls or the number of stitches in the quilt on the bed? I guess that holding a trial would at least pass the hours until Allie got here, or I'd be climbing the aforementioned walls and fretting I hadn't done enough for Mr. Bathurst.

"I need access to the witnesses. I need access to my client. I need access to the porters who might have seen anything, because it can't be just about the visitors who the jury doesn't know. I can't be confined to quarters if I'm to put on a trial first thing in the morning."

"Work it out with the White Rabbit," she said, starting to walk away.

I had two more questions, but I didn't get to ask it before she was too far gone. How was I to prove to her the American justice system worked if she was tying its success or failure to the outcome of the trial? And how was I to know if the jurors would feel free to vote based on the evidence, rather than trying to please the Queen, who could possibly make their lives hell for, well, the rest of their lives?

CHAPTER THIRTY-TWO

I was escorted back to the room and told the White Rabbit would be in to speak to me as soon as he got instructions from the Queen. Aiden was nearly purple and apoplectic when he saw me.

"Are you insane?" he screamed. "Have you lost your mind? We have been trying to come up with a plan for what to do next, and you decide to risk yourself, Bert, me, and all of our friends to have a trial you can't win for a guy you don't know to liberate people who can't stand up for themselves? Tell me why this is worth it. Tell me why you're doing this! I don't get it, and I can't even help you with it!"

Bert didn't say a word.

I started yelling back. "This is me. This is what you fell in love with. This is what worked in dealing with my stepmother: a fair trial, in front of her own subjects. It's what I do; it's what I am. This is why I wouldn't give up on Mia or her father. This is why I couldn't turn away from Allie when she first showed up and why Bert's still here.

"Maybe it's just because I grew up in Ohio. I'm a good, old-fashioned, red-blooded American who just can't fathom a justice system that doesn't have the presumption of innocent until proven guilty. Would my ancestors have done the same? I don't know. They're not here. I am. This is something I cannot bring myself to close my eyes to and then just sit here drumming my fingers for the next twenty-four hours when I can do something to prevent a horrendous miscarriage of justice!"

"Well, if you could stop tilting at windmills for just a few minutes, maybe we could figure out a way out of here!"

"You think I'm not? You think this trial is just about Mr. Bathurst and whether or not he can keep his head? It's not. It's about getting the Queen to realize locking people up and demanding obedience does not work as well as listening to what they actually need from their leaders! It's not pretty, but it's way more effective at actually making things better."

Aiden ran his hands through his hair, leaving it sticking up at all turns, and started pacing back and forth. It was quite an outburst, but it would have been more effective if he had been able to pace without tripping three or four times on the rug. The last frustrated lap left him landing on his knees, as if he was hoping I wouldn't notice him at my feet.

"Find a way to walk this back. For me, Janie," he begged. "Don't put yourself on the line for this."

I went over to him and ran my fingers down the curve of his jaw. "Aiden, I love you. But how is this any different than you putting yourself in danger to come rescue me when I was kidnapped by my stepmother? How is this any more dangerous than you being willing to step into the fray to help me protect Mia? How is this any different than you wanting to talk to your father to get information? Or start researching swords or magic or any one of a number of things you've done lately in a bid to keep the house safe? You think I don't worry every single day that you might get hurt while doing some experiment, trying everything you can think of to keep us all safe?"

"Someone's got to! Sometimes I think Tobias is the only other person around who really understands just how dangerous all of this is!"

We kept ranting and yelling at each other for a while, until I heard Bert telling us to shut the hell up. What I didn't expect was what Bert said next.

"Aiden, she's right. Janie has to do this. I've been around for multiple centuries, and I will say this: Democracy works. It's way better than a monarchy in the long run. A monarchy, with a benevolent leader, is just fine, but as soon as the leader isn't responsive to the people, you have chaos, and chaos is bloodier and more unstable than a democracy designed to respond to the will of the people."

I started to nod and smile, but Aiden wasn't done ranting. "What do you care about the will of the people in Wonderland? You don't live here! With any luck, we're heading home as soon as possible!" If I hadn't been convinced Aiden was in great physical shape, I'd have worried he was about to stroke out as he delivered that statement.

I took a deep breath. "You mean like the people who are here? I'm sure they all felt the same way when they first arrived. I want to go home. I want to get back yesterday. Time can't go fast enough until Allie gets here with whatever her plan is."

Aiden took a deep breath, but before he could say anything else, I heard another thump on the door. Bert looked up. So did Aiden and I. The guards who had dragged me down to the courtyard were at the door, and they'd brought someone to see me.

His head was down, and he was staring at the floor. I couldn't quite tell who it was at first, because all I could see was the top of the man's head. It looked like he'd been beaten, if not by a blunt object, than at least by lost hope. His vest was unbuttoned, and his shirt was dirty with clumps of soil and grass still sticking to the buttons. His shoes were scuffed, and his hair was mussed. The guards shoved him inside, into Aiden's arms, and the man slumped, nearly knocking Aiden to the ground.

"You have one hour," the guard intoned in the same monotone we'd heard earlier.

"One hour for what?" I asked.

He snorted. "You're the do-gooder, counselor. I assume you'd know what to do with him."

I had a sinking sensation I knew what was going on. "What happened to him?"

"He had been put into the stocks to await his punishment. Could be worse. Looks like there was only dirt and mud around. I've pulled those out of the stocks who have been pelted with rotten fruit and vegetables. They've used horse droppings before, too. And the worst? Sour, spoiled milk. You don't know just how disgusting that is." He shook his head and pulled the door behind him shut with a bang.

I helped untangle Aiden from the man who'd been thrown into the room on top of him.

It was Benjamin Bathurst, my client.

CHAPTER THIRTY-THREE

I got a towel from the stack left by the porter while we'd been out at the market and wet one corner of it to wipe the smudges of mud and dirt and grass from Mr. Bathurst's cheeks.

"You okay?" I asked.

He nodded, slowly and painfully clambering off Aiden and rolling over to sit on the floor.

Bert hopped over beside him and sat down. "I have a question," the frog said.

"Ask away," my client replied. "It's not like I've got anything better to do."

I heard the desperation and loneliness in his voice. It struck me as odd; he was the one who seemed to be repeatedly standing up to the Queen, as if he still had plenty of fight left in him, but he sounded as if he'd given up. I wanted so badly to promise him everything would be okay, but I just couldn't. Any lawyer who promises their client a specific outcome of a trial isn't doing their job. The judge or the jury makes the decision, not the lawyer, and promising something outside one's control didn't do anyone favors.

Bert looked up at him. "Sir, did you try to leave Wonderland after you found yourself here?" Apparently Bert wanted to leave just about as much as Aiden and I did. Which, of course, meant he was homesick . . . like we were.

I wondered about that for a second. Bert had been turned into a frog at least four hundred years ago, and I wondered if he felt, at times, just like Mr. Bathurst. It appeared to me they had a lot in common: two men stuck in times and places that weren't home with little to no chance of ever going back. I wondered just what that would do to someone's psyche. Of course, I had two prime examples of it right in front of me.

"Mr. Bathurst, my name is Janie Grimm. Apparently, I'm your legal representative." Never mind that I hadn't finished law school yet. I wondered if practicing without a license was a crime in Wonderland?

I had to suppose it wasn't, since the Queen hadn't questioned my qualifications. I was guessing she planned to be the judge at this trial, yet she hadn't even asked about it. Of course, I wasn't sure I even had my student ID with me. I'd left my purse and my wallet on the counter in my kitchen back in Dayton, Ohio. I couldn't even prove I was Janie Grimm at the moment.

"A female barrister?" he asked, incredulous. "I've never heard of such a thing."

Well, if Bert was right and Mr. Bathurst had lost something like two hundred plus years, he certainly would have missed the suffragist movement. Heck, he had missed most of the history of the United States.

"Something like that . . . Look, like it or not, I'm your only hope. The Queen kind of wants to cut off your head."

"Do you have any training in oratory, in legal theory, or in logical fallacy?" he asked.

How did one answer that? "Yes." If he asked for more detail I'd explain, but I felt fairly certain he would much prefer me to the dodos I'd met the day before on the walk into Wonderland. It wasn't like he had much in the way of options.

"Not only that, but I've argued a case in a realm other than ours before."

That got his attention. "What case? Where did you argue? What was the outcome?"

"I defended myself against my stepmother, in a faerie realm."

His eyes grew wide. "What do you mean? You're that girl? The American girl who argued her way out of a lifetime in a faerie court?"

"You've heard of me?" I asked. Had word of the trial spread outside of my stepmother's realm? And if it truly had, was it a good thing or a bad thing?

"The Queen was told of it. I overheard a conversation between her and the White Rabbit about it."

Curiouser and curiouser, I thought. "Does the Queen have any idea that was me?" It raised my concern for getting out of Wonderland even higher, but now I had another concern. How would I defend my client without causing the Queen to figure out I was the "American girl?" Would I even be able to get away when Allie showed up?

Mr. Bathurst shook his head. "We heard the Queen ranting and raving about mortals and their tricky ways. She wouldn't let it go. It was the most excitement we'd had around here for months."

I had a really bad feeling about this. "How long have you actually been here in Wonderland-time, Mr. Bathurst?" I knew he had disappeared a couple hundred years before in real-world time, and I was hoping for some clue as to how fast or slow time could be running.

"About five years," was the answer.

Yikes. I didn't want to spend another five days here, much less five years. And who knew just how long I'd have to wait to get home, or how much time would have passed in Dayton. "Tell me how you came to be here." Even though we didn't have a lot of time, starting at the beginning is never a bad thing

"Don't you want to know about whether I'm guilty of the crime I've been accused of?" Mr. Bathurst asked.

"Yeah, but I'm getting there. I want the whole picture," I replied. "I'll be honest; I need the information for two reasons. I want to know what happened, to know if there's any more information I—or my friends—can add when putting together a plan to potentially get us out of here. Second, I have a theory about the Queen, and I want to find out if I'm right. If I'm wrong, then I don't want my theory getting out, especially if we're stuck here. That said, it may also figure into your defense. So I want it all. If I need more time to prepare, I'll ask the guards for it, though it might mean you staying here and talking to us into the night."

"I'm good with that. But why are you standing up for me? It only draws attention to you, and if you're considering trying to leave, I would think that would be the last thing you might want," my client said, straightening his wrinkled and stained waistcoat before attempting to stand up. His lip was split, and he was going to have one heck of a shiner in the morning from the look of his face, but there was a glint in his eye. It wasn't malicious; it wasn't a mean glare. Instead, it was as if there was life there that hadn't been before.

I swallowed hard, sitting down on the bed, and gave him the answer I hadn't yet given Aiden, who was listening to the entire exchange with a worried look on his face. "I'm dong this because I was once dragged through a magical portal against my will and I had no hope to get back out again except someone came after me. I always thought if I saw the same situation and felt I could help, then I couldn't just walk away, because someone else didn't walk away from me. I'd hope if I help someone, they, in turn, would help others, and so on and so forth, until we no longer find ourselves in such situations."

I heard a strangled noise, and Aiden got up from where he'd still been sitting on the floor due to Mr. Bathurst's unceremonious entrance into the room. He walked over to me and put his hand on my shoulder.

"I get it, Janie," Aiden murmured. "And I'm one hundred percent behind you."

That was exactly what I needed to hear from him, especially since Aiden had been the one who came for me. I just hadn't known how to articulate it earlier, but it sounded right at that moment. And now I needed to hear from my client.

"Mr. Bathurst, can you tell me how you came to Wonderland? I need you to start from the beginning."

He sighed and stood up, helping Bert onto the coverlet of the bed, and then he sat down in the wooden chair where Aiden had curled up with a sick Bert the night before. "Well, I disappeared on November 25, 1809. I was in Her Majesty's diplomatic service and had been for a number of years when I was promoted to the post of Secretary of the British Legation at Livorno, Italy. In 1808, I was dispatched to Vienna by the pro tempore Secretary for Foreign Affairs. The mission was to assist in the reconstruction of Britain's and Austria's alliance and to encourage Emperor Francis II to declare war on France. He did so in April, but it didn't last long. The Austrians' advance and military action was unsuccessful, and I was recalled to London. I decided to travel north and take a ship from Hamburg, Germany, to try to put some distance between myself and the Austrians in order to avoid any connection that might cause issue on the way home."

"Are you saying you believe you were waylaid because of your actions in the diplomatic service?" I asked.

"I don't know," he replied, "but I never made it home."

CHAPTER THIRTY-FOUR

"What happened?" Bert asked.

"Well, I stopped at an inn, along with a German courier, in Perleberg, which is just west of Berlin. We were traveling under assumed names, but my German wasn't as good as my Italian. The courier ordered us fresh horses, and we retired to the inn. I had an early dinner and spent some time writing a letter to my wife while we waited. The horses kept getting delayed, and then the carriage needed work, so I started to get suspicious, believing we were getting set up. I still think I was right."

I was immediately enthralled by his story. It wasn't like he'd been going on for long or that he was an elaborate story teller, but he told his story in such a matter-of-fact way that I could imagine myself right there with him. Worrying about a set-up, worrying he wouldn't get home to his wife, and worrying he wouldn't be able to get to report what he knew about the Austrians to his superiors in London, even though I already knew the outcome.

Mr. Bathurst continued. "I started packing up my things, having realized I needed to hit the road on my own. I had no idea if the courier was the one setting me up or not, so I had to get away from him. I changed into fresh clothes and picked up my bag, but someone banged on the door. I didn't recognize the voice. I left everything behind and went out the window."

"How long before you found yourself in Wonderland?" I asked.

"Minutes," he said. "I climbed out the window of the inn, using the stones of the wall as footholds, and then headed through the pasture behind the stables. The inn was at the edge of the town, so I headed out into the countryside, away from the townspeople who might have reason to report on my whereabouts. At the time, I believed the townspeople and those working at the inn were Napoleonic agents; the more I think about it, the more I don't know. They might just have been poor peasants who would have reported me for the extra coin to feed their children."

"You sound as if you aren't angry at those who could have reported you. That's very forgiving. I'm not sure a lot of people could do it," Aiden said.

Mr. Bathurst rocked in the chair for a second. "I'm not angry with them. I am angry with those who took advantage of them. How can you be angry with a parent for wanting to feed a hungry child? I can't, but war doesn't distinguish. Germany might not have been at war, but they weren't far from it. They were being affected by a lack of trade coming in from England and from France, and the political pressure from Austria wasn't helping. It wasn't completely desperate, but there were plenty of people who weren't quite making ends meet."

He'd obviously had a while to think about it.

"What happened next?" I asked.

"Well, I got about three or four miles outside of town, when I saw a white rabbit. It came up to me and acted like it wanted attention, some affection, as if it was someone's pet. It was a nice distraction from the cold, from my tired brain, and from all of my worries that Napoleon himself was right behind me with a firing squad. I wasn't sure whom to trust, but I knew I had to keep going forward, and the distraction of the rabbit helped an otherwise drudge of a walk. It seemed as though I was following the rabbit, even though I wasn't really trying to. Suddenly, I was falling. I'd stepped into a hole when I wasn't looking, and I'd plummeted through to Wonderland."

What I wouldn't give for a legal pad and some way of taking notes, yet I didn't trust having notes someone else might pick up and use against us. I had no idea if attorney/client privilege applied here, but I was pretty sure the presence of Aiden and Bert would probably invalidate it. It was probably safer if I didn't have stuff written down anyways. Hopefully Bert and Aiden would make sure I didn't miss an important detail. I'd have to remember to ask the Rabbit if I got a staff, or assistants, or whatever the Queen might want to call them. I had a feeling no one would know what a paralegal was in this realm.

I didn't yet know what to say to my client, so I just nodded and hoped he'd keep going. He did.

"When I finally realized I was no longer in Germany, I wandered around for a while and ran into one of the Queen's guards. This was before she instituted many of the rules about visitors. She asked all kinds of questions about what was going on in our world, and I answered as honestly as I could without compromising the security of the mission I'd been on or revealing any of the diplomatic information I might know from Italy.

"I told her about the revolutions in America and the war that followed. I told her about the revolution in France and how it died down and was taken over by an emperor. I told her about the different countries and rulers that existed in our world, and she seemed appalled at there being so many rulers. She seemed to be concerned that if I spoke to any others, I might put ideas in their heads."

"What kind of ideas?" I asked.

"Revolutionary   overthrow-the-government-and-cut-off-their-heads kinds of ideas," he replied.

That might be the explanation for the whole "Off with their heads!" routine I'd read about and the Queen had displayed in the courtyard a bit ago.

"As I was saying," Mr. Bathurst continued, "I did give her a basic overview, not anything nuanced or detailed. She started asking more questions. I tried to answer as best I could, but she didn't want explanations, or rationales, or even to try to understand what was going on. She could only understand from the point of view of leaders who were being targeted by their people. She had sympathy for King George. She had sympathy for King Louis and Marie Antoinette. When I talked about Napoleon, she believed the French people had turned to him because they lacked a monarch."

Oh, wow. Maybe the Queen had started believing all the suck-up courtiers who told her only what she wanted to hear. "Did she listen at all to your explanations?"

"Well, she listened when I told her the people were angry that the rulers seemed not to understand their problems, so she started asking Wonderland citizens about what their problems were. They told her visitors were competing with them and they were losing business, so she started instituting rules to limit visitors' ability to trade for goods and services for their business. They told her a visitor had stolen food from their families, and she began limiting where visitors could obtain food.

"And then visitors were the ones talking about liberty, fraternity, and equality. She remembered what I'd told her, the little bit I'd explained about the French Revolution and the Napoleonic rule, and she decided the way to handle this was to prevent us from going home and to prevent us from interacting with her people without supervision. In short, the Queen was afraid the citizenry would become as unhappy as the people she'd heard me talk about with regard to the American Revolution and the French Revolution. Her answer wasn't to invite debate; it was to shut it down."

He wasn't answering as many questions as I would have liked. In fact, it brought up more questions than answers. "So how does that lead into whatever was going on today, Mr. Bathurst?" I asked. "How does it lead into allegations you stole tarts from the Queen?"

He took a deep breath. "First of all, if you're going to try to save my life, you should really call me Benjamin. Second of all, I didn't steal tarts because I was hungry. In fact, I didn't steal tarts at all. I packed up the tarts delivered to my room because I *wasn't* hungry. I'd been packing up food for the last couple of days, trying to put together provisions to leave, but every time I feel like I'm ready, I end up eating the tarts I've set aside. I've packed up provisions while eating the tarts and then fallen asleep before I could do anything about it. I think there's something in the tarts to keep us all passive."

That would explain why Allie's note had said not to eat the tarts. I wondered how long it had been since he'd had something other than tarts to eat.

"What if we offered you something to eat that isn't a tart?" Aiden asked.

Benjamin's head snapped up. "What do you have?"

I opened up my backpack. We still had Pop-Tarts, but that was probably too close to what he was used to, day in and day out. I had a can of Chef Boyardee spaghetti and meatballs, as well as a plastic fork. Aiden had a pocketknife with a can opener. I yanked off the label, and opened the can, setting it in the coals of the fire to heat up. Benjamin watched every move I made. I let it go a few minutes, waiting to see if it would heat up, and then used the poker to slide it back out of the ashes. I used the towel as I would a potholder to pull it out. The metal was hot, but it wasn't bad. I handed him the plastic fork and the towel-wrapped can.

He peered inside. "What is it?"

"Spaghetti and meatballs," I said. "It's not gourmet food, but it'll fill your belly and keep you going. And if you get sleepy, it's because your stomach is full, not because you've been drugged or enchanted or whatever you might want to call it."

He dug in. "This is somewhat like the food I had while I was in Italy. It's wonderful." He began shoveling noodles into his mouth, leaving red tomato sauce stains on his face. "You don't know how much you miss real food when you are stuck with the same thing day after day for years on end."

I wondered what he'd think of a McDonald's. *What I wouldn't give for a Big Mac right now,* I thought as I took stock of our supplies. We didn't have much food left, but we had enough for another day or two for just Aiden and me if we stretched it. And then we'd be, like Benjamin, stuck with the Queen's tarts.

I pulled a granola bar from my bag and opened it up, breaking the bar in half to share with Aiden. We chewed slowly, rationing the food we brought from Ohio as Benjamin was practically licking the inside of the spaghetti can.

Benjamin and I kept talking, fleshing out what had happened and what had been happening in the last few years, but I still had unanswered questions not related to his case. "Benjamin, someone mentioned a visitor had left at one point and returned many years later. Can you tell me about it?" I asked.

He nodded. "Well, it's more complicated than that. I think there might be a second one, but the second one would be the daughter of the first. They are the only ones who ever left. They're probably the only ones who know how."

Allie. And her mother. But didn't she tell us her mother was dead? If so, Allie was the only one who knew how to get us out of here. I hoped I hadn't screwed us up by going all Atticus Finch on the Queen.

CHAPTER THIRTY-FIVE

"So, what about the tarts? Did you ever steal any tarts that had not been provided to you by the Queen?" I asked.

"No," was the answer from Mr. Bathurst.

"Why is she suddenly claiming you have?"

He shrugged. "I'm not sure. She might be just trying to get rid of me. If you came in and started talking about due process and equality and rights and such, she might think I've been poisoning others against her. It doesn't matter if we hadn't met before, and it wouldn't matter if it doesn't make sense to anyone with a shred of common sense. She sent guards to search my room and found a stash of tarts I'd put aside from the morning. I'd wrapped them up, and I'd intended to take them with me when I left. I intended to leave, but I'd been called in to the dinner we had the other night and . . . I can't believe I'm saying this, but I forgot all about my plan.

"I was frustrated last night, and then we got stuck in the hall. You saw what happened there. I got back to my room, and that was when the guards came in. Remember how we weren't allowed to eat while we were there? Well, they came in and found the stash I'd set aside from breakfast that morning, and they reported to the Queen that I'd stolen them."

Yikes. That was going to be a hard one to defend. While it was true he had tarts and had seemingly been caught red-handed, it made no sense as to why the Queen was so odd about when they could eat and when they couldn't. But it wasn't like there were witnesses who could exonerate him.

This was going to get ugly.

The guards showed up faster than I expected. When they pounded on the door, we scrambled to hide all evidence of contraband food. It wouldn't do for Aiden, Bert, and me to also be arrested due to a can of Chef Boyardee. Once the room was cleared, Aiden went to unlock the door and let the guards in. The head guard peered suspiciously around the room, but found nothing to cause concern. He demanded Benjamin go with them back to his room, where he would remain under guard until the trial started.

I stood up to face the sentry before they could take Benjamin away and began making demands, ticking off each request on my fingers as I talked. "You need to tell the Queen that, after discussing the matter with my client, I need to talk with the guards who searched his room and the porter who brought the tarts that morning for his breakfast. I need to see his room for myself."

The guard nodded and took out a small notepad. He began taking notes, so I kept going. "I need to talk with the White Rabbit about procedures for the trial. I need to know what the evidentiary rules are regarding procedure and who will be sitting on the jury. I need to know whether anyone has questioned my client about what happened, the circumstances of the interrogation, and any statements that might be used against him. I want to know what rights he might have been afforded prior to being questioned, and I need to know if he was restrained in any way, before and after the questioning."

The guard nodded. Apparently he was used to taking orders from someone who rattled off a laundry list of instructions. "I will take your requests to her. I'll be back with a response as soon as I can, after I take this man back to his room and speak to her."

"Thank you," I said.

The door swung shut behind the guards and Mr. Bathurst with a soft wooden thud of finality. My brain was burning with all the things I wanted to know, and I knew I had a long night ahead of me.

Bert piped up. "What kind of a defense do you think you can mount when he's practically admitted it?"

"What?" I asked.

"He's admitted it. He told you he took the tarts and hid them away, eating them when he wasn't supposed to."

I didn't answer right away. He had a point. I wanted more information.

Aiden didn't say anything.

A few tense seconds went by. "I think there's more to the story, guys. I don't think this is a cut and dried case of theft, and even if it was, I don't believe the punishment fits the crime—and that's part of the problem. I'm not going to start spinning theories for the defense until I've finished talking to the witnesses and formulated everything in my own head. We have a luxury here that you and I didn't have in the faerie realm, Aiden. We have the time to plan, to interview witnesses, and to put on a well-reasoned, thought-out defense. We didn't get that last year."

"You did fine without it," said Bert. "I don't get why this is a big deal. You know what you're doing. You just have to open your mouth and do it."

"Just do it. Your big strategy is a *Nike* ad? Lawyers don't do that. They teach you in law school that you never ask a question in a courtroom you don't already know the answer to. Last fall, I thought I knew the answers to the questions I was asking, but with every question I asked, I had no guarantee they would actually be answered in the way I thought they were supposed to be. If my stepmother or her son had lied, I wouldn't have been able to prove otherwise."

Aiden nodded. "You're right. But you can't stop any witness from lying! Anyone could get on the stand and lie. They could deny knowing anything about it. They could make up anything they wanted. You can't prevent it."

He was right. "Yes, that's true. But even though it's true, if I've talked to them about it ahead of time, I can at least ask them about that conversation should I catch them changing their story. Even if I can't prove the lie, I can at least show the inconsistency. And that affects their credibility, even if I can't show which one is the lie."

Bert nodded. "What do you need us to do?"

"I need you to start brainstorming about what you guys might or might not know about legal procedure or protocol with other realms. You two are my research team. What do you know about trials in Wonderland?"

They both shook their heads. Nothing.

"All right. Where do we go for more information on Wonderland?"

Was it sad that it took us all a few minutes to remember that Aiden had packed the books from my father's library?

He pulled the books he'd brought out of his backpack and started flipping through the pages. The guards knocked on the door again, presumably to take me away to talk with my witnesses.

"I need you guys to figure out whatever you can from those books. I'll be back after I talk to everyone and see what the Queen is willing to tell me about the trial. You guys need to find out what I need to know from the trial in the Alice books so we can compare notes before morning."

Aiden nodded. So did Bert. From the way they snapped to, I almost expected a salute.

"Thanks, guys. I appreciate it," I said as the guards dragged me out the door to start prepping for trial.

CHAPTER THIRTY-SIX

I spent several hours with witnesses before being told it was too late to discuss procedure with the Queen. "You can bring it up with her in the morning prior to the trial, and I'd seriously advise you do wait until morning. If you wake her up now, she is not likely to be receptive to anything you might want her to capitulate to. In other words, let her sleep. *You'll* sleep better for it," the deep monotone guard, who had been with me all night, warned. He'd stayed fairly quiet through the process, but I believed he'd started to understand what I was doing.

It turned out he was the guard who had searched Benjamin's room on the orders of the queen. I talked to him for a bit, and then he returned me to my room.

When I got back, Aiden and Bert were asleep. There were no clocks in the room, so I had no idea how late it was. My guys were sprawled across the bed with the books out in the midst of the original story. I pulled a book from under Aiden's face, careful not to disturb him, and glanced over the pages he'd been reading when he fell asleep. Sure enough, the book showed that, during Alice's first trip here, there had been a trial against the knave of hearts for stealing tarts. I read through the section and put it aside, curling up myself in an empty corner of the bed to grab whatever sleep I could find.

My brain was still spinning, though I was tired. I discarded arguments and tactics as I lay there, watching the rise and fall of Aiden's chest. I fell asleep while silently auditioning winning strategies and arguments as my eyelids drooped.

I woke up with a start as someone was banging on the door. We were all up and moving in a hurry. Aiden opened the door on the same guard who had taken me to my interviews the night before, which meant the man had gotten less sleep than I had. He looked fresh and ready to go; I probably looked like I'd combed my hair with a pitchfork. Or a hay rake. Whichever would have worked the least.

I asked for five minutes to get myself together before we went down. The guard nodded and pulled the door shut behind himself, presumably to allow me to get ready. Aiden dug a comb out of his backpack, and I used it to do what I could with my hair. He nodded at me, but I knew I didn't look quite like the professional I wanted to be.

I wanted my hair dryer. I wanted a curling iron. I wasn't a frou-frou kind of girl, but at the same time, it was technically my first trial with an actual client. I'd had a suit put together for my first trial. I had picked it out a year ago and saved a dollar here and a dollar there to buy it on a clearance sale the minute it was discounted. I had shoes I'd been drooling over for months; I'd set them aside as well and saved every spare penny I could after I'd bought the suit. But now . . . I didn't so much as have nylons. And I didn't have makeup.

I wasn't vain. It wasn't about that. But much like the first day of school or a prom or my wedding day, I'd been looking forward to suiting up and going to court, fighting the good fight. I'd also looked forward to this moment for a long time. And here I was, wearing the same jeans I'd worn two days ago, without a shower, and my hair yanked back in a ponytail—more for getting it out of my face than arranging it to look professional.

My face felt grimy for not being washed better, and I was almost glad I didn't have a mirror to be able to see just how disheveled I looked. I wanted coffee. And I wanted somewhere I'd be able to throw up that coffee.

Yeah, my stomach was churning from adrenaline and nerves. I'd thought I'd start my first trial day at a desk, with a pile of law books and notebooks and highlighters and notes and binders. Instead, I had a rather sad display of just the Alice in Wonderland books we'd taken from my father's study when we'd left.

And I was going to yak in the corner before I went down to the courtyard.

Aiden offered me a granola bar, and I turned it down. "You look green," he said.

"If I eat something, I won't even look green, because it'll come back up."

Even Bert got in on the act, begging me to eat something.

"Guys, I don't think it's a good idea. It's nerves. It'll be fine. Let's pack up the backpacks and take them with us. We need to be ready to go in case Allie's message is actually more of a distraction to allow us to run away. I'm going to be concentrating on the trial. I need you two to be watching for whatever she's trying to do. You are the eyes and ears; I can't take mine off the Queen or off of Benjamin or any of the witnesses to be watching anything else.

"I also need you watching the jury, if she still lets me have one. You need to be studying the citizens, if she allows any of them to be there. I need you guys to let me know, quietly and discretely, if you see something I need to be aware of, but it needs to be understated." I threw some water on my face between words, hurrying, yet trying to feel less grubby. The guard banged on the door again. That was a quick five minutes.

It wasn't the guard. It was the Queen and the blind woman from the night before. The blind woman was carrying a tray of tarts, and I hurried to help her put it down before she could stumble. Why in the world would the Queen have the blind woman serving her? That just seemed unusually cruel to expect someone without vision to carry a tray without tripping or spilling.

The Queen did not look happy. I bobbed my head and curtseyed as politely as possible, but I couldn't wait forever for her to feel completely warm and fuzzy about my deference to her as a monarch. I felt like my nerves were about to jump out of my skin with the desire to get started. And yet, I didn't want to disadvantage my client by pissing off the likely judge.

I was so worried I was going to screw up that I almost didn't realize the Queen was waiting for someone to talk, and that someone was me. "My apologies, Your Highness. I've got a lot of details swirling in my brain as I get ready for today."

She gave me a benign smile. "You don't really believe your own hype, do you? All that dreck about a free society? You weren't just pandering to an audience? Our people need a strong leader to rally behind, or they would run around willy-nilly and cause problems."

"Ma'am?" I asked automatically. It was probably the wrong title, but what could I do? I was too worried I'd forget to ask about some arcane rule or that a procedure I didn't know would come back to bite me later. I had to struggle to pay attention. What was going on?

I suddenly smelled peppermint and old books. It was magic. I shook my head. I hadn't smelled that scent in months, not since the Seawitch had been taken—in restraints—from my house by her own sister.

Sister.

Son of a *bitch.*

I'd dropped my guard because I hadn't noticed magic in Wonderland before just now. I hadn't thought there was any magic here, because we hadn't seen it. I jerked my head around to see Aiden's eyes the size of dinner plates and his eyebrows had risen so high they were almost to his hairline.

Yup, he'd caught it, too. I turned the other way, and looked down at Bert. His froggy little mouth was hanging open, almost down to the floor; he'd also caught it. There was not only magic at home, but in Wonderland as well as in the faerie realm.

Euphegenia, the Queen of Hearts, was related to my evil faerie stepmother. She was her sister. Which also, by marriage, made her my step-aunt.

Which means my reputation preceded me.

I was so royally screwed.

CHAPTER THIRTY-SEVEN

The Queen gave me a long, lazy look. "So you're the little American girl who handed my big sister her lunch in a trial in front of her own court? How in the world did the last living descendent of the Grimm Brothers find herself in my court, under my control, after being so savvy, so smart, and so determined? How in the world did you screw up that badly?"

So she had known. She'd probably known within minutes of my arrival, and I'd been floundering around without understanding the game she had been playing from the start. The only question was what she wanted; I needed to know how to bargain with her. So, instead of beating around the bush, I asked.

"Ma'am, I'm sorry. As you've already stated, I'm an American, and I don't have a lot of experience in addressing royalty. Please believe me when I say that any protocol I missed, or disrespect I might have incidentally caused, was not my intent."

"You knew the rules well enough to navigate my sister's court and trap her in her own machinations. I have a hard time believing you didn't know what you were getting into by coming to Wonderland. Who brought stories of Wonderland to your world such that you found yourself compelled to come here and wreak havoc in a world not your own? What could possibly have drawn you here?"

I considered my words carefully, but I hadn't told her anything I would change. "I told you true when we first met; we came here after a friend who ran to Wonderland. We believe our friend has been here before. We came after our friend because we believe our friend has made the wrong decision in coming here. We came for our friend, not to make changes in Wonderland, but we cannot walk away when we see injustice, either. I myself was once dragged into a faerie realm against my own will and a friend came for me. I had to do the same for this friend."

The Queen seemed to consider what I said. "I do not think you know just what kind of reputation you have gained in the other realms. You defeated my sister, Eva, on the brink of returning to her full power. You have defeated the Seawitch and have damaged her ability to return to power. And now you are here. You are in my realm. I cannot but believe you are here to either imprison, endanger, or to harm me. You are allied with Tobias Andersen, whose name I know even here, as one who does harm to those not from the mortal realm. So why would I believe you wish to go about your business without plotting against me?"

Yikes. What could I say? I didn't want to do anything that could jeopardize my client, but right now, we were talking about me. Was this a conflict? No, not yet. They hadn't asked me to compromise my client to save myself. So far, I was good.

I just had to keep it that way.

Aiden grabbed my hand, and I squeezed back. I could do this. I was not going to back down. "You ascribe too much ambition to my actions. I am not here because I want something from you or because you hold power in this realm. Your situation is not the same as that of your sister, or of the Seawitch. Both of them were dangerous, and both of them were seeking power over and beyond what they were able to handle. Both were attempting power grabs and were willing to kill people to do so. You seem to be different, in that you are willing to hear others out on opposing viewpoints."

She was listening, but I wasn't sure just how much was getting through. *In for a penny, in for a pound.* I'd heard Doris say such in the past, and it was true. I was too deep in to stop now, so I had to keep going, pushing my point, or I might as well have given up before I started.

"I believe you actually care about your people. I believe you are not trying to gather power for power's sake, but trying desperately to hang on to power because you believe it is in your land's best interest. Instead of trying to better yourself, I believe you may be actively attempting to protect your land. The problem is, of course, that your people are not benefiting from your current mode of leadership. They do not see you as a benevolent leader, because they are struggling every day. Their lives are so hard that they no longer think about how wonderful it is to live in Wonderland. They just worry about getting through the next minute, the next hour, the next meal, the next day."

"Are you saying they blame me for their own hardships?"

There was no way to sugar coat it. "Yes."

"That's it? Just yes?"

"Look, in all my studies, I've had to look back into the history of politics in our world. Our world isn't perfect, but we've had to learn a few fundamental truths. One of those truths is that the leader gets blamed when the people are floundering in a difficult economy. It doesn't matter who the leader is. It doesn't matter what they've done, what they've tried, what they want, or what they believe. It only matters that the everyday person can't feed their kids or they are losing out on business. The more widespread the problems, the more the blame gets heaped on the person in charge."

She nodded. "There is truth in your words. I can sense it. And with what I have seen, I cannot disagree with your assessment, but I do not agree it is inevitable to do so."

Aiden squeezed my hand again. "Your Majesty, we truly came because we wished to help our friend. We have no claim on your court or your lands and have no desire to make one. In the case of your sister, and in the case of the Seawitch, there were others ready to step into the void. I am not aware of any such power struggles in Wonderland and have never heard tell of any such struggles."

She stepped closer, scrutinizing Aiden closely. "There is truth in your words, yet I sense there is something about you that is more than meets the eye. Do you have a secret, or is there something else you need to tell me?"

I looked at Aiden back over my shoulder. It was his secret to tell, not mine. It had to be his call to tell it or not. Possibilities of how we could get tangled up in secrets, the danger of Aiden's heritage, and whether it could be used against him had to be weighed against the danger of lying by omission. Could Wonderland work like my stepmother's realm, where a lie could be seen as the ultimate crime?

"My mother is mortal. My father is of your sister's court. I am, as they have called me before, a half-blood. I knew of your sister's court and advised Janie of the protocol because I lived it. I grew up in it, learning of court procedure and protocol, etiquette, and politics as I grew to manhood. I learned all of that until it was as second nature as breathing," he said. "I've had the pleasure of helping Ms. Grimm as she learns such things as well."

The Queen swept across the room to look out the window. "You really don't understand what I mean, sir. Neither of you seem to understand . . . . Ms. Grimm, are you really that clueless? The entire magical community is watching you to find out who you're going to target next. Everyone is worried they are next on your list of targets, and I can't say as I blame them. I visited my sister a month ago. She still has ink stain burns on her face from you."

I shook my head. "I could tell you she abducted me against my will and I had the ink in my pocket when she took me. I could tell you she attacked me, even after she'd lost her case before her court. All of that is still true. I threw the ink in self-defense."

The Queen raised one eyebrow at me, but didn't say anything.

"Here's the thing, though. All I had asked for was a fair trial. I knew I had a case that was fairly persuasive. I was pretty sure I was going to win. Most lawyers don't go to trial unless they have a pretty good idea of what's likely to happen. I took a calculated risk. I did not expect her to attack me, to ignore the rules of her own court, or to be such a bad loser."

"Are you saying you would abide by the results of a fair trial, without attacking or seeking retribution?" she asked.

"Of course I want safe passage back home. I want all my friends who came here the same day I did to have safe passage back home. I'd like you to consider allowing the visitors here the opportunity to do the same, but right now, my biggest concern is not allowing a man to be executed for a crime I do not believe he committed."

"How can I allow visitors to leave? The safety of Wonderland is at stake!"

"Well, you can make stipulations. You can strike a bargain with your prisoners, because that's currently what they are. I'm sure any who wish to leave would promise not to speak about Wonderland to any who have not visited previously. You could agree to help them leave for a promise not to return, if you wished. Or you could impose certain trade restrictions on the goods and services that can come in from other lands and open up your markets and your economy and your technology to ideas from other realms."

"That's an awful lot to ask," she said, but she looked thoughtful.

"I've said it before. I'll continue to say it. I don't want your throne. I don't want *any* throne. I'm not going out of my way to obtain power for myself, or I would not have returned to my world after defeating my stepmother; I'd have looked into taking her power for myself. I negotiated with the Snow Queen on closing a portal that was in my house, *not* allowing me more access to magical lands."

"I will have to consider this. If what you say is true, then you may not be a danger to Wonderland. I may not wish for you to return, but I may be able to trust you to protect yourself and your friends without causing undue harm to my people or my lands."

I nodded at her, but I had a client to defend. "We have a trial this morning. We promised it to the people. We could stand here all day and talk political history, but it doesn't get this trial started. And after the trial, regardless of outcome, I'd like to engage in negotiations regarding the visitors."

"Convince me your system works, and we will talk," she said.

I'm not sure I could have asked for more.

CHAPTER THIRTY-EIGHT

We were escorted back to the courtyard behind the Queen and, of course, behind the courtiers who were carefully carrying her train just above the ground so it would not be soiled on the dirt and cobbled street. The guards did not restrain us. I carried the books I'd brought and wore my backpack. Aiden had his as well, with Bert perched atop the top closure, just above Aiden's shoulder.

Two tables had been placed in the courtyard, and the White Rabbit sat at one of them. Aiden, Bert, and I sat at the other one. Benjamin was already in a chair at the table where we sat.

Someone had dragged a throne into the courtyard for the Queen to sit on, and there was a small stool in front of it. The throne was facing the two tables. Unsurprisingly, it appeared the Queen herself was planning to preside over the trial. She led the way to the throne and sat down with a flourish. The courtiers arranged her train on top of a small rug to further prevent soiling, and I watched her daintily placed her slippered feet on the stool.

A court announcer called us all to order. "Oy yeah, Oy yeah, all who have business before the crown step forward."

Well, that might be a bit formal, but nothing unexpected.

The Queen sat forward and announced, "This visitor is accused of stealing tarts that belong to the Queen. The punishment for this is death. Instead of proceeding directly to sentence, as is our usual, the visitors have requested a hearing on his guilt. We have agreed to do so."

Looking around, I saw that some of the merchants in the stalls had perked up at the last statement and had started to inch their way forward. They were definitely paying attention, and that could only be a good thing.

I realized there were no seats for a jury. Where were we going to get one? I didn't see enough merchants around to draw from. Something suddenly seemed very odd.

"Your Highness, I was under the impression that this was to be tried directly to a jury of Wonderland citizens. I do not see them present here, and I'm wondering if there is change in the procedure we had discussed."

The Queen gave me a smile. "You have noticed, have you? Well, if you are attempting to prove to me that your system of trials and due process is more fair than just a monarch deciding the fates of their citizens, then how better to convince me than to argue and win on the strength of your own case? Two birds with one stone, and all that?"

"May I have a moment to confer with my client on this change?" I asked. "I would like his input before I agree, since it is his head we are discussing."

She nodded, and I turned to Benjamin. "Look, here's the thing. I've been trying to convince her not only to change how she governs, but also to potentially allow the visitors to leave if they wish. I cannot promise this decision is a good one for you and your case individually, but it may well be a good idea for the visitors in Wonderland as a whole. I can try to argue that it flies in the face of the point I'm trying to make to change the rules just before we start the trial, but if I do, we may predispose her to be unhappy with us before we even start arguing your case. What do you think?"

He gave me a weak smile. Aiden looked very concerned from where he sat just behind me, and Bert was actually silent. I didn't know what to make of it.

Benjamin took a deep breath and said. "Look, I didn't expect to get a trial. I was almost wishing for an execution, just to have a different day than every day I've had since she instituted all of these rules restricting visitors. If you can negotiate on behalf of the others, do it. Even if I lose my head, then I'll at least know there was some purpose to it. Besides, she's got a point. If you've got to convince her, why not just try the case to her and let her know the reasons why England and America have chosen this way of governing. Besides, if we prevail, maybe I can help you convince her that she can still be a monarch and allow the people some freedom."

I had to give it to him. He was right. It took a lot of courage to come to that conclusion. Or maybe it was desperation. But either way, the Queen had to see why we thought it was so necessary to be fair in governing. And the hope was that if I proved it to her, maybe she'd help all of us get home.

Hey, it could happen.

CHAPTER THIRTY-NINE

"The White Rabbit may call his first witness," the Queen intoned.

"I call the captain of the guard."

There was some shuffling and scuffling behind us, and one of the courtiers brought out another table. This guard appeared to be a rhinoceros, with a pointy horn on his head. He looked like something right out of the Disney version of Robin Hood, with all of the animals as the characters. I had to stifle a chuckle.

The White Rabbit began and asked what he knew of Benjamin.

"I don't really know him, per se. I don't walk the rounds in the visitors' rooms. However, I was told he ate tarts he did not have permission from the Queen to eat."

"Who told you this?" the rabbit asked.

"The men under my command."

"Your witness," said the rabbit.

Was he kidding? I was looking forward to this. "Captain, maybe you can tell me what kind of tarts were eaten?"

He shook his head. "There were several baskets delivered that day. I don't know which ones went to which rooms."

"Maybe you can tell me how many were eaten without permission?"

He shook his head.

"Were you the guard who searched Mr. Bathurst's room when the tarts were found to be missing?"

He shook his head.

"Did you order the search of his room?"

"Yes."

"On whose orders?" I asked.

"The queen ordered me to search his room."

"Is it unusual for you to be ordered to search a room?"

"It's happened before. It doesn't happen a lot."

Light bulb. "Wait a minute. The Queen ordered you to search the room?"

"Yes."

"But you ordered someone else to do it?"

He nodded. "I had several other duties that morning to attend to, so I sent one of the guards the visitors were more comfortable with."

"Have you ever had a security issue with regards to the visitors?"

"Not for a long time," was the answer.

He was being honest, and I was treading carefully. It was time to go in for a bit more detail. "Have you ever had a security issue with regards to Benjamin Bathurst, my client?"

"Not that I can recall. He's said a few things from time to time that were not complimentary to the Queen, but he didn't push the issue."

"Does the Queen ever visit the visitors' area of the castle?"

He shook his head. "I've never seen her in the visitors' section, other than this morning when she visited you in your chambers."

"If she never goes to the visitors' chambers, then how did she know the tarts found in the visitors' chambers were missing?" I asked.

Everyone in the market fell silent, as if they were all holding their breath waiting for the answer. I knew this was a question I wouldn't be allowed to ask in a normal Ohio court, much less any other court in mortal lands, because it asked him to testify about someone else's motivations, but the Queen seemed to be allowing it, so I rolled with it.

"I assumed the head porter told her."

"Nothing further from this witness," I said.

The White Rabbit called the head porter. I could have seen that one coming. She testified that the morning of the theft, there had been baskets of tarts delivered to all of the rooms for breakfast. I went through a similar line of questions for her. She also had no idea what kind of tarts were in the basket. She had no idea which tarts had been delivered to each room because she hadn't been the one to deliver them. She didn't normally go to the visitors' area because she was overseeing the servants for the entire castle.

"Did you report missing tarts to the Queen that morning from Benjamin Bathurst's room?"

"No," she said.

"So how did the Queen know to send someone to search them?" I asked.

"I don't know. I assumed the porter in the visitors' section had, without passing the information through me. If that's the case, they know better."

"They know better?" I asked. "What happens if they don't go through you?"

"They could be fired from their position, or they could be put in the stocks. Depending on the severity of the report, they could be found to be an accessory to theft and could join the thief in their punishment."

"So, beheading," I said, "if they don't report such issues through you. I'd say that's a heck of an incentive to report every movement and every detail, don't you think?"

She agreed.

Things were coming together in a reasonable fashion. So far, no witnesses to say Benjamin had actually stolen anything. No witnesses could actually describe what it was he stole. And no one so far could tell which room anything was actually stolen out of. I was liking what was going on so far.

The White Rabbit called various servants and merchants to report they'd been aware of the allegations, but no one could testify to actually seeing anything in Benjamin's room, or seeing him actually take anything that didn't belong to him. He finally rested, sitting back in his chair with a smug air of self-centered satisfaction and wiping his spectacles with the tail end of his waistcoat.

He might be feeling confident, but it wasn't like he'd proven anything. So, I stood up and did what any attorney in the mortal realm would have done. I asked for the charges to be dismissed on the grounds of insufficient evidence.

I should have known it wasn't going to work when the Queen started laughing.

CHAPTER FORTY

She laughed and laughed, but I was serious. I waited until she stopped, and then I launched into my argument.

"Your Highness, the witnesses against my client have not witnessed him stealing anything. They don't even know what kind of tarts were delivered to his room. No one knows where the allegation of theft came from. I would submit that without knowing what kind of tart was stolen, and, you know, actually seeing him take them, we can't find him guilty. There's no evidence of a crime actually being committed!" I finished with a flourish, gesturing to emphasize my point.

She shook her head. "Of course there is."

"Your Majesty, where I come from, the burden is on the government to prove someone guilty of a crime beyond a reasonable doubt. Not all doubt, but beyond a reasonable doubt. The amount of doubt someone would rely on to make decisions in their everyday lives. In a case like the one here, where the government didn't produce any witnesses to say this offender was seen with the stolen goods or even what the stolen goods are, most charges would be dismissed."

"Even if they're guilty?" she asked.

"Even if they're guilty," I confirmed. "You see, there's a rule of law that presumes everyone is innocent until it is proven otherwise. No one deserves to be punished—especially stringent, permanent forms of punishment—without there being enough evidence to be able to say beyond a reasonable doubt that the crime occurred and this is the person who did it. So far, no one has proven anything."

"I'd like to hear more," she said. "Why are you so concerned? Show me your evidence."

"In our world, the defense is not required to put on evidence and the accused is not required to take the stand in his own defense. He has the right to keep his mouth shut and not incriminate himself. I do, however, have other evidence I can present."

"I don't see how you ever get to the truth with all of these rules that prevent someone from being able to do their jobs, so please present your evidence."

I asked to call the actual porter who brought the tarts the morning of the alleged theft. I asked her what tarts she brought to Benjamin the morning in question. "Strawberry," was the answer.

"Is there a reason you're so sure they were strawberry?" I asked.

"The kitchen wanted to please the Queen, and the strawberry is her favorite fruit. They wanted to show her that a heart-shaped fruit could make a heart shaped tart. They made extra that morning, and it was the extra that was sent for the visitors' room baskets."

"Were there other kinds of tarts made that morning?"

"Yes, but strawberry was the only kind sent to the visitors' quarters. The other ones ran out before we got to the baskets for the visitors."

"Did you deliver the basket to Benjamin Bathurst yourself?" I asked.

"Who's that?"

I pointed to Benjamin, where he sat at the table. "That is Mr. Benjamin Bathurst. He's lived in the visitors' section of the castle for several years. Do you know if you delivered strawberry tarts to him on the morning he was accused of stealing them?"

"I delivered strawberry tarts to every occupied room in the visitors' quarters, including yours, miss."

I nodded. I didn't remember her, but she might have come in while I'd been asleep. The tarts had been there, even though I hadn't seen her. I leaned over to Benjamin. "The tarts in question were all strawberry, right? That's what we talked about."

He nodded. "We get strawberry more than anything else. I'm sick of strawberry, but it's what I had set aside, because I knew if I chickened out, I'd be less likely to get in trouble for stockpiling them in my room if they were the ones we got all the time."

Made sense to me, I thought. "So were you there when Mr. Bathurst's room was searched?"

"No."

"Did you see him steal any tarts?"

"No."

"Are the tarts taken to the visitors for them to eat, or for the Queen to eat?"

"Well, they are for the visitors to eat, but only if the Queen has given her permission."

Fair enough, but I wasn't done. "So, how do the visitors know they have permission to eat if the tarts are brought to their rooms and the Queen does not visit their rooms on her own?"

"If she has not given permission, then no tarts are taken to their rooms," was the answer.

"So is it fair to say that once the treats are taken to the visitor's room, it is intended for use by the visitor in the room with the permission of the Queen?"

"Yes," was the answer without hesitation.

I could use that. "Thank you," I said and excused her before calling the guard who'd actually searched Benjamin's room.

He wasn't able to tell us much. Much like all of the other witnesses, he hadn't seen Benjamin steal anything. He didn't know what the arrangement was regarding the tarts in the rooms, as he wasn't involved with the porters at the time they delivered meals to the visitors, and admitted he didn't have much to do with the visitors and their meal arrangements. At most, he was involved with ferrying visitors from their rooms to the hall whenever the Queen decided to have them all together for a dinner or an event, which wasn't often.

I learned that no one remembered a report to the Queen about stolen anything. No one understood why anyone would suspect a theft and not report it to their superior, as opposed to directly to the Queen.

No one saw Benjamin steal anything.

No one saw anyone take anything from anyone else's rooms, and there were no outstanding theft complaints from the day before or the day of the alleged theft.

I thought I'd set up my argument fairly well. The queen asked if I was done presenting evidence, and I indicated I was, but I needed a few minutes to prepare my final argument for her on the evidence. I don't think she was expecting that.

"Is this how they do things in your world?" she asked.

"Yes. Normally there's an opening statement, then the evidence, and then a closing argument. That's when the government and the accused have a chance to tell the court what they believe the evidence has shown. The court is not required to agree with them, but it is their chance to try to convince the court they have interpreted the evidence correctly."

She waved at me.

"May I have a moment with my client?" I asked. "I'd like to make sure we're on the same page. It is his life that is affected by what happens here today."

She nodded.

I took a deep breath.

CHAPTER FORTY-ONE

I got a few minutes to talk with Benjamin. He liked where I was going. And as I looked over his shoulder, I saw the crowds of merchants and shopkeepers and patrons in the market had completely abandoned the premise of keeping up with commerce. They were paying attention to us, to me, and to the case itself.

Whether they agreed with me or not, I had no idea. I just knew I couldn't give up. In the time it had taken for us to get through most of the evidence, the sun had gone from early morning, to directly above us, to heading farther across the sky. I had no idea what time it was, but most of the day had been eaten up with the minutiae of the trial. And no matter what the stakes had been, I was enjoying every single minute of it.

I realized I hadn't eaten all day, but I was still so nauseous from adrenaline and nerves that I thought I'd throw up if anything went into my stomach. And yet, at the same time, I felt completely calm because I knew exactly what I wanted to say.

As we'd taken a few minutes to discuss strategy, I heard the hubbub of whispers and hushed conversations. If we'd done nothing else, I'd gotten them to see an example of a trial with due process and safeguards for the accused. Even if we failed, maybe it would plant the seed among the townsfolk to start to demand their rights. I hoped so. Or maybe I was just naïve.

And if I was naïve about anything, I hoped it would be because I believed in the desire of all people to be free. I knew that had been my motivation in the trial against my stepmother. It had been why I'd stuck by Mia when the Seawitch had been after her. And it was why I had refused to stay home when I could help Allie. Maybe it was a character flaw if I couldn't leave situations of injustice alone, but at the same time, I wanted to help those who would stay here even after I left.

When I stood up, I was ready to present my argument.

"Your Majesty, this is a case of too many people quick to point fingers at an outsider, with no proof of actual wrongdoing. My client is accused of stealing tarts that were provided to him for sustenance by the Queen. He is a guest in her castle, and she does not allow him to eat anything other than tarts. Tarts are not provided to visitors unless the Queen has given permission. There are no other reports of any stolen items from the castle area around the time of the so-called stolen tarts.

"There are no witnesses claiming Mr. Bathurst stole anything not provided to him for his own use by the castle. There is no evidence he was being charged anything for his living expenses. There are no witnesses who saw him with any stolen property, or that the property was actually stolen. I think the only thing the evidence has shown is the only supposed crime here is Mr. Bathurst not being hungry at the time breakfast was brought to his room. If he wasn't hungry, he didn't eat. He kept his breakfast to eat later.

"As much as some might want to him to appear guilty, the evidence doesn't show it. At most, it implies visitors are only allowed to eat the moment in which food is provided, or it is not longer theirs. But food is not retrieved from the rooms when time is up."

I stood up from the table and walked around to the front of it, leaning one hip against it, casually making my point and projecting an aura of confidence even as my heart banged away painfully in my ribcage, pounding with the adrenaline and rush of a well-reasoned argument paired with the drama of a trial.

"There is no evidence that anyone who might have had any actual knowledge, or any eyewitness testimony to prove this offense exists. No evidence exists that anyone who might have had this information actually reported any theft-related offenses to anyone who was to report it through the chain of command to the Queen. In fact, the only evidence of who made the allegation is the Queen herself, although there is no evidence she had any direct knowledge of any of the facts of the case itself."

"Are you accusing me of lying?" she asked.

"No," I said. "I'm not. I'm concerned there is no credible accusation here, no credible means of determining why Mr. Bathurst was accused. There's no evidence he is guilty of anything other than waiting to eat until he was actually hungry.

"If Mr. Bathurst is found guilty, then he will be punished for failing to eat food given to him for his own use. This is the type of uneven justice and heavy-handed governing that leads people to revolution. A free people, who believe in their system of government, will fight to uphold it. Those who feel their government is unfair, unbalanced, or otherwise unable to address their concerns will not engage in it and will avoid any and all dealings with it. They will do one of two things: they will either actively try to overthrow it, or they will put their heads down and just try to get through each day with the minimum level of attention being paid to them."

A glance at the market goers showed them all staring very intently at their own belly buttons. Either that or their shoes had suddenly become highly fascinating.

"Your Majesty, if you execute this man for the crime of stealing his own tarts, you don't win this case. You lose. Even if you find him guilty, against the evidence, it's still a loss for you and your realm. And that's the beauty of this system as well. The peoples' reaction to the public events of the government will tell you what they think. And that's valuable information. Before we got to your castle, it appeared to me that Wonderland is a beautiful world, but I didn't see many of its people out in it. It made me wonder why. Are they allowed? Do they wish to branch out from the castle? Or is there some reason why they cannot?"

She looked at me, very thoughtfully, and drew in a deep breath. "This is not germane to the trial itself. Issues of negotiating with me regarding the visitors is within your purview, and representing your client is within your purview. But you exceed your brief when you begin lecturing me, in front of my vassals; it is not within your power or your authority. Unless you've suddenly taken on representation of all of them since I last spoke to you in your room?"

I had to shake my head no. She'd been with me the whole time. She knew better, and I did too. If I overreached too badly, I'd undermine my own argument.

Aiden tugged on my sleeve as I took a minute to reassess what I'd been about to say. "You're winning, I think. You've definitely got her listening to you and parsing out your argument if she's narrowing the focus, but did you see the people in the market? They're hanging on your every word! And I think I just saw Allie among them. Keep going. You're almost done."

My heart leapt. I needed to finish this trial and get back to the room so we could get Allie's message and figure out the next part of the plan, but I wasn't done.

"Madam, my point is very simple. There is insufficient evidence here to even hint that my client is guilty of anything more than delayed hunger and fulfilling hunger with tarts that had become his own property upon being delivered into his possession. Therefore, we are asking this court, and Your Highness, to rule in the proper, equitable, and correct manner and find this man not guilty. As he is not guilty, he should therefore not be punished for a crime he did not commit.

"If this court should find him guilty, then I would submit to the court that the punishment comes nowhere near fitting this crime. There are certainly more appropriate manners of punishment for a man who is accused of theft. He has hurt no persons. He has hurt no citizens. No party is economically burdened by the alleged offense; none of your vassals have been disadvantaged because of it. There is no history of such offenses in his past. In our world, Mr. Bathurst was well-known and served a monarch himself. He was well-respected and given sensitive matters of public trust to the Crown. There is much to mitigate against a harsh punishment against a man who has never had such an issue in his own background."

"Are you finished?" she asked.

I nodded. What else could I say? I was clicking my arguments off on my fingers, but absent a ton of notes and access to a legal pad, I couldn't be a hundred percent sure.

She nodded and indicated she had already reached her verdict, asking Benjamin and myself to rise to hear it.

CHAPTER FORTY-TWO

If my heart had been trying to beat its way out of my chest before we'd started, it currently felt like it had stopped. As I stood there, waiting for the Queen to pronounce judgment, I felt it drop to my ankles, leaving me light-headed and somewhat dizzy.

"I still find Benjamin Bathurst guilty of the crime of theft," she started. "And unlike my normal routine, I shall explain. Mr. Bathurst has put himself in debt to me. He did not earn the value of the tarts he ate without my permission. As they were not earned or otherwise purchased, the crown had the right to dictate the terms under which he was able to eat the tarts."

I opened my mouth to start to object, but Benjamin grabbed my arm. "She's not done yet. See what she says about punishment before you object. I'd rather lose the battle and win the war," he hissed into my ear.

He was right.

Before I could respond further, she continued. "I do, however, believe the visiting counselor has a point she wishes to make, and I can make it for her. I have not allowed visitors to earn their own coin or keep. Therefore, they have become dependent upon me. They do not have a choice but to eat what they are given and hope they have permission to eat when they are hungry. Therefore, the crown is somewhat complicit in the circumstances that have led to the charges before the court."

I saw Allie in the crowd, her mouth hanging open in astonishment. I don't think anyone expected the Queen to admit the unfairness of the situation. Most of the other market denizens had the same look on their faces that Allie displayed. I started to gesture to get Aiden's attention, but I stopped myself for fear of giving her away. Thankfully, no one noticed my reaction.

The Queen continued, unaware of the stir she was causing, even as the crowd muttered around her. There was an electric excitement in the air, as if the crowd itself was suddenly abuzz with the very possibilities the Queen seemed to be open to.

"The visitors have some lofty ideas. I look out upon my subjects, and I realize they are no longer looking at the crown as a means of protection from forces that might hurt them, but as a force itself to be frightened of. It strikes me that the power of mitigation, the impact of mercy, can do more to stabilize a kingdom than an iron fist. This is a first for me, and for Wonderland.

"Therefore, I would suspend any punishment against Mr. Bathurst, other than time in the town stocks whilst his counselor and I discuss other matters of importance. Counsel, you may have a few moments with your client, and then you and your assistants shall join me in the throne room for further discussions."

Benjamin let out a huge sigh of relief.

"Are you kidding?" I hissed at him. "You're relieved at a sentence that found you guilty of a crime you didn't commit?"

"She couldn't find me innocent. It would be a massive loss of face, and there's no way she could handle it and keep her head up high. The people may yet pay for this, but right now, if you can convince her to release the remaining visitors and possibly help some of us to return home, I'm happy to spend a couple of hours in the stocks. If that is how I can do my part, I am happy to do so. Besides, I don't believe there will be very aggressive vegetable tossing today. I think the merchants and their customers will be more concerned with talking about the events of today than worrying about pleasing the queen by hitting me with tomatoes."

He was likely right. And those who would have thrown things in his face to appease the Queen would be less likely to do so if they thought the Queen would not be watching from a window. Besides, he might have a point. Would I agree to stand in the stocks for an hour or two to give someone time to negotiate my freedom? Absolutely.

Some of the guards took Benjamin away to the stocks; the rest of the sentries shuffled Aiden, Bert, and me back into the castle. I had no idea what time it was, but it did appear as if the sun was going down. I looked sideways and noticed two of the guards looked awfully familiar, even if I couldn't see their faces. One of them turned to me and laid a finger over his lips. It was Tobias. The guard on the opposite side grinned at me. It was Jonah.

My mind spun. I hoped they had a plan for getting us out of here, because I had no idea what the Queen intended. I could almost predict there would be some kind of retribution for making her look bad in front of her people. It then struck me as awfully funny to consider her subjects as people . . . as many of them weren't. They were hedgehogs and mice and rabbits and dodos, but they talked and acted like humans. I let out a bit of a giggle, which earned me a harsh look from Aiden.

I wasn't sure if he'd seen the others, so I figured I'd better get a handle on the ridiculousness of the situation before I had to play negotiator again. I started to say something to him again, but he shushed me before anything came out of my mouth. He was probably right that silence was best.

Four guards, including our fake-guard friends, took us into the throne room. Had Tobias and Jonah done any reconnaissance before they'd gone into character, or were they just following the lead of the other guards? Either way, I was impressed; they didn't seem to be raising any concern from the others. Upon entering the throne room, it seemed like we'd come full circle. This was where we met the Queen when we'd first come to the castle, and this was where I would negotiate to leave it.

I waited, trying to be respectful, for the Queen to speak, but she allowed the quiet to continue. She sat on her throne and allowed her courtiers to arrange her train and her robes in a flattering manner, the fabric trickling down the stairs of the dais as if they were water instead of cloth. I wondered just how much she spent on her wardrobe. I wondered what Aiden's father, Geoffrey, the court tailor to the Queen's sister, would think of how the fabric fluttered and draped as the courtiers arranged it. If nothing else, it was a topic of conversation if we ever got out of Wonderland and I needed small talk with him. I filed it away for later.

One would think I'd have been completely focused on the task at hand and ready to go, but my stomach was empty. We'd been rationing food, unsure of how long we'd have to keep going without eating the Queen's tarts, and I hadn't eaten all day for fear of the adrenaline making me yak all over my shoes. The nerves were wearing off and I was getting dizzy again, although this time, it was probably because of a low blood sugar issue, rather than nerves and stress. I was starting to develop a wicked headache, as well.

Thank goodness the Queen didn't wait too long to get going. "Well, I don't quite know what I think, but you made some interesting points. I believe it might be worth exploring further to determine if you might be correct in relations between a monarch and their subjects."

"I am not trying to take your power, Your Highness," I said. "I'm trying to show you a better way to wield it, one that might do more to make your subjects loyal and happy. It might benefit your economy and take the burden of visitors off of your royal budget."

"I'm definitely interested."

"I can't show you all the ins and outs of a capitalist, democratic society in one day. I can tell you that if you give your subjects the chance to truly give you constructive criticism about your government, to give you honest critique, you will learn more about what works and what doesn't in the lives of the people who are subject to the rules you want to impose.

"The merchants will tell you how trade restrictions affect their businesses. Those who teach the young will tell you how any education restrictions affect those they teach. The guards can tell you how effective your rules and laws can be in practical effect when they try to enforce them. You don't have to agree with them, but if they are terrified of you, they will never give you the honest information you need."

She nodded. "Of course, it's my understanding that you want more than just a listening ear from me; you want safe passage."

"I want more, actually. I want safe passage out of Wonderland for any of the visitors who wish to leave. I want any visitors who choose to stay to be allowed to stay without being restricted to living within the castle walls. I want them to be able to be a part of your world, a true citizen of Wonderland. Allow them to earn their own food, whether they eat tarts, or meat, or vegetables, or whatever. You'll save money in the end because you will likely not have to support them, and if they do stay, they'll contribute to your economy.

I want safe passage out of Wonderland for all those who came to Wonderland with me and for my friend, the one I came here to help, if she wishes it."

"She?" the Queen pounced.

I hadn't said that before? Come to think of it, I don't think I had. Did that mean I'd just given away Allie's identity? That could be bad, since I'd just seen her in the marketplace.

CHAPTER FORTY-THREE

"So, I believe I've determined who your friend is, and I'm not convinced she should have safe passage. I believe you have convinced me that the visitors should participate in our society, though there should still be rules to protect them from the dangers of our world. There are things here that they are more susceptible to than those who are native to Wonderland."

How could I argue that she shouldn't restrict movement that could be dangerous? "I'd only ask any restrictions be related to their safety and there be some provision to allow them to elect to leave Wonderland down the road. If you institute more provisions regarding the visitors after I leave your realm and they are stuck here, they may feel as if they were not presented with all the information when they made that choice."

"No, I will not allow an open-ended policy to allow them to leave at any time, but I will allow a period of time after you leave for them to determine if they wish to leave. If they decide they do wish to leave after that point, I will ask them to apply to me, their chosen sovereign, for permission to leave, and I will evaluate their honest application for any signs that they might seek to harm Wonderland before deciding."

I stepped forward, feeling hopeful at the way the conversation was going. "I believe this may be acceptable, but I would ask that, if there is no evidence or indication of harm to Wonderland, their application be successful. I would also ask that they be directed to report to me and only return through the passage in my backyard. I'm willing to work with you, and them, to help their return to life in their own realm, as well as to have a contact to remind them to keep things from Wonderland separate from our realm."

She nodded. "I would appreciate it, but you are not immortal, are you?"

I had to consider what she was saying. "Are you wanting a permanent arrangement?"

"As near to it as I can get," was the answer.

I didn't like that. I didn't like the idea of committing any future children of mine to a lifetime of service to the Queen of Wonderland and to any visitors who might pass through, but at the same time, I felt it was a risk I might be able to work with in order to obtain the freedom of the people who were stuck here in Wonderland. "Well, I'm willing to assist the visitors who are from the human realm. I can't pretend to have any knowledge or experience on how to help any visitors from other realms, and I'd rather not invite danger onto my own property that isn't welcome."

"Understandable," she said.

"I am willing to promise myself and my heirs in this service until and unless another arrangement is negotiated. If there should be no heirs, as I do not currently have one, there will be a representative from the mortal realm who will contact you to renegotiate beyond that point."

"This is acceptable. But what service do you exactly provide?" she asked.

"I will advise visitors in leaving Wonderland and in reintegrating themselves into our world. I can help to advise them on how to remain out of Wonderland in the future. Time runs differently in our world, so there may have been big changes since they left."

"This is reasonable. But what if they wish to return?" she asked.

"Then I will contact you myself, on their behalf, to negotiate prior to their return."

She considered it. "They will not return on their own prior to the conclusion of those negotiations?"

"They will not return under their own power. I would ask you not to hold it against them if they are brought here against their will."

We negotiated further and were left with an agreement that I would be the point person from the human realm, and I might be contacted to assist in negotiations with other realms if I was available, but I was the one who would determine my availability.

I thought we had it settled. I was wrong.

"Well, there's just one item left to settle, and then you and your friends can be on your way," she said.

"What's that?"

"The only exit from Wonderland that is currently accessible is guarded by a being we do not have the military might to defeat."

"What is it?"

"The Jabberwocky."

Shit. Double shit. With sprinkles on top.

CHAPTER FORTY-FOUR

"I was under the impression the Jabberwocky had been defeated several years ago," I said. Wasn't that what I remembered from the books? I was pretty sure it had been killed.

The Queen laughed. "The Jabberwocky of old had in fact been killed, but it had apparently laid eggs on the other side of the Looking Glass. I don't know how many there are, but I know there's one there. When it crossed through, looking for its parent, it had immediately grown to full size and sat in front of the Looking Glass, refusing to move until we gave it to its mother. Well, we couldn't do that, because its mother was dead."

"Have you sent others to clear the way?" I asked. I was a bit afraid of where this was headed.

"I've sent many of my own personal guards, as well as some dear friends who wished to help. I've sent visitors in the past who were seeking a way home. Part of confining them to the castle was to keep them alive, because any who went in search of a way out of Wonderland were killed by the Jabberwock. We do not have a weapon in our world that is effective against the thing."

One, two! One, two! And through and through
The vorpal blade went snicker snack!
He left it dead, and with its head
He went galumphing back . . .

The lines of the poem echoed in my head. We had a vorpal sword. I was sure of it. I glanced over at Aiden, who had been quietly allowing me to take the lead on all of this, and I saw the recognition in his eyes. He knew it, too. The problem was, we did not have it; Tobias did. And we couldn't give it away without giving away Tobias, and likely Jonah, in their undercover capacities.

"I'm a lawyer, not a soldier!" I exclaimed. "What do you expect of me?"

The Queen smiled. "There is no other way out of Wonderland except through the Looking Glass, and the new Jabberwocky is blocking the way. If you truly wish to go home, you must clear the path in order to do so."

I had a sudden thought. "Have all of the visitors you've sent against the Jabberwocky been killed?" I asked.

"All the ones I've sent, yes. There are one or two visitors who tried on their own. There is one survivor of such an action."

"Who is the survivor?" I asked, but I was pretty sure I already knew.

The Queen confirmed it. "Her name is Alice. She is also the only visitor who has left and returned. Maybe she can tell you more about the Jabberwock. She was disfigured in the attack and would have died if others hadn't dragged her out of the way. I'm not sure if she knows quite how she got away, but then, she was unconscious. She may have more information for you."

The blind woman must be Alice. It had to be. Alice, who left Wonderland and returned again to look for a life that was no longer the same, to find herself with child and dragged back. But why would anyone be dragged back to Wonderland? What was she doing here? Alice, Allie's mother. I wondered if Allie knew her mother was still alive.

"I have concerns," I said. "I'm sure you can understand this."

"I'm sure you do, yet I am not able to answer all of your concerns. Alice likely can tell you more than I can."

"May I speak with her in private?" I asked. "With no restrictions and no eavesdropping from any castle personnel?"

"If you are looking for combat advice, would it not make more sense to speak with one of the guard?" she asked.

"Possibly, but I'm not looking for combat advice. I'm looking for information about the Jabberwocky. I want to know what drove her back to your court if she had been so enamored of getting back to her own family." There was something else bothering me, nagging at me, and I wasn't quite sure how to ask the question.

"Is there anything else I can help you with?" I asked. "Removing the Jabberwocky from the pathway to your world would allow us to cement our bargain and would likely allow you to come and go in order to negotiate pursuant to our arrangement . . ."

Something just didn't seem right. I was missing something.

And then I got it.

"Your Highness, if the Jabberwock is blocking the path to our world, then how did we have signs that someone in your world had visited ours?"

"You can't be serious," she said.

Aiden spoke up. "She is. We had donuts that made one large and wine that made one small strategically placed in and around our home. We noticed a white rabbit in our backyard disappear down the rabbit hole that brought us here. And we also had a Jabberwocky appear in our backyard. We thought it was going to damage our home because it seemed to be looking for something or someone."

"That's impossible," she said. "I've forbidden all traffic into your world by Wonderland residents without court permission, and no one has been allowed to leave in many years."

"If someone had left, without your permission, would you have fought to bring them back? Would someone in Wonderland fight to bring them back, believing you wanted it? Would someone have followed them into the mortal realm and snatched them in order to return them to your control?"

The Queen looked genuinely puzzled. "Why would I do that? If someone has left, then I no longer have to feed, clothe, and shelter them. If someone has left, what would I gain by sending my people into other realms to drag them back?"

Silence.

There had to be a clock somewhere, because I could hear it ticking the seconds away. I wondered if there was a faucet dripping, too, because it seemed like any sounds one wouldn't ordinarily hear were what I heard . . . which was to say I didn't hear much.

The Queen looked agitated. Had I exposed some secret of hers, or had I gotten someone else's conspiracy exposed that shouldn't have been?

I didn't dare look at Aiden or Bert, and I certainly didn't dare look back at Tobias or Jonah, in their guard uniforms, hoods drawn over their eyes enough to shade their identity. What was I risking by even asking the question?

Was I throwing our almost-freedom under the bus to get answers on our, and Allie's, future security? She was sure it was the White Rabbit's minions looking for her.

The White Rabbit.

Who had acted as the prosecutor for Benjamin's trial.

Who had been the steward in the castle, keeping all of the visitors in line.

Who Allie was so convinced had been looking for her in the mortal realm.

And I knew the Queen wasn't the biggest obstacle to our getting home.

CHAPTER FORTY-FIVE

I glanced around. The White Rabbit was nowhere to be seen, but who knew who might be in his employ?

"May I approach the throne?" I asked. "I have something to say that is only for the ears of the Queen."

She nodded, a distant, shocked look on her face. "Of course, approach."

I carefully stepped away from my friends and walked toward the Queen, my steps small and deliberate to avoid stepping on her dress or its train. I climbed up the dais to her throne and whispered in her ear.

"I have reason to believe the White Rabbit might have been tracking visitors and attempting to drag them back against their will."

"There's only been one person who was a visitor who left this realm. There's only been one person who you could possibly be talking about," the Queen said.

"That's possible," I said. "I don't know how many are in this situation, merely the one person whom I've spoken to. This person said they were constantly seeing delegates from the White Rabbit, as if they were spying. This person indicated to me that they were hiding from the White Rabbit."

I looked into the Queen's eyes and saw something I wasn't used to. She looked scared. What in the world could be scaring the Queen so badly?

"Is she okay?" the Queen asked.

Huh?

"If we are talking about the same person, I believe so."

"When's the last time you saw her?" The Queen grabbed hold of my sleeve.

How did I answer that? If I admitted to seeing her that day, in the courtyard, I was afraid she would be somehow endangered. I didn't quite trust the Queen, even if she was putting on a good face on the concerned front.

"I hope you understand if I won't answer. I don't want to inadvertently cause this person harm or otherwise jeopardize their position." There was pain on her face. It seemed she actually cared. "I don't know what to tell you, ma'am. This person is highly concerned for their own safety, and I'd like to honor their privacy. They have been a good friend."

From somewhere near my toes, a voice spoke up. "Why don't you tell us what your concern is for the person you are thinking of, and we can determine if we can tell you more." It was Bert.

"What are you doing?" I asked.

"Look, the person you're talking about wouldn't want to stand in the way of getting the rest of us out of here if they could. They'd want to figure out the way back themselves, and getting caught up in too much personal drama prevents us from doing what we need to do. If there's a way to get past this, I'd think we would all be able to do something about it."

The Queen looked concerned. "Let's move this to the anteroom behind the throne. It's my private sitting room."

"Is it safe for discussion? Will the White Rabbit know what you're talking about?" the frog asked.

She shook her head. "I don't think so."

I nodded. Maybe she'd be okay with me getting a bite of something out of my backpack if we were going to a private sitting room. I was getting dizzier.

We stepped back to allow her to rise and followed her to a back room. There were no windows and no other doors than the one we'd come through. It didn't appear as if there was a way for anyone to spy on us, but there could always be a pinhole somewhere that someone could be watching through. It was Wonderland, after all. There could be all kinds of ways to eavesdrop that we weren't aware of. Where was Stanley when we needed him? I smiled. He'd eat this up, with all of this clandestine dealing and backroom secrets.

The room was shabbily ornate, as if it had been designed to be featured in one of those vintage home decoration magazines I saw all the time at the grocery store back home. It was cozy, yet well used, comfortable, yet classy. It looked like a home, if that home had been

Victorian without a huge budget. There was faded damask fabric I thought had a paisley design, but with closer inspection, it appeared to be elongated hearts in rich deep maroon.

There were heavy, dark wooden bookshelves holding multiple paperbacks from authors in our own world: Tom Clancy, J.K. Rowling, Stephen King, Janet Evanovich, Nora Roberts, Neil Gaiman, and Ken Follet among others. How in the world had she gotten those books if no one had been able to go into our realm, past the Jabberwocky?

When the door closed behind us, the Queen let out an audible sigh. She reached up and lifted a wig off her head, gently setting the elaborate red beehive monstrosity of a hairdo on a stand where it wouldn't get mussed. She had dishwater blond hair, which was cut short to her head. If she wore wigs on a daily basis, I wouldn't blame her for keeping her hair cut short. But why the disguise?

"What's going on?" I asked.

She laid one finger over her mouth and walked over to a painting on the wall, allowing it to swing open to pull out a bottle of scotch and four glasses. She poured a finger of scotch in each glass and passed them around. Aiden sipped at his, and Bert began sticking his tongue into his, almost like a cat sucking up milk. I made a show of sipping at it, but I had no desire to drink any. Scotch wasn't my drink of choice, and I was afraid alcohol wouldn't much help the headache I'd been fighting off for the last couple of hours. I desperately just wanted a Coke, a bacon cheeseburger, and my bed, preferably in that order.

What in the world was I missing?

Aiden must have wondered the same thing, but he was thinking faster than I was. "So who is the real Queen?" he asked.

My jaw hung open. She wasn't the Queen?

Bert nodded at me. He'd figured it out too? Where had I been? I'd been a bit distracted, but at the same time, I wasn't *that* out of it, was I? How had I missed it?

She sighed. "I was one of the visitors here. Most of the visitors have forgotten about it or have otherwise ignored it. It's the White Rabbit's plan, and his secret, keeping us all under control."

Oh. My. Goodness. I knew exactly who she was. I'd been wrong before, but now I was certain.

"Benjamin was here when I came the first time. He doesn't remember me, though. I was just a kid, and I was absolutely in love with him. I didn't know what to do. The White Rabbit was watching, though, and making his plans for later. I had friends among the visitors. When I'd finally found my way home again, he'd already planned what role he wanted me to play. He wanted me to help him stay in control of a world that could very easily go to hell without a figurehead that wouldn't be questioned, and he didn't believe he could be that leader."

"What happened to the Queen herself?" I asked.

She cleared her throat. "The subjects of Wonderland tried to overthrow her. The White Rabbit stepped in, and he promised he would be the go-between for the people to the court. He saw an opportunity to grab power, and he took it."

Wow. Suddenly, it all fell into place, and I understood why things were so difficult to understand about Wonderland. The woman we had thought was the Queen wasn't actually in charge. So how in the world could we trust any promises she made? Would we actually be able to leave Wonderland if the White Rabbit had a vested interest in keeping us here?

CHAPTER FORTY-SIX

Well, damn it.

Damn, damn, double damn, with a side dish of we-are-screwed.

I was still wrapping my head around the latest turn of events. "Let me get this straight," I said. "You're not the Queen. Somehow, the citizens of Wonderland had to be convinced you were. How did that happen?"

She didn't answer.

I pondered a moment. "It's the tarts, isn't it? That's why the visitors only eat tarts. The Wonderland denizens weren't ever close enough to the Queen to know the difference, and the White Rabbit could be sure no one got close enough to truly question it. He probably replaced all the castle staff. The tarts are magical, enchanted to control the visitors who might know the truth about the real Queen." No wonder Allie's note told us not to eat them.

"Yes," she said. "The White Rabbit wanted anyone who could actually figure out the bait and switch on the throne to be too apathetic to object. He had your stepmother show him how to enchant tart filling in order to control people by turning them into compliant, docile inhabitants of the castle, rather than agitating for change. He thought I would help him do that, but I wouldn't."

"So, what about the person who left?"

"Technically, there are two who have left and, if I read between the lines, two who have returned to Wonderland, even after they got out. I think you met Allie," she said. It didn't take a rocket scientist to figure out she had genuine caring feelings for our friend, as it was written all over her face.

"It was you," I said.

Aiden and Bert looked at me with uncomprehending looks on their faces.

"You were the one who got Allie out. You were the one who wanted her gone from this place. You were the one who knew how dangerous it was to remain here in Wonderland." I had finally pieced it all together.

She didn't say anything for a moment. "The White Rabbit was terrified I would let it slip, that Allie would let it slip. Allie knew the truth, as she was coming of age at a time when the Rabbit was first implementing his plan. She's the one flaw in his otherwise fairly comprehensive chess game. He wanted control of the court, but he didn't think he'd be able to take over the throne himself. He believed, and I think rightfully, that the people of Wonderland would never follow him. There had been too much infighting, too many conspiracies, and too much in the way of shady dealings. He wasn't trusted. But if he put someone on the throne he could control in some way, someone he could use as a prop, he could wield the power of the throne to do whatever he wanted."

Talk about a cat's paw. He was definitely one to watch.

"Does he have access to this room?" I asked. "There's a lot we can probably guess, a lot we can likely piece together. Is this going to cause you problems with the White Rabbit? How much trouble are you in if you get caught telling us all of this?"

She saluted me with her glass and sank heavily into a well-padded overstuffed horsehair chair. "I don't care. I need to help Allie in any way I can. I've tried to do my best for her, but I just don't know that I've been able to do much except cause her grief. Tell me, though. Did she find happiness in the mortal world? Has she been able to get herself settled?"

How was I supposed to answer that one? If I was right, she really didn't want to know about all the things Allie had been through lately. She probably didn't want to know about the boys, the customers, the mattress in the corner, the Seawitch torturing her, or any of the other negative stuff I knew of the life Allie had led in Dayton.

"She has friends," I said. "Ones who care deeply about her and want her safe. What can you tell me that I can use to help keep her safe?"

The fake Queen sighed heavily and set her glass down on a small wooden table beside her chair. "What is the White Rabbit doing in your world? I thought he was only going to make sure the passages were safe and no one was able to come through. After that, he was to tell me if Allie was okay, and he brought me books to pass the time. He wasn't supposed to be doing anything else . . . so what was he really doing?"

"I'm not one hundred percent sure; I can only tell you what I know." And I proceeded to tell her about the donuts, the wine, the normal-sized rabbit in the backyard, the Jabberwocky showing up, and Allie running away to protect us. "Why in the world would she run back to Wonderland if she was trying to stay away? Why would she believe she was in danger if he was only supposed to check on her?"

The Queen still had a regal bearing, sitting up straight in her chair, even though she wasn't the real royalty. Or at least she had until I asked the question. Her shoulders slumped. "So it is her," said the Queen. "And she's the one that's had the White Rabbit in an uproar. I should have known."

I motioned for her to keep talking.

She did. The rest of us sat. Aiden and Bert sipped their Scotch, while I wasn't even trying. I wondered if I could sneak a granola bar out of my backpack. It wouldn't be much, but I really wanted some food. The more I thought about it, the more my stomach growled.

"It was hard trying to hide the truth from Allie, even though she was just a kid when all the tarts started being served and as the White Rabbit's plans were suddenly coming to fruition. It took years for him to feel like he was getting control over everything. The real queen was slowly losing her mind. The Rabbit tried to convince me she was sick, but I always wondered if he was poisoning the Queen.

"As Allie grew up, he kept using me to stand in for the queen, and I was able to negotiate with him for different things to ensure my silence and cooperation. I bargained for books, real food for Allie and myself, whatever might make Allie's life a lot more bearable than it would have been otherwise. She grew up into a smart, well-educated kid."

I knew I was right. "So Allie wasn't affected by the magic in the tarts? What about other magic? Is there another magical being in Wonderland?"

She laughed. "The White Rabbit has been attempting to suppress all uses of magic here in Wonderland. It's having an effect on the environment, as well as on the people."

I thought about Alfred the Hatter, the mushrooms in the forest, the looks on the faces of the Wonderland residents in the market. I thought about the lady who'd given me the letter from Allie. I thought about the porters, the guards, and the dodos, the Caterpillar with his mushroom, as well as everyone and everything else I'd seen since I'd been in this realm, and it all started to make sense. Had I sensed the magic in the tarts when she'd had the blind woman bring them into our room? Maybe that was what I smelled.

"You're worried Wonderland is fading, that the control the White Rabbit is exerting is somehow eating away at the very fabric of Wonderland and all it is. You're afraid the more he tries to isolate you, the worse things get. You want to make the kinds of changes I was suggesting, but something's holding you back. It's the Rabbit. He's got some kind of hold on you that prevents you from making the kind of changes you believe would do the most good. It's why you ruled the way you did in the trial. It's why you made public statements about negotiating. And it's why we're here now."

She nodded.

"It's Allie," Bert said. "She's your daughter."

"She's all I have left."

CHAPTER FORTY-SEVEN

"Let me get this straight," I said. "You're the Alice from Alice in Wonderland, Allie is your daughter, and you're trying to protect her and everyone else?"

She nodded again.

"I thought you were dead," Bert said. "Allie told us you were dead."

"She probably thought I was. The deal was that she not return. The White Rabbit was supposed to help me get her out in exchange for being his puppet monarch. I don't know what Allie was told. I only know I packed her a bag on the day she left and gave her a big hug. I told her I loved her and had negotiated for her to go home. I gave her instructions on how to find her grandparents' house, the address, and I fully expected her to go there."

"Except she came through in Dayton, Ohio, rather than in London, England, and it was more than two hundred years after her grandparents died," Aiden said. "She didn't have anyone on the other side to help her, and life has sure changed a lot since you were in the mortal world."

"I didn't know what else to do. It wasn't safe for her to stay here. The real Queen was suspicious of my relationship with Benjamin because she was getting paranoid and thought we were going to hurt her. She was suspicious of my conversations with the White Rabbit, and rightfully so. As it was, I refused to help the Rabbit with his schemes until Allie was safe. He told me he'd bargained with the Queen. He told me he'd found a way to strip away magic from Wonderland and promised not to use it on the Queen if she helped get Allie out. She figured Allie being taken away from me would make me less vulnerable to the White Rabbit."

"How do you know that?" I asked.

"The Queen told me."

I heard a banging noise on the other side of the door. She rose, grabbed her wig from its stand, and settled it back on her head. It slid right into place, as if it had been made to slip on and off like a hat. I had a funny feeling it probably was.

Two guards were outside of the door, and no one else was around. Both of them had their hands up, both of them looked shocked. And both of them weren't actually guards. It was Jonah and Tobias.

"What is going on?" the Queen demanded.

The White Rabbit was standing behind them. "Are you plotting against me, my dear? You had to know your ruling in the courtyard was wrong. You had to know I'd be watching for anything that may appear to be a conspiracy. You've messed up."

What were we going to do now? I wondered. I'd started to get enough information to start piecing the whole puzzle together. The really real Alice, the one in the Queen costume before me, was pure vanilla mortal, just like me. She wasn't magic in any way. And it appeared as though the Rabbit had been stripping magic from Wonderland. He wouldn't have wanted a magical queen if he wanted to control the land.

Therefore, Alice, despite her statements to the contrary, couldn't be my stepmother's sister. The real Queen was, which would explain why she was dangerous and why the Rabbit couldn't control her. But if it was her magic that kept Wonderland growing and prosperous, was it the lack of magic causing the proliferation of the nightslip mushrooms we saw in the forest? And why hadn't the Rabbit realized this was hurting Wonderland? Too many questions, and not enough answers, nor enough time to sort it all out.

We were all dragged unceremoniously out of the private sitting room and back into the throne room. The real guards seemed embarrassed. I bet they were. Tobias and Jonah had fooled them, as well as everyone else, for an entire day. Nevertheless, the eight guards were armed with wicked-looking curved swords and stood ready to use them.

The White Rabbit was holding a gun.

A regular, garden variety, non-magical kind of six-shooter Colt. The kind of gun I'd seen in old Westerns. I wasn't even going to try to guess how the Rabbit managed to get his hands, um, *paws* on a gun.

"Now, why don't you tell me one good reason why I shouldn't

shoot all of you on sight?" the Rabbit asked.

"Because," said Alice, "if you shoot these folks, I have no incentive to continue with the farce we've been involved in for years. You need me to stay on the throne. The people aren't going to stand much longer for your type of iron-fisted rule. They needed to see reasonableness being considered, or they were not going to continue to be subservient to your regime. They needed to see that the crown actually cares about them, or they would have started to organize against you. I've given your actual time in control a longer length, a longer life, and more time before the people start to demand something different."

He seemed to consider this. "But if that's the case, what stops me from going after your daughter? What stops me from making sure she can't stir up trouble?"

Alice laughed. "She thinks I'm dead. She ran back here because of you, Mr. Rabbit. You stalked her while she was in the mortal realm, despite your promises to leave her alone. You chased her, so she was not able to have a normal, productive life. You violated the spirit of the arrangement we had when I agreed to take up this sham. Tell me why I should trust your word again."

"Because we need each other," was the answer. "Your daughter is back in Wonderland, and I know it. For you to be assured she gets back out, unharmed, you need to work with me to make all of this go away."

She didn't say anything, and I didn't have much I could add. I wanted to know what the Rabbit's price was for her silence and her cooperation. I wondered what he wanted out of us. And I wondered just what the Jabberwocky had to do with all of it. Was Alice putting us on when she brought up the Jabberwocky, or was it truly the only way out? And she had mentioned that one of the visitors knew about fighting it. It had to be the blind woman. If that was the case, and if Allie didn't know about her mother being alive, then who was the blind woman to my friend? Who was she to the fake Queen?

Suddenly, I had a strange thought.

The more I thought about it, the more I was convinced I knew more of Alice's secrets than she realized. I thought I knew more about what had really happened. And I thought I knew just what had brought the White Rabbit to this pass.

Boy, he really hated Alice to have gone to these lengths. I shook my head to clear it.

"Let me be the first to say, Mr. Rabbit, that I think we can come to some kind of arrangement. I think we can all get what we want out of this."

He raised the gun and pointed it directly at my face. My head swam, and I felt faint. Was it because of the imminent danger, or the lack of food? I swayed on my feet and felt Aiden put his hand on my shoulder. It steadied me.

In the times I'd faced magical shenanigans—a trial for my life, a battle-hungry Seawitch, a Jabberwocky in my backyard—I'd never been as scared as I was facing down the barrel of that gun.

CHAPTER FORTY-EIGHT

He waved the gun, and I put my hands up. I wondered how long I could keep them up. The headache started to go away with a new wave of adrenaline coursing through me, but at the same time, I was getting sick to my stomach. Food was going to have to happen soon.

"Sir, I don't know if you realize, but I have some experience at negotiating between realms. I was serious when I was talking about negotiations to allow the visitors to leave. I was serious when I was talking about being a contact for those who leave and to be the one they come to if they ever decided they wished to come back. That was all legitimate and before I realized who was truly in charge. I agree with the Queen. I believe it is only a matter of time before the people want something different, but I believe her public decisions today may have bought you some time to consider your next move."

He stood there, motionless, but he didn't pull the trigger. The others didn't move. I didn't even hear them so much as breathe.

I continued. "We can all go about our lives and go back to the way things were. There's no reason to think anyone else is aware of the conversation we just had, behind closed doors. Your secrets are safe, and we are all willing to keep them that way. We just want those who are stuck here to have hope and a chance to go home again. And of course, we'd like to get there ourselves. We're willing to offer our services to help facilitate this. You tell me what else you might be in need of, and we might be able to do a deal."

Tobias was shifting back and forth on the balls of his feet, as if ready to spring into battle. Jonah's hands were in front of his body, in preparation to jump forward if need be. I couldn't see Aiden, but I heard the intake of his breath behind me, and Bert spoke up before I could tell him to let me handle it.

"People and anthropomorphic citizens can live together in harmony, sir. They're not better or worse than each other. They're just citizens sharing the same world."

Where did that come from? I wondered. And then I saw the look on the Rabbit's face. He was listening to Bert's statement.

The Rabbit's stone-faced expression cracked. "You don't understand. For years, we were in service to the Queen. For years, we've had to endure her insults and her orders and her insanity. It's time one of us was in charge. But to overthrow the Queen, we'd have to also deal with the prying eyes of outside realms. Better to make it appear that the Queen was still in charge so as not to raise suspicion from other magical beings." He lowered the gun.

I got it now. Part of the prevention of visitors from leaving was to prevent the secret from getting out. If the real Queen's sister was my stepmother, what would she have done if she learned her sister's reign was in trouble? But my stepmother was safely ensconced in Søborg Castle, behind lock and key. The Snow Queen, who had taken over my stepmother's throne, wouldn't be interested, would she? I didn't know of any relationship between them, but it wasn't completely unheard of.

For all I knew, all the Queens in all the realms were close in age and had grown up like sisters together. That kind of bond could run deep, so it was always possible there were other rulers in other realms I didn't know about who could have an interest in the real Queen's plight.

How was the White Rabbit to know who might start asking questions and come around if someone did get out of Wonderland and start talking? What assurance did he have that any one of the visitors wouldn't say exactly the wrong thing at exactly the wrong time when the wrong person might be listening? It could make his carefully constructed world crumble down around him like . . . well, like crumbs. No wonder the Rabbit was restricting and medicating the visitors who would have reason to go elsewhere and complain.

And no wonder he had tried to follow and watch and scare Allie; he was afraid she was out there spreading word that he was exerting control over the throne. And there was no way he was going to allow any of us to leave, because then the jig would absolutely be up, as there was no way I could even hope to keep my mouth shut. I knew I'd be trying to get a hold of someone, anyone, to let them know what was going on in Wonderland, because I knew the people were so unhappy.

It wasn't as simple as just getting us home.

If we were able to escape and go home, we would all be spending the rest of our lives wondering if the White Rabbit would show up and try to scare, intimidate, bully, or kidnap us to prevent us from toppling his regime. I refused to live like that. We had to find a way to knock him off his perch, rather than just go home—as much as I was ready to go eat my way through a large pepperoni pizza and crash in my own bed—or we'd never be rid of him.

I realized I'd tuned out the White Rabbit. He was no longer pointing the gun at us, and he was saying something. "I'm sorry, can you repeat that?" I asked.

"I said, you'll be escorted to your quarters in the visitors' annex, and you'll be provided tarts for dinner. I expect you to eat every bite, and if you refuse to do so, you will answer to me. As for you, my dear 'queen,' you will join these visitors in their quarters. If you speak to your daughter, then your job is to convince her to take your place. You are finished on the throne, my dear."

"Will I have a chance to speak with my client?" I asked.

"No," said the Rabbit. "He is being removed from the stocks as we speak and is being served with a triple portion of tarts with orders to eat every bite."

I guess that was better than having one's head chopped off, but I couldn't worry about him at the moment. I was more concerned about not wanting Allie to be blindsided by the White Rabbit's plans. I had a funny feeling she wouldn't want to be the next Queen of Hearts, regardless of what she'd gone through in Ohio.

We were escorted back to the same room we'd started out the day in. A large silver platter, as wide as the span of my arms, sat on the foot of the bed. It was piled high with tarts of all kinds, and they were still warm. I could see the steam rising off them. I was starving, so I was definitely tempted.

The room had seemed relatively large the night before with just Bert, Aiden, and me, but now there were three more people. There was one bed and one chair, and the Queen's large dress with train took up quite a bit of room. It was going to be a long night.

Then again, we were still waiting for Allie.

I took one look at the Queen and yanked my pack off my back.

"We need to get you out of your dress and into something that allows you to move around easier. Actually, we need to get all of us ready to get out of here if Allie shows up with a plan."

The Queen protested a bit, but I shushed her. It looked like she'd fit into the spare pair of jeans I had in my backpack, and Tobias had an extra shirt that would fit her. I didn't have a bra for her, but we could at least get her out of the dragging train, the heavy dress, and all the rest. It wouldn't be safe to leave her here, and I knew Allie would want to take her with us. Escape would be easier if Alice's outfit didn't scream her public identity, as well as make running in general possible.

I made all the guys go stand by the window while I helped Alice out of the dress and then the corset, the underskirt, and all the rest. Without a good idea of what to do with it, I piled the dress in the corner of the room farthest away from the fireplace.

She seemed appalled at first by the jeans. I wondered if Alice had ever worn pants, given the era she'd come from. The Victorian period hadn't exactly been known for practical wear for women.

I knew there was a zip-up hoodie in Aiden's bag, and I pulled it out for her. She wasn't exactly a small-chested woman, and I figured she'd be less self-conscious with another layer to make her feel more secure. I was right. She stopped hunching her shoulders forward quite so much after she put on the sweatshirt.

Alice looked like a modern suburban soccer mom once we got her into her new clothing, her short hair spiking around her head and the club team logo on Aiden's sweatshirt. The only thing we couldn't provide for her was footwear.

"I'm used to the slippers," she said. But they were awfully noticeable and clashed with the casual nature of the clothing we'd lent her. Still, we didn't have another choice. I hadn't packed additional footwear, and none of the guys had extra shoes that would fit her.

She'd have to stick with the jeweled red satin slippers. I made a mental note to have her slip them off if we were sneaking around anywhere, for fear they might reflect a glint of light.

The guys turned back around, and our next problem was what to do with the tarts we'd been mandated to eat.

My stomach started growling on cue.

CHAPTER FORTY-NINE

"All right, I've got to get food in me," I said, but before I could do anything, five voices rose in unison to argue that I shouldn't eat the tarts.

I laughed. I wanted nothing to do with those damn tarts. "Relax, folks. We've still got some food in the backpacks. I think I've got some ravioli in here." I did, in a now-dented can at the bottom of my pack, which was much lighter without the extra pair of jeans. That gave me an idea.

"Alice, how well do the tarts pack?"

She looked horrified. "Are you seriously thinking of repeating Benjamin's mistake?"

"No," I said. "I don't intend to ever eat them myself, which was his biggest mistake. I intend for us to take them with us when we get out of the castle." I wanted every single advantage I could come up with, and the Jabberwocky might like some tarts. I opened the can of ravioli, pulling out the fork I'd let Benjamin use the night before, and started to eat. "Sorry, guys. I haven't eaten all day, and the adrenaline of the trial's got me a bit nauseous." I didn't even care that the pasta was cold. If I didn't get food in me soon, I was going to throw up.

Aiden pulled granola bars, Pop-Tarts, and some other odds and ends out of his backpack. Jonah and Tobias each had a couple of smooshed candy bars in their pockets. I had a couple of caramel apple suckers stashed in the bottom of my bag that I kept available to tide me over if I got hungry in between meals while I was at school. I decided to save those for later, though, because they weren't quick to eat or very filling.

It represented the last of the food we had brought in, but it was enough to at least take the edge off grumbling stomachs and low blood sugar mental fogs. It wasn't like we were passing around a sufficient amount of food for a sit down dinner, but it would keep us all thinking clearly. Aiden still had a bottle of water, and we passed it around; the bottle had enough for a few quick swigs to wash our meal down. The tarts on the tray had stopped steaming by the time we finished our snack.

We all finished up and then cleaned up the debris of our food. It wouldn't do to leave evidence that we were planning to disregard the White Rabbit's orders. Then again, we were in the room with the Queen. If she got back into her dress, she could officially give us all permission to eat whatever the heck we wanted. I tabled the thought; it was better to have her in clothing that would let her sneak out with us.

Just as I thought it, a rope of bed sheets tied in knots fell over the window, and I saw it shaking, as if someone was climbing down it. It didn't take long before Allie appeared.

"What the heck is going on here?" she asked.

I shrugged. "We've picked up some stragglers," I said with a grin. "And the White Rabbit has put us all together in the room for the night with orders to eat the entire plate of tarts."

"You haven't touched them, have you?" she asked.

Aiden shook his head, and the rest of us followed suit. I don't think Allie noticed, though, nor did she recognize her mom yet. She was too focused on her plan of getting everyone out the window, and no one knew how much time we had to do it.

"Good," she said. "We're breaking you out and getting all of you home."

You. Not us.

She wasn't planning to go with us.

I wasn't planning to leave her.

I grabbed the underskirt from the Queen's dress and enfolded the tarts in the material, tying the ends into a knot someone could sling over a shoulder. We packed up everything belonging to us and followed Allie, one by one, up the knotted rope.

My arms burned as I climbed. I hadn't been to a gym in a long time, and I was definitely out of shape. Why was it that the idea of getting in shape, or getting more martial arts and weapons skills, only came to mind when I actually needed them, as opposed to before magic stuck its nose in my business all over again? I'd have to make sure to do something about that when we got home, because this was now the third time I'd landed in deep magical poo. There's no way I could believe, or delude myself, that it wouldn't happen again.

It took the better part of half an hour for each one of us to shimmy up the bed sheets to the roof. Allie seemed ready to roll, but the rest of us, except for Tobias, were grunting and out of breath, clutching our sides. Yeah, we definitely had to get to the gym when we all got home. It's not fair; the Avengers never acted like they got stitches in their sides or as though they'd pulled a muscle. Why couldn't they show that in the movies?

Allie gave us a few minutes and then silently motioned for us to follow her. We did so, slowly, one at a time. Night had fallen as we had gotten to our rooms, and now it was dark on the rooftop of the castle. Allie picked her way slowly across the battlements and suddenly disappeared over the side.

We were slower. We didn't know the way and weren't quite as nimble as she was, but when I got to where Allie vanished, I saw where she'd gone. There was a stepladder up the side of the castle and no guards in sight. We slipped down quickly, with Jonah carrying the tarts, Bert hitching a ride in my backpack, Tobias attempting to help Alice, and Aiden doing his level best not to trip and fall. I couldn't believe we were getting away; we weren't exactly *Mission: Impossible* material.

Our luck only held for so long, though. And of course, it was Aiden to end it.

He tripped while descending the ladder, the rung cracking under his foot, and he slid the rest of the way down. Two guards must have heard him. I wasn't sure if it was Aiden's muffled curse, the sound of the cracking wood, or the thump he made when he landed.

"You okay?" I asked in a whisper.

He nodded, holding his hands out of in front of him. I saw splinters embedded in his palms, but I didn't have time to do anything about it when guards were sounding the alarm of our escape. We were off and running into the forest, puffing with exertion as we went. There wasn't a lot of quiet to it, but there sure was a lot of hurry.

I had to hand it to Tobias; he thought of something I hadn't. Our rubber soled tennis shoes were a great protection against the nightslips, but the Queen's shoes weren't. He grabbed at her, throwing her over his shoulder, and ran for the woods. Aiden and I ran after him, with the others just ahead. I kept turning around to look, but the guards weren't gaining on us. They'd stopped at the edge of the tree line where the nightslip mushrooms had begun to grow.

We weren't being chased anymore, but that didn't stop us. We kept running, following Allie through the forest, until Tobias called out. In truth, I was surprised he'd been able to run as far and as fast as he had with Alice slung over one shoulder. When Aiden and I caught up to him, he was breathing hard.

Allie called back, "It's not too much farther. Mia and Doris are waiting for us."

"We gotta slow down," Tobias said. "I'm not as young as I used to be."

I thought he was looking pretty spry. He might have a grown daughter, but he wasn't exactly ready for the nursing home yet. I smiled at him and wished I could help, but Alice actually weighed a few pounds more than I did. I was afraid I'd drop her. Yet another reminder that I was getting awfully flabby from too many nights of spaghetti and case law.

We got to a clearing in the wood where the mushrooms didn't seem to grow, and I found Mia and Doris stoking a low fire with something steaming away on top of it. They had our blankets covering parts of the ground, laid out around the fire as pallets ready for us to spend the night, but there was no way I was going to stay another night in Wonderland. I wanted out. I wanted real food. And then I wanted a plan for how to unseat the White Rabbit, once we'd marshaled our strengths.

Of course, what I plan and what takes place aren't always exactly similar.

CHAPTER FIFTY

Mia grabbed me in a huge hug when I approached, while Doris reached for Allie, crushing her in an embrace that nearly smothered the girl.

They'd opened a few cans of beans and vegetables and had them heating over the low flames of the fire using a grate they'd fashioned out of twigs and leaves and such. We all dropped our bags and sat down, resting weary feet and backs. Alice stood at the edge of the group and stayed silent as she watched Doris fuss over Allie. I saw the heartache on her face and stood up, going over to Alice while Allie was distracted by all the hugs and laughter from the others.

"Go to her. Let her know you're still here and you're okay. Take it from someone who doesn't have living family around. Even if she's upset with you for some reason, she'll be happy to know you're alive and well. Everything else can come later." I squeezed Alice's hand, trying to reassure her.

She swallowed hard and headed over to her daughter. "Allie," she said softly.

Allie looked up from Doris's shoulder and the food bubbling slowly over the fire. "Mom? What's going on? How are you here?"

She reached out to touch her mother's arm, as if she didn't believe it was real, and then ran into her mother's embrace, crying and laughing. I looked up and saw tears on Doris's face, and Aiden leaned over to awkwardly hug his own mother, still being careful not to bump the palms of his hands on anything.

"Allie, honey," Alice started, but dissolved into tears before she could say anything more.

Between the sobbing and hugging, the story slowly came out. Allie really did think her mother had died and hadn't recognized Alice in modern, mortal-realm clothing. She had been too distracted by getting us out of the castle and fleeing through the woods to realize we even had an extra person with us. Allie had believed her mother was killed when helping her escape Wonderland and had thought the White Rabbit had a hand in it.

I wanted my own mom. But I couldn't have that. I would never have that. The only thing I could do was to keep pushing forward. I put my arm around Aiden's waist and drew him away, sitting him down and pulling the first aid kit out of Mia's backpack. There was a set of tweezers inside, and I began pulling the splinters out of his hands while everyone else was watching the reunion. I'd learned over the time I'd been with Aiden to do that kind of thing . . . finding ways to treat his bumps and bruises from his klutz moves when people weren't looking. It also served to give me something to focus on other than my own thoughts about missing my mother.

I overheard the conversation between the mother and daughter clearly as I worked, turning Aiden's hands sideways into the light to make sure I'd gotten all the wood fragments. There was some kind of antibacterial ointment and gauze, so I spread a thin layer on his hands and wrapped up his palms for protection.

There was plenty of pain in their conversation. "I had no idea," Allie started. "I really thought you were dead."

"That was the price for getting you away," Alice replied. "I had to let you think that."

"What really happened?"

The story that came out was the same as Alice had told us earlier, with a bit more detail. Alice was heartbroken that all the visitors who had been her friends had their memories affected by the tarts the White Rabbit insisted on feeding them. Her closest companions no longer remembered who she really was, and none of them treated her well. She'd started trying to go amongst them in disguise, but the White Rabbit had caught her and had punished one of the visitors for her disobedience.

That was how the blind woman had gained the scar on her face, or so the story had been told by villagers who had taken in my friends while Aiden and I were at the castle.

"The blind woman," Allie said. "I knew who she really was."

"What do you mean?" asked her mother. "She wasn't placed with the visitors until after you left."

"No, she actually was put in the visitors' annex a week or so before my leaving. Remember how I was always climbing in and out of windows, taking messages to everyone?"

Alice laughed. "Yes. I always worried you'd fall, but you were far more nimble than anyone I'd ever met."

"She was a sweet lady. She gave me some sweets and told me that if ever I had a chance to get out of Wonderland, I should do it and never look back. I kept checking on her every day, and I told her I wasn't planning to leave."

Alice had a horrified look on her face. "Did you make her any promises?"

Allie sat and thought for a moment. "I promised I would always think of her. I promised that if I came back, I would try to get a message to her, and I did try. I left a note for Janie with a message for her."

Alice's head whipped around to me. "Did you deliver the message?"

I shook my head. I hadn't seen the blind lady since that fateful dinner party where Benjamin had gotten in trouble for talking back to the Queen, er, *Alice*, except for when the two of them brought in those tarts before the trial. There wasn't exactly an opportunity to pass on Allie's message at that time.

That reminded me of a question I had for Alice. "Why were you singling out Benjamin at dinner? And why did you bring the blind woman in with you before the trial?"

She sighed. "I brought her with me to see what she'd do; I wondered if she might try to get a message to you about what was really happening in Wonderland. As for Benjamin . . . He and I were once great friends. He was the only one who would talk to me when I was brought back. He was the one who held my hand when I realized I wouldn't get back home. He was the one who held my hair when I was throwing up with morning sickness. He delivered you, Allie, into this world."

Alice kept talking, softer now. "Benjamin doesn't remember our friendship. The White Rabbit and his magic tarts have seen to that. I keep trying to say things that might trigger him to remember something, anything, about the past—he has resisted the magic fog more than any of the others. The hope was that he would remember me."

Something in her voice had me wondering why she was so focused on Benjamin.

"Alice, what aren't you telling us?" I asked.

She looked up from her daughter with a pleading look. The expression I saw on her face seemed like she wanted me to reel back the question, as if I could suck it back into my mouth and go on as if it was never asked. I almost wished I could do that for her, but I couldn't.

We needed to know. The time for understanding family issues was way behind us. We were camping in Wonderland, who knew how far from the Looking Glass, the Jabberwocky, an army of soldiers and guards led by the White Rabbit, and heaven only knows what else, in a clearing surrounded by deadly nightslip mushrooms. We didn't have time to sugar coat it.

"Benjamin is Allie's father, isn't he?" I asked.

CHAPTER FIFTY-ONE

A llie was paying attention, her mouth hanging open, but no sound coming out.

Her mother slowly nodded, tears coursing down her face. "He is."

"You weren't pregnant when you went home from Wonderland, were you?" I asked, repeating the story Allie had given me back in Dayton.

"No. I was truly just a little girl trying to go home. But the White Rabbit did come looking for me. He didn't want me to get away, because he believed I was going to spread word that the Queen was losing control. She had been manipulated into believing the citizens loved anything she did, for any reason, and would blindly follow her no matter what. She couldn't accept that I had questioned her authority, and the White Rabbit fed into her delusion."

Allie looked stunned. Something told me this was a version she hadn't heard before.

"The White Rabbit told me if I didn't go back with him, the Queen had decreed that my parents, my sister, and all of my relatives and loved ones would be killed. I was a teenager. I didn't know who, if anyone, I could have gone to. I wouldn't have known who could help. And I had no way of asking anyone."

Tobias cleared his throat. "What about Reverend Dodgson, the one who wrote your story down?"

She shook her head. "He was a good guy, but he didn't know anything about all of this."

Tobias walked over to Alice and laid a hand on her shoulder. "Actually, he did know about it. It's why he was asking you so many questions about Wonderland. The files compiled by various organizations studying magical realms were highly lacking in information about what was going on in the courts of Wonderland. He was looking to get more information; he would have known who to call and how to help."

She shook her head. "If he'd actually known someone, they

would have tried to come after me, and whoever he sent would have learned what was going on. It would have been worse; the Queen would have killed them, too. This way, more people were safe."

His shoulders slumped, and he shook his head. "They did send someone after you disappeared the second time—several someones, in fact. They were told you were not in Wonderland. Those sent were not allowed into the castle, and no one they spoke to reported seeing you. I called in and checked the files when I was on the way over to Janie's house the other day, before we came here. Your account of Wonderland didn't give anyone cause to suspect the White Rabbit of anything other than being one of the Queen's underlings. They assumed you ran off somewhere with a boy."

Alice screwed her eyes shut and made a muffled sound of frustration. I heard the anguish as she tried not to wail loud enough to give away our position. I felt for her, yet I had to ask. "Alice, we've taken your word on a lot, and what we've seen supports it, but if the people who came looking for you way back then had no reason to know what was going on with the White Rabbit, then they wouldn't have looked any further. Why hadn't you told Reverend Dodgson about the White Rabbit and his plans?"

I sat down next to her and patted her hand. Hey, I'd seen my stepmother do it before, and it had worked for her. It felt awkward, but it was an etiquette move Alice likely would recognize, as she had grown up in the formality of the Victorian era and had been sitting on a throne for the last several years.

She sniffed hard. "You're right. The problem, though, is that the White Rabbit was exactly as I described at the time I was describing it. He was a toady to the Queen and constantly worrying about pleasing her. He wasn't the same as he is now."

"So, you were telling the reverend the complete truth?" Mia asked.

"Mostly," Alice said. "I didn't tell him about the mushrooms, but they weren't as bad as they are now. They used to be easily avoidable, and now it seems they are growing out of control. I didn't know you could walk on them when so many have stepped on them and died."

I lifted my shoe. "This is one of those things I was talking about that other worlds could offer: the soles of our shoes are a technology developed after you left. It's practically impervious to things that could soak through and contaminate the skin. We were warned about the mushrooms by a citizen of Wonderland—I didn't want to give him away—but the rubber soles on our tennis shoes seemed to protect us."

She hung her head. "So many things could have gone differently, but there are some I wouldn't change even if I could. One of those things is here, in my arms, and I never thought I'd have that again." She squeezed Allie tightly.

"Mom," Allie started, leaning back. "You always told me you got pregnant with me while you were home, that you were already pregnant when you came back."

Sighing, Alice stood up and wrapped her own arms around her chest, staring at the clearing. "I told you that because by the time you were old enough to ask the question, Benjamin had already forgotten about our relationship due to those tarts. I told you not to eat them for a reason. Benjamin had forgotten my name. He'd forgotten things about when we'd gotten together. He'd forgotten about giving me roses from the Queen's own garden, and he'd forgotten about buying me a hat from Alfred the Hatter."

"Was it just you he was forgetting?" Tobias asked. I saw his face, and he looked very tired. I wondered just what exactly he was thinking about when I saw him look furtively at Mia, but she wasn't watching him. Mia was too busy paying attention to Allie.

Alice continued. "He forgot a lot, but mostly things from Wonderland. Some of those were the most important. He could tell you about his parents or how he came to Wonderland, but his daughter? Nothing. He constantly forgot Allie's name, and he forgot how old she was every time he saw her," she said, talking to the rest of us.

How heartbreaking, I thought. I wondered what I'd do if it had been Aiden. I reached for him, and he gave me his hand. I ran my hand up to his elbow so I didn't bump his sore palms, and he drew me closer to him, hugging me tight. Apparently he was thinking the same thing I was.

"He forgot about the times we shared before the White Rabbit's plan fully went into place. We'd been allowed out of the castle for supervised outings, and one of the places we came was right here. We packed a picnic lunch, and he bribed the guard to leave us alone. We'd eat, relax, and feel like normal people again, rather than slaves or captives."

I looked around. "What was so special about this place?"

Alice smiled. "This was the Queen's croquet grounds, where I'd beaten her in a croquet game with flamingoes just before I went home. It had been Benjamin who'd helped me figure out how to actually play by her rules. I left that out of the story I told to Reverend Dodgson, because I wasn't sure how to get Benjamin out of Wonderland. He missed his family and wasn't sure how to get home. I wanted to give him that since I'd been able to figure out how to go. I'd been trying to figure out how to go back for him when the White Rabbit showed up."

"And you went back so you could protect him as well as your family from the White Rabbit and the Queen?" Jonah asked.

"I thought it was best. And I ended up with my Allie, so I have no complaints about it. I just wish I could have helped him more."

I didn't know what to say. A big part of me wanted to promise her that we could fix it, that we could go back for him, but if he ate another round of tarts, there was no way to know if he'd even remember I'd been his lawyer. And what would I do with him? I had already figured we'd be bringing Alice to my house with Allie and helping them to get back on their feet, but I wasn't exactly set up to become Janie Grimm's Home for Wayward and Reformed Wonderland Refugees.

I shook my head. "It's something we can look into, but first, we need to get the two of you out of here. Which means dealing with the Jabberwocky, doesn't it?"

She nodded.

CHAPTER FIFTY-TWO

"We can't just sit here," I said, pacing back and forth by the fire. "We have to keep moving. I don't know what the White Rabbit might do to keep us here, because you heard what he said: he can't afford to let us leave. He needs us back under his control, and he needs to be able to fog everyone's memories with those damn tarts. He's not going to let any of us leave. And even if the White Rabbit was willing to let us roam the countryside, he's not done. He's going to put up a fight. And he's not going to make it an easy one."

"She's right," Tobias said. "We've got to get moving and get away from this fire. We've eaten and had a few moments of rest, but we've got to keep going. We need to clear the Jabberwocky from in front of the Looking Glass so we can go home. Best case scenario is that we can clear the way, get home, and fight on our own territory. Worst case, we have to fight here. Either way, there's going to be a fight, and we're completely exposed where we are."

We packed up the remnants of our dinner, and Jonah, Mia, and Tobias kicked dirt over the ashes to snuff the fire. Mia and Jonah handed me the sections of mushroom that the caterpillar had given us when we'd first arrived in Wonderland, as we shuffled everyone's things around to put all of our trash together in one bag.

"Besides," Mia said. "I don't think we should be keeping them in the same bag that we're carrying trash in, and Jonah's been taking some samples for Stanley. I don't think we should mix up the mushroom that we might need to use with things we've grabbed to study later."

I nodded. It made sense to keep things organized. I put the different pieces of mushroom in different pockets of my pack, keeping them in the right order so I'd know which piece was supposed to be for making things larger and which for making things smaller.

"Where's the Jabberwocky, Alice?" Tobias asked. "The White Rabbit will be looking for us. If we work on clearing the way home, then maybe we can take care of all of it at once."

Alice picked up a stick beside the still smoking fire and began poking in the ashes. "I've not heard of the Jabberwock leaving Wonderland, though, and the fact that it appeared in your world is concerning. I can't promise we'll find it where I've described."

I shrugged. "We've got to try. We can't just sit here and do nothing. Doing that means the White Rabbit will just find us faster and will trap us, forcing us to eat tarts until we forget what we're trying to get back for." I scuffed more dirt over the fire, hoping no one who found the clearing later would see it and be able to follow us.

We started walking with Alice trying to lead the way, but she stopped before long. "I can't see where I'm stepping. Either we need to get to the path, or I need to figure out a better way to get there, because I don't trust these slippers over the nightslip mushrooms."

She was right. And it was getting dark, making it harder to see. We'd only walked about a mile or so when she'd stopped, and there was no way I would push her any farther. If she, who knew the land better than the rest of us, couldn't see well enough to know where to step, then it wasn't safe. Tobias tried to carry her farther, but he was tiring rapidly. Jonah took a turn as well, and he made it farther than I would have expected. When I raised an eyebrow at him, he grunted something about heavy set pieces and boxes of props. Knowing that his day job was with the theater in Dayton, I didn't doubt it. He was the constant understudy, and I was sure they probably made him earn his keep with physical labor since he wasn't getting much stage time.

We got closer to our destination, and I started getting nervous. We didn't have a good plan for dealing with the Jabberwocky, and the guys were getting tired. I knew I was, and I wasn't even helping carry Alice. I finally decided we needed to stop for a rest when I saw a rocky outcrop that was free of the nightslips.

"What causes the nightslips to grow, Alice?" I asked.

"Lack of magic," she said. "The Queen used magic on a regular basis. Several of the other residents had mild versions of it at their disposal, mostly used for the household or in their businesses or just to maintain their lands. When the Queen wasn't able to use magic and the White Rabbit restricted its use outside of the castle, the mushrooms grew out of control. They grew and they grew; they killed off visitors, they killed off Wonderland denizens, they killed livestock. Farmers couldn't grow food. More and more came to live at the castle, but the Rabbit wouldn't allow more magic, no matter how they begged. The Queen, the real one, would probably have a good laugh at all of this if she could remember enough of what happened to piece it all together."

"The Queen is still in the castle?" Tobias asked.

"Of course she is," said Alice. "She's the blind lady in the visitor's ward. The Rabbit's kept her under control and wouldn't let her get medical treatment for her eyes. He didn't want her to be able to look around herself and try to break the enchantment of the tart filling. She's been kept isolated, only allowed around other visitors at large meal gatherings, so the castle staff watches her and prevents her from comparing information with anyone. It's why I asked Allie if she'd made any promises to her."

Because she was faerie, I realized. And promises to faerie had a weight of their own. I'd learned that myself in dealing with my evil stepmother. I'd used her promises against her to free myself at one point. And Allie's promises appeared to be fairly innocuous, but that was, of course, why Alice had asked about them.

But the real question was whether or not the Queen remembered enough of herself to enforce promises. I hadn't heard of any Allie might have broken, but how easy was it for a teenaged girl to make promises she didn't remember later? What promises might a fifteen-year-old with few friends and fewer trusted confidantes have made? I shuddered. I hoped there weren't any more we didn't know about. Promises to a faerie being related to my stepmother carried their own danger, a kind of danger I didn't want to think about.

I asked Alice if there was any more information we needed to be aware of. I hoped she could tell from the wording of my question that I was giving her an ability to keep some of her own secrets, but also told her I wasn't going to be kept in the dark.

She sighed, sitting down heavily. "The White Rabbit couldn't force anyone to kill the Queen, nor would he do it himself, either. If she dies, the other faerie realms have ways of knowing. In order for the White Rabbit to remain in control, he's got to keep her alive, but I have no idea how much she knows or remembers."

Allie nodded. "It's why I tried to send her a message."

"I'm sorry?" I asked. "What did you hope to accomplish with that?"

The mother and daughter looked at each other, and Allie shrugged. "I figured there was some kind of mental fog going on. Mother kept me from having to eat the tarts, so I knew who she was, even though she wasn't wearing her wigs and other finery. She seemed to recall more if someone reminded her of something, but every time she took a bite of the tarts, she'd forget again. I was hoping a message from me might jog her memory. Even if she's not the best ruler out there, she is a bit more free with her subjects than the White Rabbit, and I hoped she'd help topple his regime. I was trying whatever I could."

Alice nodded at her daughter. "You're not wrong. Many a time I've prodded her in a way that might spark some kind of memory to give her cause to stand up to the Rabbit. She had been strong enough, but I don't know if the tart's enchantment would interfere with her magic."

I had more questions, but I wasn't going to get a chance to ask them at the moment. A loud, ear-splitting, thunderous shriek of anger reverberated through the air. I winced and saw the others jump at the noise. That didn't sound good, but I had an idea what it may have been.

It was the Jabberwocky.

We were apparently closer than I'd thought.

CHAPTER FIFTY-THREE

I could see the creature through the section of trees just in front of us, and it looked like there was a mirror directly behind the monster. Was that the Looking Glass? I hoped so. The idea of getting home, ordering a giant mountain of pizza, and taking a long hot shower was appealing. But how to get past it?

Apparently I wasn't the only one thinking we needed a plan. Aiden and I looked at each other, and I shrugged. "I'm not the combat guy. I don't know anything about tactics."

Tobias leaned forward, studying the creature for several minutes. I started to ask him a question, but he shushed me.

After a few minutes, Tobias grinned. "Well, I am and I do. Come here." He squatted down, grabbed a stick from the ground, and used it to draw Xs in the dirt to show us where we were to go. He had a plan, one all about distraction and confusion. In fact, it had me confused. I asked him to explain it more than once before I finally realized I didn't have to understand how each part of the plan worked; I just had to know what part I was supposed to play. I had to trust that Tobias, with all of his years of experience, actually knew what he was doing.

He had put Aiden and me on the creature's left, with instructions to keep the Jabberwocky's attention while he and Jonah tried to attack from the right. But there was also something about Alice and Allie trying to distract from the front, and all of us sneaking around behind the creature to slip through the Looking Glass. There was more, but that was what I understood about it.

"What about the tarts?" I asked.

"That's our fallback plan," Tobias explained. "If this doesn't work, we'll back off and regroup, try to wait him out."

"I'm not sure we've got that kind of time on our hands, do we? I mean, aren't the guards going to figure we're going straight here?" I asked.

"Well, here's the problem, Janie," Tobias explained. "The Jabberwocky is awake and agitated. There's no way we're going to get close enough to leave food without becoming a meal ourselves."

"So the best course of action is getting even closer to fight it?" I asked, a bit panicky. "Who thought up that suicide plan?"

He smiled. "You've got a point, but this is the fastest way I can think of to get past him. We don't have time to do otherwise without a guarantee that the tarts are enough to work. And remember, we only have reason to believe it would cause a mental fog. There's no reason to think the tarts would make the Jabberwock go to sleep so we could slip past."

Put that way, fighting the creature made more sense than feeding it. Tobias was right; we had no evidence that the tarts would put the thing to sleep, just that the Jabberwocky would be confused. It already sounded angry, so confused and angry did not seem like a good combination. We had to go with the most direct approach.

I followed Aiden as he picked his way slowly off to our designated battle station. I watched him closely as he tried not to trip when he walked. On our way through the forests earlier, he'd used the tree trunks to prevent himself from falling onto the nightslip mushrooms, even though his hands were still bandaged and sore. It was hard to sneak up on anything when one was crashing into tree trunks and trying not to fall on poisonous mushrooms. I didn't know what was going on, but he seemed even more clumsy than normal. I wondered what was wrong with him, and as we got closer to our post, I looked closer.

Oh, crap. Aiden's eyes were glassy and his face looked flushed. Did that mean his hands were infected? Had he been poisoned by mushrooms? "What is going on with you?" I asked in a barely audible whisper, but he shook his head. I reached up and touched his cheek. Sure enough, he was burning up.

We didn't have time to wait out the Jabberwocky. We had to defeat it *now* so I could get Aiden to a doctor. I waited until he wasn't looking and then brought out one of the empty cans we'd had food in and scooped up some of the mushrooms. If he had been poisoned, I wanted to have a sample to give the doctors at the emergency room. I wrapped it carefully in my extra T-shirt, and put it in the outermost pocket of my backpack, where it wouldn't even come close to touching my skin or anything else in my bag.

We didn't need two people sick.

I could see where Alice and Allie were approaching the Jabberwocky, and it roared. I saw Tobias sneaking around, away from them, and Jonah following him, ducking around the legs of the animal and getting behind it. Tobias had the sword out, in two hands, and as I watched, I heard a sigh beside me.

"What?" I whispered.

Aiden shook his head. "I saw myself with that sword, saving the day. Instead, I can only sit here and watch and wait for you to see someone else come to the rescue."

"Haven't we had this conversation?" I asked. "It's not a big deal. I don't need to see you 'save the day' right now. You already did. You saved me when I needed it the most. Now it's Tobias's turn to show his daughter what he can do."

He coughed, barely catching himself in time to muffle the noise against his fist. This was not good. What had he done to become so sick?

"I love you, Janie, but that doesn't mean I don't need to keep saving you. I need to always show you what you mean to me. And in the world—or rather, worlds—we live in and those we visit, I think you need to understand that I'm always going to try to save you. I just don't know how long I'll be around to do it."

He sounded like he was starting to get hoarse. Was Aiden truly sick, or was there something else going on? Was it just Wonderland itself? Had he somehow eaten a tart without realizing it? Had the Rabbit found some way to poison him? I had to shut off that part of my brain for a moment, or I'd panic. I found a place with no mushrooms in the vicinity where Aiden could sit down and lean against a tree while I jumped out and waved like a mad idiot in front of a creature who seemed convinced we were out to kill it . . . because, of course, we were.

I saw the monster starting to turn toward Jonah and Tobias and knew it was my turn to create a distraction. "Aiden, stay here and out of sight. I'll be back."

He saluted me, and I knew he really wasn't feeling well when he didn't argue. "Stay alive. We're almost home," he said.

"You, too. I love you," I replied before leaping out of the woods and grabbing some rocks from the ground.

I'd played softball for a number of years as a kid, and the motion came back fairly quickly, although my aim could use more practice. It didn't matter how good my aim was, as I just needed to get the monster's attention and keep him from trying to eat Tobias and Jonah. I ducked and dodged, running closer as I continued picking up rocks and chucking them until the Jabberwocky finally turned its attention away from the guys and started toward me.

That would be the whole idea of the plan, but the last part I hadn't thought through very well. I hadn't considered what to do in order to keep myself from being eaten once I had the Jabberwock's notice. I chucked the last couple of rocks in my hands and turned tail to run.

The monster thundered after me, flailing and screaming its unholy shriek, stomping and shuffling as it moved. It appeared as though there was something wrong with it, but I couldn't tell right away.

And then I saw it.

The Jabberwocky had been chained by the leg to an iron post driven deeply into the ground right in front of the Looking Glass. We hadn't seen it before because the creature was standing directly in front of it, blocking our line of sight. I wouldn't have noticed now if I hadn't run in exactly the wrong direction, away from Aiden and the others, toward the Looking Glass. Which meant we had no choice; there was no distracting the creature long enough to let anyone through. We'd have to kill it or contain it, and we didn't have chains big enough to secure it.

What were we going to do?

CHAPTER FIFTY-FOUR

I turned again and ran for the stake, sliding under the creature toward the metal spike holding it hostage, with one foot tucked under me as if I were sliding into second base. I had my hands up, like I'd been taught as a kid, holding them high above my own head to keep them from getting skinned up in the dirt under the seat of my pants.

The Jabberwocky seemed confused, as if it couldn't figure out where I'd gone, but Allie and Alice were next up for diversionary tactics. They threw rocks and twigs and other things as fast as they could, fighting to keep the creature's attention on themselves and away from Tobias. The Jabberwocky swung out with its sharp claws, but it consistently missed.

I'd discovered the Jabberwocky hadn't planted itself there as everyone thought. I reached for the chain, thinking that if I untied the animal, maybe one of us could lead it away from the others so they could get through, but then I smelled it.

Stale peppermint and old books. The scent I remembered of my father, the scent of home and love and everything else I missed about Dayton. It was the smell of magic. I looked down at the post and realized three things.

First, the post had been enchanted and likely would not let me remove it. If I was able to remove the post and chain, I'd eventually get killed from standing still long enough to become a morning snack. Sooner or later, the Jabberwocky would realize where I'd gone, and I would very much prefer not to be at that very spot when the Jabberwocky figured it out. Being somewhere else, anywhere else, was infinitely more appealing.

The second thing I realized was that there had to be way more to the story than we knew. We'd suddenly gotten very concerned about getting home and hadn't done much of anything about preventing others from following down the road. The White Rabbit had obviously been able to get in and out of Wonderland repeatedly without the Jabberwocky being a problem. He'd been able to send scouts to find

Allie. He'd been able to get in and out to drag Alice back. How long had the Jabberwocky been here?

The third thing was that most people and subjects in Wonderland didn't actually have magic. The Queen did. The reports we'd gotten indicated the only magic the White Rabbit had access to was the tart filling, and that recipe dated back far enough that it was hard to tell if it was magic or some kind of potion with its own power.

So who had enchanted the chain and post, and why? And had the same person placed the Jabberwocky at the opening in order to prevent us from leaving? No time to ponder any deeper than that. At this point, we'd engaged the Jabberwocky, and its scaled head and catfish-like whiskers were whipping around, trying to scent me and follow where I'd gone. I took off at a spring, almost willing the thing to follow me as I ran, away from Aiden and toward the others, yelling as I went.

The others nearly stopped dead in their tracks as they saw me, running on almost the exact opposite side of the creature, nowhere near where I was supposed to be. Only the howling Jabberwocky behind me jumpstarted them back into action.

I was yelling, screaming at them all to stop, to retreat and listen. Tobias had the sword cocked and ready to swing at the creature when he saw me, staring briefly as if I had lost my mind.

Of course, it was very possible I already had.

We slipped back away from the creature, and it did not follow us, though it watched carefully. As we retreated, I grabbed Jonah's sack of tarts from his bag and flung it to the ground in front of the creature. Pastries spilled out and distracted the Jabberwocky. It began snuffling around at the bag and started sucking down the tarts one by one. There must have been thirty of them, meant to feed the five of us humans plus Bert—more than enough to put anyone into oblivious fogginess and kept like an animal in the zoo, forever.

I saw it. The telltale feature that told me I'd gotten it exactly right. I knew the truth now about the Jabberwocky and what it was, although I wasn't quite sure why it was chained there. I turned away, herding the others to Aiden's hiding spot in the woods.

Aiden's breathing was labored when we got back to him, but he refused to let me fuss too much. "Janie, what is it? What happened?"

I had to gulp air, my lungs burning from the exertion and unfamiliar physical work. Yup, the gym had to become a top priority. I was a lawyer, or almost, but that didn't mean I could settle for a lifetime of sedentary work behind a desk. Heck, I couldn't even get through law school without running for my life, and more than once. If I was going to make a habit of this, and it was starting to look like I would, I had to do something about it.

I nodded at the others. Doris began to fuss over Aiden, who was looking worse and worse for wear.

Tobias looked livid as he turned on me, shouting, "Why did you do that? I was in position! The plan was working, and we'd have been home!"

Jonah and Mia and Bert all jumped in, asking the same thing, until I put up one hand to shut them all up. "You don't get it," I said.

"What?" asked Bert. "Did you discover some new fact no one could have figured out?"

I laughed. "No. *Any* of us could have figured it out. I just happened to get there first. The creature has appeared and disappeared on its own; it has appeared in our land and disappeared again almost instantaneously. Disney made a big deal out of it when they made the movie so that it's fairly synonymous with the story now, but it wasn't always. I can't believe I hadn't thought about it before."

I paused, but the others still looked at me blankly. "That creature is magically chained in place," I explained, waving an arm in the direction we'd just left. "There's something else going on here, something we've missed until now."

"What is it?" Allie asked. "I don't know the book or the movie. I've only ever lived it."

"There is only one other character that could have some possibility of magic in its veins, one who used it in the original story to thoroughly confuse your mother." I turned to look at the Jabberwocky, and I saw it again, the distinctive cheesy grin marking exactly what the Jabberwocky actually was. It was a character that always kind of creeped me out.

"That creature has been enchanted to look like a Jabberwocky. It's a Cheshire Cat."

CHAPTER FIFTY-FIVE

The others all stared at me, somewhat in shock.

"Why would anyone do that?" Jonah asked.

I tried to explain. "The real Jabberwocky was slain in the books. Unless Alice was right about Jabberwocky eggs, there is no actual Jabberwocky any longer. And yet, we'd seen it. It had shown up in our backyard. It was sitting right here in front of us. So how is there a second one?"

"For all you know, the first one laid eggs before it was killed," Mia said, shaking her head.

"True, that's possible," I said. "And Alice told us this was the case; I just thought it unlikely, especially after I saw the spike and shackle. Why would anyone chain the thing right in front of the Looking Glass unless it was a trap? If they need to come back and forth to our world, it wouldn't be through the Looking Glass, as it merely opens up to another realm that's a mirror image of the one we're in. Setting us up like this means we'd likely waste time, allowing the guards and the Rabbit's forces to catch up to us."

I turned to Alice. "Where did you hear that the Jabberwock was guarding the pathway to the mortal realm?"

"The White Rabbit, of course." She looked absolutely mortified. "I haven't been out of the castle since well before the Queen was deposed. I'd been told I'd have to go through the Looking Glass to go home since the other pathways had been sealed due to the Rabbit's policies on visitors."

"So what happened to the Cheshire Cat, the one from the story you told Reverend Dodgson?" I asked. "That's something I never heard you say."

Alice looked stricken. "There was one specific Cheshire Cat I met when I first came here; I haven't seen him for years. I wondered when he disappeared, but I was still a kid. I figured he'd gone off to do whatever it is that Cheshire Cats do."

Well, cats were finicky, picky, fickle creatures if I remembered right. I'd had a kitten when my mother was alive, and the thing had loved me desperately; it would only go to my mother or father when I was asleep, not around, or otherwise occupied. Yet, the kitten wanted nothing to do with me when I wanted to play and always wanted to play when I was doing my chores.

We'd given the cat away when my father remarried, because Evangeline had claimed she was allergic to them. Who knew what the truth really was on that score. I'd been sad, but I thought I was getting a new mommy in the bargain, so I hadn't complained. And then my stepmother had tried to fog my memory for years in a similar way the tarts had been affecting the White Rabbit's prisoners. I felt a renewed sense of urgency to help all the visitors to Wonderland, but we had other things to figure out first.

"Okay, so it's not a Jabberwocky; it's a Cheshire Cat. What do we do?" Doris asked.

I peered out of the woods at the grinning Jabberwocky chowing down on the brain-fogging pastries we'd laid out in front of it. "We can't kill it," I said. "It's as much of a victim as we are."

"But the Rabbit doesn't have the power to enchant something like that. The only reason he has the tarts is because he got the recipe from the queen before I gained her throne," Alice said. "Something else is going on, and I don't know who might be involved in all of this."

It appeared to me that she was as clueless as the rest of us. She hadn't heard anything about further magic use, but I knew I was right. The Cheshire Cat was the only other magic-user in Wonderland, and something had turned it into a Jabberwocky, chaining it right in front of the Looking Glass. The White Rabbit had to have another route in and out for him to have been constantly chasing Allie. This couldn't be it. And while the Cheshire Cat/Jabberwocky was a problem, it wasn't our biggest problem to date.

"So what do you actually know about other routes out of Wonderland?" I asked. "This is very obviously a trap. We need to find another way out of here."

She nodded. "I know of other ways out, but I was told they were blocked or otherwise closed. The Rabbit kept telling me for years that this was the only route in and out of Wonderland. I don't know why I didn't realize that he was lying to me."

"The White Rabbit was getting into our realm somehow, so there has to be another route. In fact, I'm thinking that many of the ways into the mortal realm are probably still around. None of us had a problem getting here. And it isn't like the passageways are always open; otherwise, we'd have fallen into Wonderland the minute we tried to mow the lawn after we moved in. Something is controlling those openings, and I don't know what it is."

The JabberCat was less agitated as we all stood farther away; nothing was bothering him, so he seemed to be okay. I saw the grin again, in a faint creepy outline, and then the Jabberwocky-looking creature disappeared, leaving the smile briefly before it vanished the rest of the way.

The Looking Glass behind him was gone.

What the hell? Was the opening to the mortal realm dependent on the mental and physical state of the Cheshire Cat? I shook my head in disbelief. What a way to hide a passage, and what a lie to tell to keep Alice from trying to leave again. The Rabbit was absolutely paranoid and was using more and more force to keep himself in power. That meant he was dangerous in a way that only desperation could be.

Of course, that gave me a heck of an idea.

"Alice, was there a passage here at one point? Notwithstanding the Looking Glass, was there another passage into the mortal realm somewhere in the area?"

She nodded. "It would be right behind where that creature sleeps. We could possibly get through it without him noticing if we tried and were very, very quiet."

"Where would it bring us out?" Tobias asked. "I wouldn't want to pop out in the midst of rush hour traffic or in some third world country. This boy needs medical attention, and he needs it now."

Allie shook her head. "I think this one will come out near the university, not far from the law school. It's where I came out when I first left Wonderland. Isn't there a hospital nearby?"

I nodded. Miami Valley Hospital was right down the road from the University of Dayton, and the law school building was on the side of campus nearest to the hospital. With any luck, we'd come through near one of the poles posted with a comm that would allow us to call for campus security. That might be the best way to get Aiden to a hospital. His lips were looking slightly blue, and his breathing was getting shallow. He was awake, but his eyes were glassy.

"Let's go. We don't have a lot of time."

Tobias started to heft Aiden onto his shoulder, and Jonah stopped him. "No, sir. You've been carrying Alice, and you might still have to carry her farther. Let me. He's my friend, and you're going to hit a limit soon."

He was right. I was actually fairly impressed Tobias hadn't started complaining about his back. I knew I'd thought it before, but Tobias kind of reminded me of a combination of Bruce Willis and Michael Caine: a sophisticated older man, but one who'd seen plenty of action somewhere out there . . . and even Bruce Willis at his most manly was going to give out sooner or later.

"Let's go," I said. "Jonah can take Aiden. Tobias has Alice. I've got Bert. We've got everyone? No one's leaving anything behind?"

They all shook their heads no, and Alice even held up her shoes, her only belongings taken from the castle.

"All right. Let's go home."

We began moving, as quietly as we could, toward the passage into Dayton. I never thought I'd be quite so happy to be going back to Ohio as I was right at that moment.

CHAPTER FIFTY-SIX

A lice was right. Behind where the Cheshire Cat was snoring, there was a small gopher-sized hole, similar to the rabbit hole in my own backyard. One by one, we stepped through. We made it through the passage, and I realized we were in Woodlawn Cemetery, near where my father was buried. The university was across the street from the cemetery, and I took off running, leaving Mia to explain. I knew there was a security pole in the parking lot behind the law school, which was just over the fence and across the road, and that was the fastest way I could think of to get help for Aiden. I left the others behind to make their way toward the road and the gate into the cemetery.

I was puffing hard when I got there, banging on the call button and yelling at the dispatcher to get me a car with an officer that could help me transport someone to the hospital. I knew they were trying to get all the information they could, but I was getting impatient as they kept asking me questions about his condition.

"Look, I'm a law student, not a medical student, but he looks bad. I'm calling for help. I don't have my cell phone with me, and this was the fastest way to find help. I know Miami Valley is right here, but we can't carry him that far. Get someone here, now!"

They agreed to send someone. I waited for the campus security vehicle to show up and then gave them directions toward where I left everyone behind in the cemetery. They offered me a ride, but I turned them down.

"You've got to go through the gate, and it's faster on foot for me to run back. It's my boyfriend who's sick. Just please hurry!" I said, taking off at a dead run before they could say anything else.

I was puffing hard and grabbing my side when I got back, and I could hear the security vehicle siren as the officers went down Stewart Street and toward the entrance to the grounds. "Not. Much. Time. How. Is. He?" I gasped.

Doris shook her head. "Not good."

Aiden was sitting on the ground, and Jonah was next to him, looking exhausted. Tobias was arguing with Mia that the group needed to separate because we weren't ready to answer questions about some of the people in the group.

Doris intervened. "Look, he's my son. I'm going with him. Janie, you need to come with us, too. Mia and Jonah, you need to decide where you'll do more good. But Tobias needs to go looking for a payphone to call Harold and Stanley to come get the others. Remember, Allie and Alice don't have IDs or social security numbers, and the police will ask for everyone's identity when we walk into the hospital. They'll be trying to figure out if someone poisoned him," she reasoned.

She gave Tobias the numbers, and he took off in the opposite direction, on foot, with Allie and Alice following him. Alice was walking under her own power with her slippers back on her feet since we were no longer around deadly poisonous mushrooms. After a second or two, Mia and Jonah followed them, reducing the number of people we'd have to explain at the hospital. I sent Aiden's and Doris's backpacks with them, but kept mine, since Bert was still perched inside. They left just before the security vehicle came around the corner, barely evading notice by the officers inside.

The gumball lights on security vehicle shone and spun as they pulled up next to us. "What in the world . . .?"

"I think he either got stung by something or he stepped in or on something that's making him sick. I don't know what's going on, but we weren't looking where we walked, and then all of a sudden, he was like this," I said. How else were we going to explain?

The cop took one look at Aiden and helped us to get him into the back of the cruiser, loaded the rest of us up, and started heading for the hospital. Luckily, it took just minutes to drive there, but it would have been fifteen minutes or more to walk—longer to carry Aiden, who was all but unconscious by the time we got to the hospital. The cop had been on his radio to the emergency room on the way, and there were medical personnel waiting for us to whisk Aiden away into a treatment room and begin bustling over him, barking orders and calling for tests.

One of the nurses came over. "What do you think he got into?" I was asked.

"I'm not sure," I said, but then I remembered I had grabbed a sample. "But when I saw him getting sick, he was right near some mushrooms I'd never seen before, and I wanted to make sure it wasn't this, so I grabbed some." I pulled the wrapped-up can out and showed them the nightslip mushrooms inside. "I was really careful not to touch them, because I don't know what happened to make him become so ill."

The nurse took the can from me, rather dubiously, and asked me where I'd found them.

"We were in the cemetery. My dad's buried there, so when we got back from a camping trip, I wanted to go there first. I try to go when I can."

She nodded. "I'll take these to the lab. I've never seen anything like this either, but that doesn't mean these mushrooms caused him to get so sick. Does he have any allergies to foods or medications?"

Doris took over, giving a rundown of his medical history. It turned out Aiden had been to that hospital quite a bit over the years, so they had a lot of his history already, as well as having his insurance card on file. By the time we were done, the nurse seemed amazed.

"If he was a kid, I would suspect abuse. If it didn't appear that every admission was legitimate, I'd think he was doing it for attention. He might be the most accident-prone person I've ever seen in my life. Has he ever had a neurological evaluation?" the nurse asked.

Doris laughed. "Yes, he did, two years ago. I took him to the Ohio State University hospital and had them run every test they could on his brain. The doctors told me he has a brain, and it's normal."

I smiled. "Look, we're used to Aiden being a klutz, and it's possible he happened to fall on some poisonous mushrooms with his mouth open. Stranger things have happened with him. But what we want to know is whether he's going to be okay."

The nurse couldn't answer, of course, because she was talking to us instead of being in with the treatment team. She left us in the waiting room and went to see if she could get us some answers about Aiden's status.

Doris wrapped her arms around me, and I felt like the floor was about to drop out from under me. I'd been so worried about getting from point A to point B that I hadn't thought about Aiden actually being sick enough that we should worry about him. In the time he and I had been together, I wasn't a stranger to emergency rooms, but this was the first time we didn't get an immediate answer to the "is he going to be okay" question. I started to shake.

She hugged me tight, and I started to cry. I knew Doris had to be as worried as I was, but the attitude from the nurse had me absolutely convinced I was about to lose Aiden. There had been just too much stress, adrenaline, and worry over the last few days. I hugged Doris back and tried to compose myself.

An hour went by, and we still didn't have an answer. I'd stopped crying, and Doris had gone looking for a payphone to call the others and tell them to come to the hospital, as we were waiting for answers.

The same nurse came out and informed us that though they had not been able to identify the mushroom, it was definitely causing the issue, according to his blood test. They asked again where the mushrooms came from, and I said they had been by a tree. When asked if there were more there, I shook my head, claiming the sample I grabbed had wiped them out. I hadn't seen any more of them. They thanked me for getting them the sample.

Aiden was on a dialysis machine and hooked up to IVs, as they were trying to flush the toxins out of his body. There was no promise he would live through the night. They let me in to see him, and there was a tube in his mouth for him to breathe. He wasn't conscious, and his red hair was mussed. Doris came in right behind me, and I knew we had to take another step; we had to get a hold of Geoffrey. He needed to know what was happening to his son.

I was exhausted, but I didn't know what else to do. Doris said she'd have Stanley take care of it, that she had a way to contact him whenever there was an emergency to do with Aiden. I just nodded.

I was too tired to be in charge any more.

CHAPTER FIFTY-SEVEN

We were home, but we weren't safe yet. There was way too much to do. Harold showed up at the hospital with Tobias and Jonah in tow. They came bearing food.

Thank God they did. I was hungrier than I'd expected. They'd shown up with several taco packs from Taco Bell and a big bag of bacon cheeseburgers and fries from Wendy's. We all sat in Aiden's room, chowing down on food that wasn't going to fog our brains or turn us into a long-dead creature from a children's story.

I wished I could have shared my fries with Aiden, but he just lay there on the bed with machines beeping. I watched the rise and fall of his breathing as I munched on greasy, non-memory erasing deliciousness. When I couldn't stuff myself any longer, I opened one of the caramel apple suckers from my backpack to counteract the fast food taste in my mouth.

We settled in for a long wait and within an hour or so, Geoffrey appeared, knocking softly on the door before coming in. The look on his face when he saw his son with all of the tubes and cords and medical paraphernalia, as well as the beeping and blipping of the machines, just about overwhelmed him. Tears started sliding down his face as he stepped into the room and crossed to his son's bed.

I stepped back to allow him space. I'd been holding Aiden's hand myself for the last forty minutes, eating one-handed as fast as I could go.

"What happened?" he asked. "Will he be okay?"

"We don't know if he'll pull through," Doris said, stepping forward and wrapping her arms around his waist.

The one thing I would always say for Doris was that she was there for whatever people needed when it came to comfort. He seemed shocked when she did it, but he hugged her close, and I saw her sigh. I realized she needed him as much as he needed her in that moment.

What I didn't expect was the look on Harold's face. I wondered if Doris knew he was in love with her. Heck, I hadn't even known until that second, but he didn't say anything. What a hard position for Harold, in love with her but thinking she was in love with someone else. Her relationship with Geoffrey had kept coming up over and over the last couple of years. Aiden was a reminder of the relationship as well. Doris always acted like she still had feelings for Geoffrey, so I assumed she was still in love with him.

Jonah and Tobias pulled me aside. "We don't feel right leaving Allie and Alice alone for too long. Mia didn't think they'd feel right without another woman present, or she'd have been here with you. She wanted me to tell you she's got Stanley digging through your dad's library for more information on Wonderland, and she's online looking for anything she can find. She sent me with your cell phone." Tobias handed it over to me, and I checked the date and time.

It was still Saturday.

We'd only been gone for five hours.

Though it felt like we'd been gone two full days, I was glad. We had the rest of the weekend to get our feet under us before we had to go back to normal life. Of course, going back to the normal life of a second-year law student and working on a moot court brief would be a nice vacation after Wonderland. I smiled.

"Thanks. I hadn't realized just how used to having my phone I'd been. I wonder what Wonderland would have done to the clock in my phone if I'd taken it."

Geoffrey heard what I was saying, and he perked up. "Wait a minute, did you say *Wonderland?*"

I nodded. "He came in contact with a nightslip mushroom."

Geoffrey's jaw dropped. "What the hell were you doing in Wonderland?"

We all looked at each other. We hadn't thought about what to say to other magical realms, and Geoffrey always had his own agenda. I stepped forward. "We met someone who had made their way to our world from Wonderland and someone from that world had come through stalking them. We were trying to take care of the problem."

He still stared. "Wonderland's been a nightmare for years."

I bet. And that would be even if they didn't know about what had happened to the Queen. "It doesn't matter right now why we went, other than we were trying to save a friend from being pursued by something from Wonderland. The question I have for you is if you know of anything, or can negotiate for anything, that might cure your son."

He started to say something, but I cut him off.

"No, I'm not the one bargaining. You are. Figure out what you can bargain with, and see what you can do for Aiden. It's not about me. It's not about court politics any more than it has to be for you to get what you need for him. It's not about the mortal realm, or the faerie realm, or Wonderland, or anything else. You're his father. Be his dad."

Geoffrey's face went pale. "Do you know what you're asking?"

"No. I don't. I don't know exactly what happened between you and your son, but he's hurting. You weren't there a lot for him. You want him to meet you halfway, but he doesn't see you as willing to meet him. Show him that he's the most important being in all the realms to you, more important than your position, or politics, or anything else."

He clenched his jaw against a bitter retort. "I used my position to help my son."

I softened. "I know. I saw that when I was trying to defeat my stepmother in your court. But he didn't see it. He wasn't in a position to be able to understand exactly what you were trying to do. He feels like he comes second for you, behind whatever else might advance your standing." I raised one hand. "I'm not saying it's true. I'm saying it's what he thinks. Give Aiden a reason to believe in you again."

He shook his head. "Even if it means going to your stepmother Evangeline to negotiate with the Queen of Hearts?"

Yeah, I was one up on that tactic. "You don't have to negotiate with the Queen. Negotiate with the White Rabbit. While you're at it, they have human visitors who are being held against their will, many, if not all, of whom ended up there through no fault of their own. We brought two of them back with us. They need to be allowed to stay here with no harassment from the magical realms or from Wonderland."

He nodded. "That will be the easy part. But what do you mean to negotiate with the Rabbit? He's not in charge. We'd know if the Queen was dead, and the Rabbit doesn't have the magic to hold the throne."

Okay, we needed to fill him in enough to be able to negotiate. "Long story short, the Queen is being held against her will and her mind is being fogged by enchanted tarts. The White Rabbit is in control, and he's the one ruling with an iron-fist behind a puppet throne."

His eyes were about as wide as they'd ever been. "Even if that's true, the Rabbit wouldn't negotiate himself. He'd still use his puppet to pull off the illusion."

I smirked. "Unless I took the person he'd put on the throne with me to the mortal realm."

"Oh, shit," he responded, using the first mortal colloquialism I'd ever heard come out of his mouth.

I couldn't disagree with his sentiment.

CHAPTER FIFTY-EIGHT

I filled in Geoffrey about the Jabberwocky, the rules on visitors, what had happened to the Queen, the mind-fogging tarts, and everything else. That I had tried to negotiate allowing us to leave Wonderland and keep the Rabbit's secrets, but we hadn't been permitted to depart. Something had to be done to protect the subjects in Wonderland and to allow the remaining visitors to go home if they wished. If Geoffrey could do that, and figure out a means to save Aiden, I'd become his biggest cheerleader.

I gave him all kinds of credit. He didn't whine. He didn't beg. He didn't try to wheedle out of anything. Instead, Geoffrey hugged Doris again and then went over to his son for a moment and squeezed Aiden's hand. He leaned over, said a few words, and kissed Aiden on the forehead.

And then he left.

Doris gave me a worried look. "Do you really think it was wise to do that?"

"What do you mean?" I asked.

"To tell Geoffrey so much about what we went through. Would that lead the Snow Queen and the faerie court to Allie and Alice? Is that safe for them?"

I nodded. "I thought about it. But we aren't in a position to do anything right now. We're tired. We're hurt. Look at Aiden. I know I'm not in a mental position to be saddling up for going back just yet, because I need Aiden to do that. I can't do it without him. And I think you feel the same way. Tobias has got to be exhausted from carrying Alice. Allie's been up and down emotionally, worrying about all of us—think about the risk she just took.

"Mia and Jonah? They've been nothing but supportive, but they aren't ready to step forward in something like this either. And I still worry about Jonah. There's something there I just don't know, and I'm not sure even he knows what things might come up in his life just yet. We're not in the shape we need to be in order to pull this off."

"What do you expect Geoffrey to do?" Bert asked from my backpack. I'd almost forgotten he was there, because he'd been so quiet.

"What do you mean?" I asked.

"I agree with you completely, but Geoffrey's not a one-man army. He's a political toady."

Doris started to defend him, but Bert stopped her.

"I'm not saying that's a bad thing. I am saying he's not John Wayne, Jackie Chan, Madeline Albright, and James Bond all rolled into one package, because that's what this might take," said the sage voice of the frog. I gave him a sardonic glare as he peeked out of the top of my backpack. He hopped out of the bag, and Harold helped him up onto a chair.

"If you think Geoffrey has made it through his entire career without racking up favors he could cash in later, you're out of your mind. There's no way he doesn't have markers to call in, and his son needs it. Doris, you can't tell me Geoffrey ever paid child support. And I think Aiden's biggest problem with his father is that Geoffrey wasn't there for him; he never felt like his father had his back. Geoffrey's been begging for a second chance with Aiden. I don't think Aiden would be able to ignore something like this. It's the chance Geoffrey's been wanting."

Tobias flinched. Yeah, he'd been listening as well, and it applied to him as much as it applied to Geoffrey, because he'd been as much, if not more, of an absentee father to Mia. I shook my head. I was sick of dealing with all the emotional stuff I had to shovel, including my own. We all had to move forward and stop reliving our own pasts . . .

Because it appeared as though we were going to have an extremely interesting future.

The more life kept going, the more I realized I'd never get away from magic. As much as I was looking forward to going to school on Monday—for a normal day of dealing with Constitutional Law, Evidence, Criminal Law, and all the rest—I knew I'd miss the challenge of dealing with all the faerie court nonsense that kept cropping up. I didn't like the constant feeling of being in danger, or of my friends and family being in danger, but it seemed to me there might be a niche for a lawyer who understood the problem humans had dealing with magic and faerie and other-realm problems. I bet Mia would agree.

It was just minutes after Geoffrey strode out of the room when the doctor came in. Harold quickly tossed his jacket over Bert on the chair before the doctor could see him. I was sure Bert didn't appreciate being buried, but even if he had been just a regular pet frog, the hospital staff would surely object to his presence.

"I don't like the results we're getting from the tests," the doctor said. "Aiden is more stable than he was when he got here, but this is one of the fastest-acting mushrooms I've ever seen. We're pumping him full of fluids and electrolytes to help flush out his system. The fungi tore up his stomach, and we had to do multiple rounds of activated charcoal into his stomach to soak up whatever we could. We also pumped a lot of blood out of his stomach, so we're trying to keep a slow IV going with a unit of whole blood to keep him stable."

I listened, understanding much of what they were talking about from all of the issues I'd seen my father go through with his cancer treatment.

"What is his prognosis? How long before he wakes up?"

The doctor shook his head. "I don't know. I have to be honest . . . There's no guarantee he *will* wake up. We've had the dialysis machine running at the highest rate we could justify because we were getting results that indicated his kidneys were beginning to fail. We think we have that under control, but if he comes through this, there's no guarantee his kidneys will come back from it. He may have to go on intermittent dialysis, or we might have to look at an eventual kidney transplant, but right now, that's not the concern."

It wasn't?

"The biggest issue here is whether he'll wake up. If he's not awake and somewhat responsive in a day or so, then we know the treatment isn't working. I'm concerned that whatever poison made this mushroom act so fast may have caused brain damage we're not aware of at this point."

We asked questions for a while, but no matter how we asked, it kept coming down to one thing: only Aiden could pull himself through this. If I could have taken on some of what had affected him, to lighten the load on his body, I would have.

I sat by Aiden's bed and held his hand, alternately praying and silently begging him to open his eyes. Doris sat on the other side, and I assumed she was doing the exact same thing.

The others milled in and out, as if watching us for some sign they should do something to help, or leave, or fetch something. Tobias finally left, taking Jonah with him, to go to the house and set up watch to protect Allie, Alice, and Mia. Harold insisted on staying. So did Bert.

We encouraged them to go. We didn't trust the White Rabbit not to try something while we were otherwise distracted. I kept wondering if Aiden had somehow been poisoned on purpose, yet couldn't figure out how it would have been done. When the medical staff wasn't present—as they came in every hour checking his vitals, taking blood samples, and changing IV bags as well as other medical necessities—we kept tossing theories around of how Aiden may have been poisoned.

Doris and I stepped aside politely to let the nurses do their work when they made an appearance, but otherwise, we were right there with Aiden, waiting for some sign that he was coming back to himself. There wasn't anything else we could do.

I hoped his father could.

CHAPTER FIFTY-NINE

There was nothing else to do but wait.
The tests kept showing Aiden wasn't improving enough to make the doctors happy, but he wasn't getting worse, either. In the absence of improvement, I'd take him holding steady while we waited for a miracle.

I finally fell asleep on the couch in Aiden's hospital room, but only after Doris convinced me that I needed to rest and she wouldn't go anywhere while I slept. Once I put my head to pillow, I was out cold.

I woke up a couple of hours later with the darkness of night casting shadows into the room. One small light next to the bed was on, casting its dim glow on Doris, who still sat at Aiden's bedside. She was holding his hand and brushing his hair back from his forehead.

Harold still sat in a corner, but he'd conked out as well, slouching on a chair with his head leaned back against the wall behind him. His mouth hung open in sleep, and he looked old and tired. I wondered just how much he'd worried while we were in Wonderland. I didn't say anything, though, because I didn't want to wake him up.

Suddenly, it got very cold in the room. I'd felt that cold before. I lifted my head from the pillow and sat up. Doris saw the movement and started to say something, but I pressed a finger to my lips to signal her to remain quiet. I stood up, shaking Harold's shoulder gently and shushing him as he awoke before going to open the door.

It was the Snow Queen coming to see Aiden in his hospital bed. Only one person could have sent her.

Geoffrey.

"What happened to him?" she asked.

There were two courtiers I didn't recognize standing behind her. They were dressed somewhat oddly in classically cut suits that would have been more at home in the 1940s. The pair might have looked overdressed for visiting an urban hospital on a Saturday night, but they weren't outrageously out of place. As a matter of fact, I rather liked the smart, mid-calf length skirt and fitted jacket the Snow Queen was wearing and wondered if I would be able to find one like that when I was wearing suits on a daily basis to work.

I shook my head to clear it. I must really be tired and stressed if I was unable to keep my mind on task. "How can I be sure you're actually the Snow Queen?"

She looked taken aback and then reconsidered. "I'm sure you've had a demanding day. Normally, I would not abide such insolence, but you are certainly entitled to be a bit on the cautious side, so I will permit it. You may ask two questions in order to determine my true identity."

How gracious, I thought. "The name of the emissary we agreed you would send to collect on a favor on your behalf?"

"Jenny," she said, correctly naming the nightingale we'd met several months ago, who could speak and who had helped negotiate our working relationship.

"The location where we first were in the same room at the same time," was my second question.

She smiled. "The ladies room on the third floor of the local courthouse," was the correct answer.

I let out a breath I didn't even know I was holding and explained the last several hours in as concise a manner as I possibly could without leaving out any more than I had to. Of course, I did leave out everything I could about Allie and her mother, referring to them only as visitors who had come back with us.

"So, you see, Aiden's on the ropes here, medically speaking. We're not exactly sure when to expect retribution from the White Rabbit. We'd like to not be in the middle of this, but at the same time, I believe that the real Queen actually not being on the throne is hurting her realm."

"Are you asking for a favor?" the Snow Queen asked.

Tricky that. "No. But I would bet five bucks Geoffrey asked you for one. And since I don't know the nature of what he asked, or the nature of the price he might pay for it, I will only ask if Aiden is going to be okay."

"Clever girl," she said, smiling at me with a wink. "You're

shaping up to be a tough little negotiator. We may have use for your services down the road. There is something we are working on that might need all your skill, but that day is not today."

I nodded and pointedly looked at the clock on the wall. The machines hooked up to Aiden still beeped and blerped and booped and hummed with no changes. The squiggly lines on the monitors were still at the same level of squiggly, and I took it as a good sign, but how long could Aiden stay like this?

She seemed to understand, because the Snow Queen nodded at me. "You're right. Geoffrey has negotiated a service to me in exchange for helping his son. I have some small powers at healing, and my court healers have indicated to me that there is a natural remedy to the mushrooms. I believe that doing what I can magically as well as providing you with the healer's remedy will fulfill my bargain with his father."

I sighed. "I hear an unspoken but."

She looked confused. "What do you mean?"

"I mean, 'providing that remedy will fulfill my bargain with his father' but . . . There's an unspoken but. So cough it up," I said, too tired and worn out to play the diplomacy game. "It's been a long day and getting longer. If there's a side effect or anything we need to know, then we need to know, but don't keep us in suspense. I'm sorry for the directness, but we don't have the time to wait."

She smiled, and I saw an admiration there for what I was saying. "You know," she said, "you have a plain-spokenness about you that is refreshing. And you're right. Your boyfriend will have some magical side effects for a short time after the treatment. I just can't quite predict what they will be."

As much as I wanted to tell her I didn't care if he grew horns from the top of his head as long as he was alive and with me, I didn't want to put the idea in her head to grow horns from the top of his head. She was a faerie being, and one thing I'd learned was that they were honest, to a certain extent, but they liked to bend their promises all over the place in order to get what they wanted while still being able to say they kept their word.

"Why can't you predict the side effects?" I asked.

"This remedy has been used on denizens of Wonderland in the past, as well as faerie creatures who wandered into that realm before. The side effects are fairly mild and predictable in humans or in faerie beings, but with Aiden's heritage, I have no idea if he will react like a human or like a faerie; if he will have both sets of symptoms, or neither. It also means I have no idea if those side effects will be as temporary as we believe, or if they will last longer. It might even be permanent. There's no way to tell."

"You've never tried it on someone with Aiden's background? He can't be the only half-human, half-faerie being out there!"

She looked at me, confused. "Of course he is. Didn't he tell you that?"

No, he hadn't.

CHAPTER SIXTY

Well, I hadn't expected that one. And while I knew Aiden's heritage bothered him, it didn't bother me. We'd already worked through that obstacle. I wasn't happy, but it was only because he hadn't told me that little wrinkle on his own.

"What are the side effects for humans?" I asked.

"Memory loss, short-term fogginess, and general confusion," she said.

"Okay, what about for faerie creatures?" Doris asked.

"Well, they have a tendency to turn into the being they most fear."

Oh. My. God.

Those damn tarts.

The White Rabbit had been using the tarts on humans for the side effects, and it was why he had to keep feeding it to them; it would wear off eventually. The Queen had been most likely to be affected like a faerie creature than the others in Wonderland, but what she most feared must be a disabled, doddering woman with no power. The Cheshire Cat had been afraid of the Jabberwocky, but had retained enough of himself to disappear when he was calm.

What was Aiden most afraid of?

I didn't know.

Did that make me a bad girlfriend? I shook my head and looked to Doris. "What do you think?" I asked. "He's your son."

She gave me a terrified glance. "So you're okay with a gryphon appearing in his hospital room?"

What the hell was a gryphon, and why was Aiden so afraid of it?

Doris must have understood my confusion, because she explained. "You know how some kids are afraid of the dark, or afraid of the monster under the bed?"

I nodded.

"Aiden saw a drawing of the gryphon in an old, classic illustration someone had given me of Alice in Wonderland, and when he saw it, he would cry. It never made any sense, but he was two. I figured it looked scary to him," she said, wringing her hands. Harold got up from his chair and went to put his arm around her. "He wouldn't let me read from the page with the drawing because it scared him so much."

I'd sent Aiden's backpack home with Mia because I hadn't seen any reason for it, but now I wished I'd kept it so I could look through the book. It would have given me some idea of what we might be facing.

"What exactly is a gryphon?" I asked.

Bert, who had been quietly sitting inside the top of my backpack, where he'd moved for easy hiding and coat-coverage prevention, and not saying much of anything, now spoke up. "A gryphon's got the head, talons, and wings of an eagle with the body of a lion. But I don't think that's what Aiden is most afraid of."

"What do you mean?" I asked.

"About a month ago," Bert said, "Aiden and I were up late talking while you and Mia were still at the school library. Allie had already gone to bed, but neither one of us were tired yet. We ended up eating a tray of brownies Doris had left and just about made ourselves sick with too many snack chips and cans of soda. We got to laughing at each other, as we were belching pretty loud, and we were having a good time. Aiden said he was ready to face just about any being out there except one. When I asked why, he said it didn't make sense."

"Why are you saying it like that?" I asked. "*That* doesn't have to make sense. We need to know what we are dealing with."

"Hold your horses," Bert said. "I'm getting there. Aiden specifically told me he was going to start researching what to do if we ever ran across this being, but he wanted to be sure he was ready to deal with it. He didn't want me to talk about it. He didn't want you to ever know about it."

I started getting a really uneasy feeling about all of this. "What was he doing to get ready to deal with all of this, as you put it?"

"He was researching weapons. He wanted to show you he could overcome his fears, that he was ready to handle whatever obstacle he came across. He wanted you to see that he wasn't afraid of it anymore, even though he was still absolutely terrified at the time."

No wonder I'd gotten the reaction from Aiden that I had. He'd argued with me about . . . oh, my. It fell into place. "He was afraid of the Jabberwocky."

Bert nodded. "Aiden was convinced we were going to run into the thing sooner or later, so he researched the heck out of how to kill it. He maxed out four credit cards to buy that damned sword off eBay."

And then I'd told him to let Tobias carry the sword. I'd had no idea Aiden had been trying to gear himself up to work out a phobia. I wondered how long he'd thought about it. And no, we weren't married, but why would he run up so much credit card debt just for a damn sword?

Oh, no.

Was I going to have a Jabberwocky for a boyfriend? Was there enough magic inside of Aiden, like the Cheshire Cat, to maintain some semblance of himself, or would he permanently and totally become the thing he feared? If so, was I going to have to use his own sword on him?

I turned away from everyone, including the Snow Queen, to look out the window, though there wasn't much to see. The window faced a wall from another hospital building and overlooked the parking garage. Yet even that was comforting, because it was a reminder we were no longer in Wonderland. Though we'd made it home, Wonderland was still affecting us.

"How do we restrain him to allow the magic of the tarts to run its course?" I asked.

"There's no guarantee it will happen in the first place," said the Queen, sitting on the chair Harold had been sleeping in earlier. "But you're right to be cautious."

Visions of the kind of chain that had kept the Cheshire Cat in place as the Jabberwocky danced through my head. How could we possibly make sure we could restrain Aiden, keep from doing too much damage at the hospital, and otherwise ensure magic was kept away from humans? I had to come up with something. And we had to get him out of the hospital before we turned him into a monster.

"We'll take the treatment," I said. "We need Aiden well enough to be discharged so we can get him away from so many helpless, innocent people before we give him the other remedy you spoke of."

She nodded. "I can help you. My magic will freeze the progression of the mushrooms through his blood. It will give his body a rest and will allow him to awaken. He will have a miraculous recovery. However, it is temporary. His own body heat will eventually melt the freezing I place on the toxin, and it will start to progress again when that happens."

"How long will we have?" Doris asked. I wondered what she was thinking, but it was probably along the same lines as my own train of thought. I was worrying I would get him back, even partially, just long enough to say a goodbye. How long could he live like this?

"Maybe twelve hours," was the answer. "Again, because it's magic and because of his own heritage, it could be more. Or it could be ten. But I would plan on less, just to be on the safe side." She pulled a large Tupperware container out of her shoulder bag. Inside the translucent plastic, I saw shapes that looked like more tarts. She handed them to Doris, who shoved the container into my backpack. It was really the only place we had to carry stuff out with.

I had some phone calls to make.

CHAPTER SIXTY-ONE

Stanley owned a field outside of town where there wasn't much traffic and where there was plenty of room where Aiden could stretch out if he became a Jabberwocky. Harold called Stanley with Doris's cell phone, and the two of them began discussing the logistics of how to handle whatever Aiden might go through.

The Snow Queen asked Doris if she could lay hands on Aiden. Doris nodded. I noticed that Doris's cheeks were tear-stained and puffy, as if she'd been crying while I was asleep. We were both pretty strung out, and Harold didn't look much better. Even so, there was hope. I just wished for a chance for Aiden, some glimmer of possibility that we weren't bringing him back just to lose him again.

She laid her hands on Aiden, one on his forehead and a second on his abdomen. I saw the rise and fall of Aiden's chest as she worked. I smelled the stale peppermint and old book scent that meant the presence of magic, and it became strong enough to almost choke me. I didn't mind because I saw Aiden's eyelids starting to flutter. He slowly came awake and jerked hard against the machines and the hands of the Snow Queen. I reached out, but the Snow Queen shook her head. I got the message. She didn't want the magic to spread to me.

"It's okay, Aiden. She's here to help. I'll explain later, but let her work. It's the best thing you can do right now, and we'll get you out of here as fast as we can."

His eyes were wide and scared, and I tried to convey a feeling of calm and composure—not the easiest thing to do while I watched him struggle.

"Really, Aiden," his mother said. "It's okay. We all talked it through before we let her touch you."

His eyes stayed wide, but he couldn't talk with the tube in his throat. His hands were free, and he pointed at the throat tube. I assume he wanted it taken out, but we couldn't call in a nurse just yet to remove it. I looked at the Snow Queen.

"Just need a minute or so more," she grunted with some effort.

Aiden watched me carefully as the Snow Queen finished her ministrations. When she was done, she nodded to me and then staggered back. Her two attendants helped her to a chair. She took a deep breath.

"I haven't done that for quite a long time," she said. "It hasn't been necessary for many years. Has it really been so long since anyone came back from Wonderland?"

I stepped forward. "I was in the midst of trying to negotiate for the release of all of the visitors who were being held at the castle against their will and fed nothing but tarts when I learned the White Rabbit was actually ruling behind a puppet throne. The real Queen, who I discovered was my stepmother's sister, was being held with them. We were unable to get them all free, but I wanted you to know we did try. I don't know what effect that has for you, nor do I know how it will affect my stepmother and the terms of her captivity, but I wanted you to be aware of it."

She nodded at me. "I did get word, but I appreciate your telling me. I actually believe you are singularly situated for such a role. Are you still willing to act as such a go-between?"

I considered. This was something that could take up significant time over the course of my career and my life. It would mean quite a lot to my bottom line if I agreed; so the next question was compensation. But the clock was ticking for Aiden, as well.

"I'm willing to discuss the terms of such representation. I'm open to it, but I can't volunteer. I can see such a role as being highly time-sensitive, plus I will have the issue of also trying to pay my bills and run a legal practice, and possibly even raise a family. I can't agree blindly without having some indication of compensation in the agreement. It would be irresponsible to do it any other way."

She nodded. "Of course. I understand. I have children myself. You are a very responsible person to be thinking ahead. I'll have the rabbit hole moved so nothing can come through behind your house while you are otherwise dealing with the issues of Mr. Ferguson," she said, indicating to Aiden on the bed. "I wish you all the best."

I swallowed hard. I could feel Aiden's gaze on me, staring hard.

He couldn't exactly respond with the tube in his throat, but how could I explain further? I was going on the assumption that he'd be okay and would be my spouse, eventually, which also meant if I had kids down the road, they'd be his. It was a good lesson in learning that human or faerie medical treatment might be different for him, as well as for kids who would have at least some of his genetic issues, but now wasn't the time to be dwelling on it. I had to get him out of the hospital and to Stanley's open field before the Snow Queen's enchantment wore off. The clock was ticking, but I had no idea how long the countdown would last.

The Snow Queen must have read my mind. She stood up, only slightly wobbly after taking a few minutes to get her bearings, but she was definitely not at her level best. She bid us goodbye and was gone almost as abruptly as she'd shown up,

Aiden was still giving me a level gaze. I wondered just what was going through his mind, but I told him to hold whatever thought it was while I ran for the nurse's station. I told the nurses Aiden had woken up, and I asked if they could remove Aiden's breathing tube to allow him to speak.

I watched the doctor question Aiden, take some blood, run some tests, and take his pulse. Aiden couldn't do much more than nod with that thing in his mouth, but I could tell he was running out of patience. I could sympathize.

They finally ascertained that Aiden was doing better and he wanted the tube removed. The doctor tried to convince him to keep it, but Aiden was having none of that. They warned him about the hoarse voice, difficulty speaking, raw throat, and other similar symptoms that could result after they removed it, but I was with him. I wanted it out so we could get moving.

Somehow, Aiden seemed to understand that time was of the essence. I wondered how much of the conversation he'd heard while he was unconscious. If he'd heard it all, there wouldn't be much to explain. The nurses pulled the tube out, and Aiden gagged his way through it, but at the end, he was breathing on his own without too much difficulty. "Want to go home," he said to the doctor who was again monitoring his pulse and blood pressure.

The doctor nodded. "With any luck, you'll be home soon. We'd like to keep you for a couple of days for observation, but if all goes well, we might let you go tomorrow afternoon."

Aiden shook his head, and I spoke up. "We don't live far from here, just a couple of miles down the road. We can get here in a hurry if he goes downhill, but we all just want to go home. It's been a very trying day."

The doctor gave me a funny look. "I don't buy the story about how he got poisoned. I'm not sure he's safe at home, so I'm not inclined to allow this. Convince me it's okay, and I'll let him go."

Aiden sat up. "Will leave. On. My own. Will sign against. Advice. If you. Want." He was definitely hoarse, and it took effort to talk for him. I couldn't blame him.

The doctor tried to talk him out of it, but Aiden was adamant. I couldn't blame him. Even if he didn't know about what might be ahead for him, I wouldn't have wanted to stay here either. I'd have wanted to get behind a protective threshold as soon as humanly possible. And that meant going home. I just couldn't actually take him there yet.

The rest of us stayed silent while Aiden tried to argue with the doctors. They wouldn't bring him the paperwork to sign himself out, but they did agree to remove all of the monitors so he could start to walk around on his own. The doctor gave me a funny look. Did they suspect me of domestic violence or some kind of coercion or intimidation? Funny that. Aiden was stubborn enough to make a mule give up when he decided to make up his mind about something, and he'd obviously done it here.

I began to ask the doctor what kinds of things we should be looking for as we sat here with Aiden. The doctor wanted me to watch for any signs of jaundice, of any of his limbs becoming paralyzed, of thickness to his speech, or any problems with his motor functions. The nurse came in with a set of test results, which the doctor seemed fairly surprised at. He told us there had been a huge amount of improvement, but he wasn't changing his mind about Aiden going home.

One look at my boyfriend's face told me he wasn't changing his mind, either. That might be a good thing. Who knew how long we had before the Queen's magic wore off? We were down an hour already.

CHAPTER SIXTY-TWO

I poked my head out into the hallway as Aiden sat up with Doris's and Harold's assistance. They had to help him put on his pants and shirt, and Harold bent down to put Aiden's shoes on him. The nurses talked amongst each other about their favorite TV shows and other mundane topics. One had a kid getting ready for Halloween, and he had decided he wanted to go as a rabbit and dress his pet rabbit up like a magician. I thought that was clever, but I hoped I wouldn't need a magician of my own to get out of the hospital.

The elevator was just around the corner from Aiden's hospital room. If Harold went out to the nurse's station and distracted the lone remaining nurse, we could likely sneak Aiden to the elevator. The question was whether he'd be able to walk under his own power, because I knew Doris and I wouldn't be able to carry Aiden far.

I spied a wheelchair in the hallway and waited until the nurse wasn't watching to snag it, dragging it as quietly as I could into the room. I relayed my plan to the others.

Harold went out to chat up the nurse. I had no idea what he planned to say, but he was a charming man in a nerdy Sean Connery kind of way. Connery was better-looking, but people responded to Harold's easy smile and good-natured small talk. He got the nurse going on the latest episode of some medical drama I didn't watch, and they were getting into a spirited discussion within minutes.

Doris and I helped Aiden into the wheelchair, and the pair was poised to go just inside the door. I helped Bert get repositioned in my backpack with strict instructions to act as a silent lookout unless he needed to sound an alarm. He nodded as if he was completely focused on the plan, and then he saluted me.

"Are we going home first?" Bert asked.

"Why? We've got to get Aiden to Stanley's field and feed him the tarts."

"You might need more help. You might want Allie and her mom there as well."

I considered his statement and said, "Let's get out of the hospital first. Then we can decide whether to call the others and who all should join us."

He nodded. "Allie or her mom might have an idea of something we can try. I'd get her response to some of this before you do it."

"Too late now," I said. "We're kinda committed. Now hush until we get to the car."

Doris and I wheeled Aiden out of the room toward the elevator when the nurse was focused on Harold. I hit the button for the lobby and felt a sigh of relief as the elevator doors closed behind us without our being caught by any medical staff.

We got to the lobby, and I wheeled Aiden out. Doris hurried ahead of us, planning to get Harold's car started and headed our way. I slowed our path, giving her time to get the car. We stopped briefly to rest in the lobby, and I saw Aiden's eyes. He looked at me very suspiciously.

"What's the rush?" he asked.

"We've got to get you out of here before the Queen's spell wears off," I said.

"It's not permanent?" he asked. So much for the hope that he'd overheard the conversation in his room before he woke up. Whispering so the lobby volunteers and other patrons wouldn't hear, I explained we had only a few hours to administer a more permanent remedy, but we had to get somewhere we'd be able to deal with the side effects.

"What side effects?" he wanted to know, in his hoarse and raspy voice.

I shook my head. "Not here," I whispered. "Too many ears around, and we're not exactly supposed to have you out of your room. Let's move."

I stood up from my position of leaning over Aiden to whisper in his ear and looked around. No one seemed to be paying much attention to us, and no one seemed to be watching. I pushed him through the doors, and we felt the cool fall breeze on our cheeks as we waited for Doris. It didn't take long before she pulled up in front of us. I helped Aiden into the back seat and then walked the wheelchair inside while

Doris called Harold. I hopped into the car, and we drove around the block to give Harold time to exit the hospital.

We picked him up, and I felt a slight thrill, the exhilaration of having a plan actually work as planned. Harold and Doris were in the front seat, and I sat in the back, carefully holding Aiden's bandaged hands. I couldn't think of any other details at the moment. My brain seemed to have stopped working properly, and I just had random thoughts firing incoherently. I had nothing else to give, and I needed a break. I leaned my head against Aiden's shoulder and shut my eyes for a few minutes.

In the absence of a good idea, go with the one that makes you feel better. Doris drove us home. She pulled up to the garage, and Harold jumped out. Tobias must have been watching from the window, because he came out to the car. Aiden looked at me and asked for an explanation. I burst into tears.

How was I going to tell him? I was so worried I was going to lose him. And if I did, I didn't know what I would do. But for now, I still had him, and I wasn't giving up.

"Aiden, why did you go looking for a vorpal sword?" I asked, sniffling. There had to be an easier way of telling him this, but I wasn't sure how.

He gave me a funny kind of look, but he didn't answer.

"Was there something you were trying to do with it?" I asked.

He didn't answer, but this time, he looked down at his bandaged hands where they lay in his lap.

"Aiden, was there something you were trying to prove?"

His eyes shot up to mine, and he reached up to his sore throat. "I don't know. What. To say," he choked out. "Was always. Worried. About magical creatures. But the Jabberwocky. Always scared me. Wanted. To be. Prepared." He coughed as he finished speaking.

"Did you have some reason to be worried about Wonderland? Did you know anything about it before Allie told us?"

He nodded. "I knew. Some."

I had to remind myself that he was probably getting tired, and the tube he'd had in his throat wasn't going to help. I explained the Snow Queen's information about the tarts.

Aiden's eyebrows rose so high, they almost hit his hairline, which was quite a trick to pull off. "Did. You. Give me. That. Treatment?"

I shook my head. "We haven't done it yet. We couldn't give you the remedy in the hospital because we were afraid . . ." I couldn't say it.

"That. I'd. Turn into. The Jabberwock."

I nodded. "We had to get you out of the hospital before we could even consider it. Stanley has some farmland outside of town where there would be fewer people who could be hurt. Less property that can be damaged. A minimized opportunity for mayhem we can't get under control."

"The house?" he asked. "What if. The Rabbit. Comes here?" He was starting to speak in longer sentences, and I thought it was a good sign.

"The Queen is moving the rabbit hole from behind the house so nothing can use it to get into our backyard."

He seemed impressed. "What was the cost?"

In other words, nothing in faerie comes free. He knew it, probably better than anyone. "So far, nothing. We didn't negotiate for it. Your father did."

If I'd thought he was surprised earlier, it was nothing compared to the reaction my last sentence had brought. He didn't say anything in response to that and apparently had no intention to address it. "Any other option than the tarts?" he asked.

I shook my head. "The Queen's remedy is a temporary one. If we don't deal with this, you will eventually end up back in the hospital, fighting off the poison of the mushrooms. And you weren't exactly winning the fight."

Aiden closed his eyes and sat silently. I didn't have anything else left to say, which was good timing because the others had started piling out of the house to welcome him back.

CHAPTER SIXTY-THREE

I stepped out of the car to fend off the others. "Look, guys. I've explained to Aiden what's going on, so now we have to figure out what we need and get out to Stanley's field before the Snow Queen's magic can wear off. We've got the tarts. We just have to get there."

They scurried off, calling instructions to each other. It was organized chaos, and it was beautiful, even more so because I wasn't organizing it. I could sit with Aiden in the back seat of the car and allow Tobias and Harold and Doris get ready to go. Poor Stanley kept calling out suggestions that everyone kept shooting down, but he insisted he come along and bring the leg irons he'd found in my dad's old trunks.

I so had to go through those at some point, get it organized, and learn exactly what I had. Of course, I'd been saying it for a year. I needed to make those trunks a serious priority. Maybe I should start a list: going through the trunks, training with weapons, going to the gym . . . but before I could start any of that, I had to save Aiden.

My friends loaded up boxes and bags of tools, nails, and weapons. Someone handed me Aiden's backpack, and I noticed that Doris had brought a picnic basket. I needed to keep my bag and Aiden's close at hand; his had the books, and I couldn't remember what was in mine, other than Bert, who had thankfully stayed quiet. Mia and Allie brought out a small tote bag with magazines, a couple of paperback books, and my mp3 player. Apparently everyone thought we might be waiting a while for Aiden to de-Jabberwocky. Stanley offered to run to the store.

"Why?" I asked.

"Because we're out of salt," was the answer. Not something I thought I'd ever hear in my house, ever since I started keeping a bit extra around. Apparently continually laying a salt line since we'd been gone had severely eaten into the supply. I guess three small boxes of kosher salt weren't enough in an emergency. I couldn't complain about the liberal use of salt on a day like today.

Finally, everyone else climbed in the cars and we headed out again. I didn't know what to do, but if I kept focusing on the next step, getting through the ordeal in front of us, we'd eventually make it out the other side. I had to keep promising myself exactly that, just to keep myself moving. I held Aiden's hand softly in my own, and I had to fight to keep from squeezing it. I wanted to reassure him—he had to be terrified—but I didn't want to hurt his still sore hands.

Stanley's car, a beat-up 1980s model station wagon, likely with a million miles on it and worth more for its scrap than as a car itself, pulled off the road when we passed a grocery store, while the rest of us kept going out of town, east on Highway 35 toward Xenia. Harold knew where we were headed and led the rest of the convoy to Stanley's land. Eventually, we pulled off the highway. I wasn't completely sure of where we were, but as we drove, it became clear that Stanley's property was enough off the beaten path that we had a place to deal with the potential Jabberwocky issue without prying eyes. I breathed a sigh of relief.

We finally pulled onto a dirt path with no other building or marked areas in sight. There were plenty of trees on either side of the road, but we did eventually come to a clearing. It looked like a corn field, one that had already been harvested. Some stalks were still visible and the rows were still there, but we managed to find places to spread out a few blankets and get somewhat comfortable.

Aiden sprawled out on a blanket. He was definitely getting tired, although his eyes were still bright and clear. I leaned down and felt his forehead. It was fairly cool, so I wasn't as worried as I could have been if he'd still been as feverish as he'd been when we left Wonderland. I asked him if he was ready.

Wounded hands and all, he grabbed me and drew me down to him. I couldn't help it. I let out a cry and bit down hard on the sob that threatened to make its way out.

"I love you, Janie. It will be okay. I will come back to you, no matter how confused or disoriented the tarts make me. I believe it is temporary. I believe, with all my heart, that no matter what else happens, we are fated to be together and nothing is ever going to keep us apart. Keep reminding me of what we have. I cannot believe in a world that would allow me to forget my feelings for you."

I heard Doris sobbing nearby. We had an audience, but I didn't care.

"I love you, Aiden. And I will always love you. You are my future, and I will do everything I can to continue to remind you of that." It occurred to me that he was concentrating on the possibility of the human side effects: the forgetfulness, the mind fog, and all the rest. But what if he turned into . . .

He was apparently reading my mind today. "Janie, if it all goes wrong, you need to know it's okay. You guys have to do whatever it is you have to do to stay safe. I get that. I don't blame anyone."

Oh, God. He was actually thinking about it. He knew what stopped a Jabberwocky. He probably knew better than we did. And he knew Tobias had it. He was trying to tell me it was okay if we had to use the sword. I didn't want to hear it.

"Janie," Harold said softly, "I think you want to get back before he does this."

He was holding the container of tarts in his hand as Stanley began to pour a salt circle around Aiden's blanket, about fifteen yards in diameter. The salt looked odd on the uneven ground around us, but it was smart. I hadn't even heard Stanley pull up. Had time started running that slowly for me? Or was something else going on?

I nodded and gave Aiden the deepest, most meaningful kiss I could. There probably wasn't anything attractive about it. Tears were leaking out of my eyes and down my face. My nose was running. I was seconds away from breaking down and was only holding it all in by sheer force of will. I didn't want his last memory of me to be of a leaky, snotty faucet. Not that he'd remember it, but still.

I squeezed Aiden's hands and stood up. He winced slightly, but he nodded. It took everything I had to step away, to go beyond the salt line and leave him behind. Stanley handed Aiden the container of tarts and had to help me walk away because I was crying and fighting not to let Aiden see it. Mia and Jonah were there, and they caught me before I could collapse. Bert was right at my feet, and Allie sat down cross-legged on the ground beside him, laying a hand on his head. I noticed him look up at her, and I wondered if there'd been something going on between them. They'd been good friends for a while, both of them out of their original lives. I wondered what kind of couple they would make. They deserved some happiness, and I hoped Bert wouldn't get his heart broken again. Heartbroken frog was not my idea of fun.

Aiden looked over at me, and I realized his eyes weren't dry either. He took the lid off the container and sat up slowly, painfully, before lifting one of the tarts to his lips and start to eat.

"This actually tastes pretty good," he said, shoveling it in his mouth.

My heart sank into my stomach as he tore into them. I knew I'd stuffed myself silly earlier with fast food that had been brought to the hospital. He hadn't had anything to eat since we'd been back. I knew he would be hungry, but I'd kind of hoped he'd be able to take a single bite and be cured. It didn't quite happen that way.

He finished off the first tart and looked at us with a vague expression on his face. He waved, as if he was unsure of who we were. Bert leaned against my leg, and I felt Doris come over and take my hand. Harold and Stanley were propping Doris up, and I saw that her face was also wet with tears.

"He's chosen well in so many ways," she whispered, choking as she said it.

I watched Aiden eat the second tart, licking the filling off his fingers as he finished it, as though it was the most delicious thing he'd ever had in his life. That's when I saw the skin on his face start to take on a greenish color and elongate with whiskers coming out on either side of his mouth, his neck stretching and his fingers growing into long, deadly talons. An inhuman scream came out of his mouth, and it hurt my heart to hear it.

It was true, then. He was going to transform into something, and we were pretty sure it was the Jabberwocky. Mia told me to turn away, but I shook my head. I saw Tobias unsheathing the vorpal sword.

Oh, shit. I didn't think I could do this. Why had I said yes to this?

CHAPTER SIXTY-FOUR

Tobias saw me looking at the sword, and he looked embarrassed. "Janie, I'm not using it yet. We're not at the point where it might be necessary."

I nodded. "But we're heading there. Is it more humane not to wait? Is he suffering?"

He shook his head. "I don't know. I do know I'm not ready to use this yet. There's more we can try."

"Like what?"

"Well, the memory thing for humans is temporary. Since it's related to the tarts being eaten, I would assume it only lasts until the digestive system gets whatever causes this to be completely through one's body before beginning to wear off. It could be that the transformation will wear off as his body digests the tarts."

He had a point. There was really no way to know unless we gave the effect of the tarts time to subside. I wasn't ready to give up. I didn't want Aiden to give up. But watching the creature who had been my boyfriend shriek and cry as it transformed into the hideous beast made me wonder if we were torturing him by letting him go through this, and if it was, what was the right thing to do?

"Okay," I said. "We wait."

Stanley had pulled the picnic basket out of the car for the rest of us to eat while we watched Aiden. Stanley had on his insulated hunter's cap with the flaps pulled down over his ears and headphones in with loud rock music thumping behind the flaps. Stanley also put on a pair of dark aviator sunglasses and a pair of earmuffs over the flaps. In short, he looked like a paranoid dork, but it was enough to make me smile a bit.

I sat there looking at Stanley, and I felt bad for him. His wife had been sick for a long time, but he was here with us instead of sitting with her. And yet, she probably knew him well enough to realize that he would regret missing all of this. It made me think about how some couples were just so well-suited to each other. I hoped Aiden and I would one day be the kind of older couple who had a relationship like that. I'd have to remember to apologize to Stanley later about his camera, which had gotten ruined. I felt bad that he was doing so much to help Aiden and me, when we hadn't brought back his camera, much less the photographs he'd wanted.

Stanley had a metal lawn chair in the back of his car. He'd poured a salt circle around the chair and sat down. The rest of us were seated on blankets in the field and watched, silently, as Aiden finished the painful transformation. Because it was a magical change, and because of his half-faerie heritage, Aiden couldn't cross the salt line, and it pissed him off. He started throwing himself bodily against the invisible barrier created by the salt and screaming as it burned. He kept looking directly at me as he did it. I wondered if he was just trying to get to the last being who had been kind to him, or if he'd decided to eat me. I didn't necessarily like either option at the moment.

I tried several times to calm Aiden, but it appeared as if he didn't hear me. In fact, it seemed as though the more I tried to calm him, the more agitated he got. Doris finally asked me to stop, and Aiden settled down a bit more when he didn't hear my voice. That hurt.

After that, no one talked. No one made a sound. We just sat there, passing back and forth bags of cold cheeseburgers, chicken nuggets, French fries, and other leftover fast food we had brought in the picnic basket. As we were shoveling greasy fast food crap into our mouths, Aiden whined and cried and attempted to break free.

After a while, it appeared he'd given up on trying to escape the magical ring. Aiden sat down on the ground in the middle of the salt circle and stared at us. It was a little disconcerting, but an improvement over the whimpering and screeching.

Stanley finally got up, wiping French fry grease from his hands on the seat of his pants as he did so. "I'm going to run another circle around him," he said. "I've just got a funny feeling we should have another barrier between us and him while we wait for the enchantment to run its course."

I nodded. Stanley broke the salt circle around his own chair with his foot and grabbed a canister of Morton's table salt in each hand.

Jonah and Harold helped Stanley encircle another salt line around Aiden, who turned to watch them with a wary, red-eyed stare, as if he somehow knew what they were doing and was reserving the right to object to it later if he chose to.

Was he actually aware and understanding, or was I just looking for a reason to hope? I wasn't sure. And if I just needed a bit of hope to get through this, I was prepared to hang on to it with both hands and my teeth if I had to.

I felt the snap of magic as their salt line clicked into place, and I wondered why it was so strong. And then I felt it. Something was inside the circle with Aiden, but I couldn't see it just yet. It must be low to the ground. I looked around, and Bert was sitting right beside me, so it wasn't him. Allie and Alice were behind Bert. It wasn't them. As a matter of fact, all of my friends were behind me, and I wasn't in the circle, either. So what was going on?

I'd stopped crying by this point, and was watching the ground near Aiden's feet. Sure enough, there was a hole developing just big enough for a, well, a rabbit. It seemed to get bigger, and Aiden himself began howling and stomping and whining like a dog who'd scented an animal in his backyard and wanted to go outside now.

I was rooted to the ground, but that didn't stop me from staring, from looking at Aiden's feet and wondering where the opening had come from. For all I knew, Aiden had created it himself with the wicked-looking feet that had destroyed the tennis shoes he'd been wearing.

"Doris? Harold? Stanley? Are you seeing what I'm seeing?" I asked and finally tore my eyes away from Aiden to look at them. Doris was mesmerized by the monster her son had become and wasn't responding. Harold shook his head, but also kept watching Jabber-Aiden. Stanley, on the other hand, was sitting on the ground with his headphones on, and he couldn't hear me. All of the others seemed to be staring, as if in a trance.

I snapped my fingers in front of Stanley's face, and he looked up. "*What?*" he yelled, obviously unable to hear me with the music blaring in his ears. I had to be impressed by the choice, though. He was listening to Rob Zombie. I wouldn't have thought he'd know who that was—the man was in his eighties after all—but Stanley seemed to be enjoying it.

I squatted down in front of him and pulled one earbud out of his ear long enough to yell that I'd smelled magic and something was going on. He glanced up with a look of concern on his face and grabbed the rest of the salt, yelling and pointing and gesturing wildly for me to help him spread the salt in another circle around all of the rest of us standing on the sidelines.

I felt the pop of the circle closing around us. Something had obviously tried to affect us. It hadn't affected me, but I was wearing the necklace Aiden had given me the year before that negated magical effects on the wearer. I'd put it on before going to dinner in Wonderland the night before, and it must have been protecting me now.

What was going on?

CHAPTER SIXTY-FIVE

Once the salt circle we were all inside closed, the others were able to see without any form of magic influencing our vision. We watched then, as the opening at Aiden's feet got bigger and bigger. For some reason, the hole's growth had been making them all foggy until we were behind the salt.

I yanked the headset off Stanley's head and ripped off his hunting cap. "Hey, did you have a secret portal on your land you forgot to tell us about?"

"No," he said. "I plant corn here. Or rather, I pay someone else to do it these days. I walk the land before each planting season and before harvest, and I've never run across even the slightest amount of magic here. There's no way I could have missed it. I've been on this land in some way since I was a kid. My grandparents owned it."

Yikes. I had to believe him. Stanley had been around magic for years, to hear Doris tell it. I'd think he'd have noticed magic on the land if he'd been here for so much of his life. I nodded. "So what's going on?"

No one answered, but they didn't need to. The hole stopped growing in size, and Aiden the Jabberwocky stopped snuffling around its edges. He was watching the hole, but he wasn't whining or crying or scratching anymore.

It was almost as if Aiden's own personality was starting to come through that of the Jabberwocky. I decided to take it as a good sign. If he was acting like himself, maybe he would eventually fade back into himself. I smiled at him, and it appeared as if the Jabberwocky smiled back. Even though that was kind of a creepy-looking smile, I forced myself to keep the same look. And then the Jabberwocky winked at me.

Well, that was unnerving.

Of course, Aiden had a better view of what might be coming through the opening than I did, or any of the rest of our friends. It didn't look like the portals to the faerie realms; it looked like the rabbit hole we'd stepped through to follow Allie. But why would one suddenly appear in Stanley's field?

The White Rabbit stepped out of the hole.

That, I hadn't seen coming.

Aiden was behind the Rabbit, staying very quiet, and went unseen.

The White Rabbit only saw all of us standing there in front of him. He took in the salt lines and laughed. "I'm not magical. This circle will not hold me, and they will not protect you."

That did sound awfully funny coming from a human-sized talking rabbit. If I was a human-sized carrot, I'd be afraid, but without a Queen and without any magical powers or a weapon of any kind, it was just kind of sad. I didn't know of anything he could do to us.

I felt some kind of vindication flowing through my veins. "Protect us from what? Are you bringing an army into our realm? For what purpose? To get back at us for leaving? Please, tell me what you're going to do."

He shook his head. "I will get you for this. I will find a way, and when you have children, I will come through this portal and find my way to your home. I will trick them into coming to Wonderland, and I will never allow them to leave. I will never allow you to come visit them. You will never have children who stay with you. You will never have grandchildren in your own realm. You will never be happy, and just when you believe you could never be punished worse, I will begin slipping some of our mushrooms into your food. You won't even know when I start; it will be subtle. Before you know it, I'll have given you enough that you won't be able to recover from it. Because there's only one remedy for it, and you will never get it because it is only in Wonderland."

Wow. He was a bit behind the times. And I had no intention of bringing him up-to-date. If I could get the Rabbit to give up and leave, we'd all be happier. Who knew what kind of mischief he was up to? I had to keep him focused on me, and talking, to try to get him to see sense. If nothing else, perhaps Aiden would realize what was going on and be able to scare the Rabbit into going along with us. It could work. Really.

"Mr. Rabbit, we have left your realm and left it for you to handle as you see fit. Why are you so fixated on us?"

"Why, you have ruined everything!" he sputtered. "You've brainwashed our new Queen and kidnapped her. Upon your escape, I have no doubt you notified other realms about what is going on in Wonderland. You've surely lied and told them untruths. I'm going to have to answer to outsiders about how our world works! It's none of their business. You're going to doom the anthropomorphic folks to be servants and vassals and lesser beings again. Mark my words, we will rise up, and we will come after you and punish you for the loss of our freedom!"

Be still my heart, there, William Wallace, I thought. Boy, was he out of tune with his own people if he thought he was some kind of passionate freedom fighter as opposed to just trying to keep his own power base intact. How desperate was he?

"Mr. Rabbit, do you understand that the people you claim to represent do not follow you? They don't agree with you. Some of them actually helped us. They helped our friends. And they helped us to avoid all kinds of things in Wonderland that would have hurt us. They gave us directions. They pointed the way when we were lost. They passed us messages we needed in order to figure out how to escape."

"You're talking about the visitors, aren't you? Of course they helped! They think they're being held for no reason, that they're being punished. They aren't, but they cannot be allowed to run Wonderland on their own. They, like you, have dangerous ideas and cannot be allowed to take over! Who helped you? I need their names." The Rabbit kept running its front paw between its ears, as if it was a man nervously running its hand through his hair in a nervous, stressed tic.

"I'm not talking about visitors. I'm talking about Wonderland residents, like you, who do not have a human appearance. They've made it very clear they are unhappy with your rule. And let's face it, it is *your* rule. You've merely put a puppet on the throne in order to hide the fact that you're the true leader. So what do you honestly think is going to happen now that your Queen is gone? Do you really think they'll follow you?"

His eyes narrowed, and he pulled two small pistols out of his waistcoat pockets. Somehow, I hadn't thought about him concealing a weapon, much less two. I put my hands up in the air, like people were instructed to do in Western movies when someone pulled a gun. The others all did the same.

The Rabbit started ranting about nosy, interfering outsiders and knowing what was best for his own people. He started down a tangent about how he knew he was the one who could best judge what was needed, and the best way to get nosy interfering outsiders out of his way would be to kill us. Both weapons were now pointed directly at my head.

I heard a roar. And then the White Rabbit was gone.

I looked up at Aiden, my boyfriend the Jabberwocky, and saw giant jaws chewing in an exaggerated motion. He swallowed hard, twice, and the White Rabbit was gone. The Jabberwocky let out an enormous burp.

"That's fairly impressive," I heard from near my toes.

Bert apparently gave the belch high marks.

CHAPTER SIXTY-SIX

The portal shriveled up, rippling the ground around it as the White Rabbit went down Aiden's throat. As the hole filled itself in, Aiden helped stomp it closed. I watched his large foot come down at the site where the portal had been and solidly land on non-magical ground. Thankfully, there wouldn't be another unexpected trip into Wonderland. If we ever went back, we'd go on purpose and be way more prepared than we had been this time.

Just then, the Snow Queen appeared in the woods, coming toward us quietly, dressed in white and silver faerie court finery. She walked slowly, but purposefully. At least until she saw the Jabberwocky. That stopped her in her tracks.

I didn't think I'd ever see a faerie queen speechless, but there she was. She began to pick her way through the field, careful not to step on any of our salt lines, and shook her head. "It always amazes me what humans are afraid of," she said, looking back at Aiden, who was settling himself down on the ground, curling up his body in a ball, as if about to take a nap like a giant cat after a large meal.

Could my life get any weirder?

I wasn't sure.

The Snow Queen nodded her head at me. "It appears Mr. Ferguson has experienced the faerie court reaction. I wondered which way it would go."

"How long does it take to wear off? Will it? Would it wear off on an ordinary faerie being?" I asked.

"Eventually," she said. "Within a couple of hours, normally, but in this case, I'd guess it would be shorter. Did he display any symptoms of mental fog or forgetfulness before he transformed?"

I nodded.

"That should wear off as well, but it might take longer," she said. "And thanks to all of you, the Queen of Wonderland has been reinstated to her throne and has expressed her gratitude for your actions. She is not overly thrilled that her savior was the person who had her sister imprisoned, but she is grateful nonetheless.

"The Queen of Hearts wished to say that she is willing to negotiate terms for all of the visitors who were living in the castle to return to their own realms if possible, and she would want you to negotiate those terms on their behalf. She indicates the two who left with you are welcome to remain here, as long as they agree not to discuss their time in Wonderland with any who have not already been there."

I turned to Allie and her mother, who had their arms wrapped tightly around each other. They nodded silently. "I think we can handle it," I said. "When are the negotiations to take place, and where?"

"She has agreed for the negotiations to happen in your world, exactly one week from now."

I nodded, and we negotiated for the Snow Queen to send an emissary to me in two days' time at my house. I figured she'd send Geoffrey and that he'd get a chance to check on his son, but I was okay with that.

I turned to Stanley. He held up his arm and pointed at his watch. In the dusk light, I couldn't see it, and I gave him an exasperated look. He looked at it and called out, "It's eight o'clock."

I looked sideways at Aiden's sleeping form and wondered something. "How are you suddenly the one who's stuck cleaning up so many messes in realms not your own? I mean, you told me some months ago that you had your own lands to run, but you took over my stepmother's court and began trying to resolve that disaster, and now you're fixing Wonderland's issues. Aren't you getting a little tired of cleaning up other people's messes?"

The Snow Queen laughed. "That's a truth. But as you seem to be finding out on your own, sometimes it's not about whether you're sick of cleaning up the messes of others, but more about it needing to be done and you're the one capable of doing it. Besides which, having a bit of goodwill yourself can't hurt down the road.

"You strike me as a very capable person, Janie Grimm. I see you as having a major role in some of the things that may transpire over the next few years. I hope you are ready for where it might take you.

You are certainly surrounding yourself with capable and caring people who have a very specific set of identifiable skills." She paused. "You are not in my debt, although you may wish to remember that I have done a service that has benefited you this day."

"I will," I said, but my sight was still on Aiden. He was making a snuffling sound that sounded a lot like when he snored in the middle of the night.

Out of the corner of my eye, I saw the Snow Queen nod at me. "You'll go far," she said before she walked back toward the woods, fading as she went. I'd have to remember that she didn't appear to need a portal to get from place to place, but right that moment, the only thing I could concentrate on was getting Aiden back to normal.

The others began packing up their things and heading back to the cars. I stayed where I was, waiting as Aiden slowly morphed back into his normal shape, even though he stayed the same size as the ten-foot-tall Jabberwocky. His catfish-like whiskers disappeared, and the talons were shrinking to their fingernails, but I still didn't dare go near him. Getting too close would break the salt circle.

Besides, he was huge. The others had been standing outside the cars watching from a distance as Aiden transformed back to himself. The only problem was that he wasn't getting any smaller. I didn't think I'd ever get him in the car, much less through my front door, unless I solved the problem of why he wasn't shrinking back to his normal size. I'd never have a normal date again.

A thought hit me. His human half was reacting to something from Wonderland that made him large in our realm, much like the donuts had made Bert large that morning. It was something from Wonderland. The wine in the "Drink Me" bottle had fixed Bert's size issue, but unfortunately, we'd used the entire bottle getting the frog back to normal. We did have something else, however.

The Caterpillar's mushroom.

I ran back to the car and ripped my backpack out of the back seat, tossing things out of my way until I found the mushroom pieces. I'd put the two sections on the same side of the bag that the Caterpillar had handed them to me. I took a second to remember what he said: One side of the mushroom made you larger, and the other side made you smaller. I grabbed a piece from the "smaller" side and raced back.

"Aiden!" I yelled, waking him up.

He sat up slowly, lumbering to his feet, though he stayed inside the salt circle. If he was back to himself, would it affect him? The fact that he was still magically larger than he was supposed to be may cause the salt to hold him in place. He wasn't a monster anymore, though, and that's all that really mattered.

"I need you to eat this. I promise it will help."

He gave me a blank look, as if he didn't know who I was. "It's me, Aiden. It's Janie. I need you to trust me. You're almost cured; I just need you to eat this."

Doris stepped forward. "If she's telling you to eat it, you should. Janie wouldn't hurt you," she assured him.

I tossed Aiden the mushroom chunk, and he popped it into his mouth. It didn't take long before he finally started to shrink back to his normal size, curled up on the ground.

Stanley pulled out his mp3 player and began playing music, only this time, it was a bit more laid-back and classic. He chose "Sweet Home Alabama," "Brown Eyed Girl," and finished off with "What a Wonderful World" before getting in his car and I could no longer hear.

It made me feel good that he'd picked such uplifting music. Aiden kept slowly shrinking back to his normal size, but when he could finally talk again, he seemed very confused about what had transpired. He took a step toward me.

"Janie, what happened?"

At least he recognized me now.

I shook my head. "Stay where you're at. We'll go home in a bit. Things are going to be okay. Everyone's safe."

"Your stepmother is Eva. She's going to try to hurt you to get her power back."

I nodded, a sick feeling forming in the pit of my stomach. "Yes, but she's no longer a danger. She's been locked up."

He seemed surprised. *Hooboy.* It seemed he was a year or so behind.

"I'll fill you in on all of it. I promise," I said. I sat down on the ground with my knees to my chest at the edge of the salt line.

Bert sat by my side. "This may be temporary. And you guys love each other so much. You'll get through it,"

"I know."

He hopped away, and I overheard him talking to Allie. A phrase caught my attention, and I turned away from Aiden, just in time to hear Bert asking Allie to go out on a date. Who better to understand the trials and tribulation of a human in a frog's body than a girl who had grown up in Wonderland? I smiled to myself and decided I would give Bert a chance for some romance. I wondered if we could serve them up a true gourmet dinner. It wasn't like they could go to a restaurant, so maybe we could bring a restaurant to them. They'd both earned it.

I looked at Aiden.

He'd earned it, too. We'd work on the memory thing. I'd always be there with him.

He stood up and reached out a hand to me.

"Are you okay?" I asked.

He nodded, and I scuffed the salt circle so I could run into his arms. He wrapped them around me tightly. "I had a few moments of confusion, and then I remembered enough to know I haven't properly thanked you for everything."

I smiled against his chest. "Not necessary. I have you," I said. "And that's all I need."

Acknowledgements

I need to thank the following people . . .

. . . To Ray and Daniel Westcott, my guys, my family, and my backup. Without you two, I would not accomplish everything I do.

. . . To Alvin and Karen King, the world's best parents, because they're mine.

. . . To Eugene and Sandra Westcott, the world's best parents-in-law, for the same reason.

. . . To Mary Jane Woodruff, grandma extraordinaire, for being one of the first, and biggest, fans of Bert.

. . . To Ashley, Jake, Blake, and Kenley Ballard, and to Alex and Michelle King, for family foibles, squabbles, and memories. I've got enough material to keep me going for centuries, and we've got years and years to go, with miles and miles of memories yet to make.

. . . To Brian, Jenni, Skylar, Sierra, Desi, Ambrosia, Mara, and Anna, as well as Alan, Chantell, Savannah, and Joran, for enthusiastically making me a part of another family and giving me even more nieces and another nephew to love.

. . . To Rebekah, Audra, Chris, Leann, Brian, Rebecca, Erin, Erin, Tara, Andrea, Heather, Amy, Martha, Breanne, Noelle, Melissa, Linda, Jane, Lisa, Ben, Steve, Sarah, Sara, and all the rest of my AWESOME friends, for keeping me sane and on course with all the craziness of the last several years. YOU GUYS ROCK. My apologies if I've left anyone off this list, believe me, it was unintentional.

. . . To Jaime-Kristal Lott, editor extraordinaire, who keeps me on track when I've gone off the rails in the story. Bert wouldn't be the same without you.

. . . To Celina Summers, Jeanne De Vita, Kelly Shorten, Kerry Mand, and all the other fine staff at Musa Publishing and the Urania line for their faith in my work, enthusiasm, and all their help in seeing these books all the way to print (or e-print). Also to James Barnes and

Loconeal Publishing for seeing the potential in these books after Musa Publishing ceased to exist.

... To the Springfield/Mechanicsburg writers' groups, and especially to Linda Johnson and Heather Angus for their help and support in keeping me focused on my writing and all the miniscule detail work that goes with making it right.

AUTHOR INFORMATION

Addie J. King

Addie J. King is an attorney by day and author by nights, evenings, weekends, and whenever else she can find a spare moment. Her short story "Poltergeist on Aisle Fourteen" was published in MYSTERY TIMES TEN by Buddhapuss Ink, and an essay entitled, "Building Believable Legal Systems in Science Fiction and Fantasy" was published in EIGHTH DAY GENESIS; A WORLDBUILDING CODEX FOR WRITERS AND CREATIVES by Alliteration Ink. Her novels, THE GRIMM LEGACY, THE ANDERSEN ANCESTRY and THE WONDERLAND WOES are available now from Loconeal Publishing. The fourth book, THE BUNYAN BARTER, will be available in 2015. Her website is www.addiejking.com